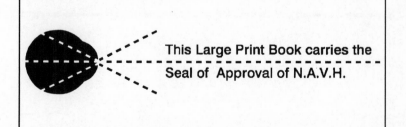

THE SILENT PATIENT

THE SILENT PATIENT

ALEX MICHAELIDES

THORNDIKE PRESS
A part of Gale, a Cengage Company

Farmington Hills, Mich • San Francisco • New York • Waterville, Maine
Meriden, Conn • Mason, Ohio • Chicago

Copyright © 2019 by Astramare Limited.
Thorndike Press, a part of Gale, a Cengage Company.

ALL RIGHTS RESERVED
This is a work of fiction. All of the characters, organizations, and events portrayed in this novel are either the product of the author's imagination or are used fictitiously.
Thorndike Press® Large Print Basic.
The text of this Large Print edition is unabridged.
Other aspects of the book may vary from the original edition.
Set in 16 pt. Plantin.

LIBRARY OF CONGRESS CIP DATA ON FILE.
CATALOGUING IN PUBLICATION FOR THIS BOOK
IS AVAILABLE FROM THE LIBRARY OF CONGRESS

ISBN-13: 978-1-4328-5864-3 (hardcover)

Published in 2019 by arrangement with Macmillan Publishing Group, LLC/Celadon Books

Printed in Mexico
Print Number: 13   Print Year: 2020

For my parents

For my parents

But why does she not speak?

— EURIPIDES,
Alcestis

But why does she not speak?

— EURIPIDES,
Alcestis

Prologue

Alicia Berenson's Diary

July 14
I don't know why I'm writing this.

That's not true. Maybe I do know and just don't want to admit it to myself.

I don't even know what to call it — this thing I'm writing. It feels a little pretentious to call it a diary. It's not like I have anything to say. Anne Frank kept a diary — not someone like me. Calling it a "journal" sounds too academic, somehow. As if I should write in it every day, and I don't want to — if it becomes a chore, I'll never keep it up.

Maybe I'll call it nothing. An unnamed something that I occasionally write in. I like that better. Once you name something, it stops you seeing the whole of it, or why it matters.

You focus on the word, which is just the tiniest part, really, the tip of an iceberg. I've never been that comfortable with words — I always think in pictures, express myself with images — so I'd never have started writing this if it weren't for Gabriel.

I've been feeling depressed lately, about a few things. I thought I was doing a good job of hiding it, but he noticed — of course he did, he notices everything. He asked how the painting was going — I said it wasn't. He got me a glass of wine, and I sat at the kitchen table while he cooked.

I like watching Gabriel move around the kitchen. He's a graceful cook — elegant, balletic, organized. Unlike me. I just make a mess.

"Talk to me," he said.

"There's nothing to say. I just get so stuck in my head sometimes. I feel like I'm wading through mud."

"Why don't you try writing things down? Keeping some kind of record? That might help."

"Yes, I suppose so. I'll try it."

10

"Don't just say it, darling. Do it."

"I will."

He kept nagging me, but I did nothing about it. And then a few days later he presented me with this little book to write in. It has a black leather cover and thick white blank pages. I ran my hand across the first page, feeling its smoothness — then sharpened my pencil and began.

He was right, of course. I feel better already — writing this down is providing a kind of release, an outlet, a space to express myself. A bit like therapy, I suppose.

Gabriel didn't say it, but I could tell he's concerned about me. And if I'm going to be honest — and I may as well be — the real reason I agreed to keep this diary was to re-assure him — prove that I'm okay. I can't bear the thought of him worrying about me. I don't ever want to cause him any distress or make him unhappy or cause him pain. I love Gabriel so much. He is without doubt the love of my life. I love him so totally, completely, some-times it threatens to overwhelm me. Some-times I think —

No. I won't write about that.

This is going to be a joyful record of ideas and images that inspire me artistically, things that make a creative impact on me. I'm only going to write positive, happy, normal thoughts.

No crazy thoughts allowed.

■ ■ ■ ■

Part One

■ ■ ■ ■

He that has eyes to see and ears to hear may convince himself that no mortal can keep a secret. If his lips are silent, he chatters with his fingertips; betrayal oozes out of him at every pore.

— SIGMUND FREUD,
Introductory Lectures on Psychoanalysis

CHAPTER ONE

Alicia Berenson was thirty-three years old when she killed her husband.

They had been married for seven years. They were both artists — Alicia was a painter, and Gabriel was a well-known fashion photographer. He had a distinctive style, shooting semi-starved, semi-naked women in strange, unflattering angles. Since his death, the price of his photographs has increased astronomically. I find his stuff rather slick and shallow, to be honest. It has none of the visceral quality of Alicia's best work. I don't know enough about art to say whether Alicia Berenson will stand the test of time as a painter. Her talent will always be overshadowed by her notoriety, so it's hard to be objective. And you might well accuse me of being biased. All I can offer is my opinion, for what it's worth. And to me, Alicia was a kind of genius. Apart from her technical skill, her paintings have an uncanny ability to grab your attention — by the throat, almost — and hold it in a vise-like grip.

Gabriel Berenson was murdered six years ago. He was forty-four years old. He was killed on the twenty-fifth of August — it was an unusually hot summer, you may remember, with some of the highest temperatures ever recorded. The day he died was the hottest of the year.

On the last day of his life, Gabriel rose early. A car collected him at 5:15 a.m. from the house he shared with Alicia in northwest London, on the edge of Hampstead Heath, and he was driven to a shoot in Shoreditch. He spent the day photographing models on a rooftop for *Vogue.*

Not much is known about Alicia's movements. She had an upcoming exhibition and was behind with her work. It's likely she spent the day painting in the summerhouse at the end of the garden, which she had recently converted into a studio. In the end, Gabriel's shoot ran late, and he wasn't driven home until eleven p.m.

Half an hour later, their neighbor, Barbie Hellmann, heard several gunshots. Barbie phoned the police, and a car was dispatched from the station on Haverstock Hill at 11:35 p.m. It arrived at the Berensons' house in just under three minutes.

The front door was open. The house was in pitch-black darkness; none of the light switches worked. The officers made their way along the hallway and into the living room. They shone torches around the room, illuminating it in intermittent beams of light. Alicia was discovered standing by the fireplace. Her white dress glowed ghostlike in the torchlight. Alicia seemed oblivious to the presence of the police. She was immobilized, frozen — a statue carved from ice — with a strange, frightened look on her face, as if confronting some unseen terror.

A gun was on the floor. Next to it, in the shadows, Gabriel was seated, motionless, bound to a chair with wire wrapped around his ankles and wrists. At first the officers thought he was alive. His head lolled slightly to one side, as if he were unconscious. Then a beam of light revealed Gabriel had been shot several times in the face. His handsome features were gone forever, leaving a charred, blackened, bloody mess. The wall behind him was sprayed with fragments of skull, brains, hair — and blood.

Blood was everywhere — splashed on the walls, running in dark rivulets along the floor, along the grain of the wooden floorboards. The officers assumed it was Gabriel's blood. But there was too much of it. And then something glinted in the torchlight — a knife was on the floor by Alicia's feet. Another beam of light revealed the blood spattered on Alicia's white dress. An officer grabbed her arms and held them up to the light. There were deep cuts across the veins in her wrists — fresh cuts, bleeding hard.

Alicia fought off the attempts to save her life; it took three officers to restrain her. She was taken to the Royal Free Hospital, only a few minutes away. She collapsed and lost consciousness on the way there. She had lost a lot of blood, but she survived.

The following day, she lay in bed in a private room at the hospital. The police questioned her in the presence of her lawyer. Alicia remained silent throughout the interview. Her lips were pale, bloodless; they fluttered occasionally but formed no words, made no sounds. She answered no questions. She could not, would not, speak. Nor did she speak when charged with Gabriel's murder. She remained silent when she was placed under arrest, refusing to deny her guilt or confess it.

Alicia never spoke again.

Her enduring silence turned this story from a commonplace domestic tragedy into something far grander: a mystery, an enigma that gripped the headlines and captured the public imagination for months to come.

Alicia remained silent — but she made one statement. A painting. It was begun when she was discharged from the hospital and placed under house arrest before the trial. According to the court-appointed psychiatric nurse, Alicia barely ate or slept — all she did was paint.

Normally Alicia labored weeks, even months, before embarking on a new picture, making endless sketches, arranging and re-arranging the composition, experimenting with color and form — a long gestation followed by a protracted birth as each brush-stroke was painstakingly applied. Now, however, she drastically altered her creative process, completing this painting within a few days of her husband's murder.

And for most people, this was enough to condemn her — returning to the studio so soon after Gabriel's death betrayed an extraordinary insensitivity. The monstrous lack of remorse of a cold-blooded killer.

Perhaps. But let us not forget that while Alicia Berenson may be a murderer, she was also an artist. It makes perfect sense — to me at least — that she should pick up her brushes and paints and express her compli-cated emotions on canvas. No wonder that, for once, painting came to her with such ease; if grief can be called easy.

The painting was a self-portrait. She titled it in the bottom left-hand corner of the canvas, in light blue Greek lettering.

One word:

Alcestis.

CHAPTER TWO

Alcestis is the heroine of a Greek myth. A love story of the saddest kind. Alcestis willingly sacrifices her life for that of her husband, Admetus, dying in his place when no one else will. An unsettling myth of self-sacrifice, it was unclear how it related to Alicia's situation. The true meaning of the allusion remained unknown to me for some time. Until one day, the truth came to light —

But I'm going too fast. I'm getting ahead of myself. I must start at the beginning and let events speak for themselves. I mustn't color them, twist them, or tell any lies. I'll proceed step by step, slowly and cautiously. But where to begin? I should introduce myself, but perhaps not quite yet; after all, I am not the hero of this tale. It is Alicia Berenson's story, so I must begin with her — and the *Alcestis.*

The painting is a self-portrait, depicting

Alicia in her studio at home in the days after the murder, standing before an easel and a canvas, holding a paintbrush. She is naked. Her body is rendered in unsparing detail: strands of long red hair falling across bony shoulders, blue veins visible beneath translucent skin, fresh scars on both her wrists. She's holding the paintbrush between her fingers. It's dripping red paint — or is it blood? She is captured in the act of painting — yet the canvas is blank, as is her expression. Her head is turned over her shoulder and she stares straight out at us. Mouth open, lips parted. Mute.

During the trial, Jean-Felix Martin, who managed the small Soho gallery that represented Alicia, made the controversial decision, decried by many as sensationalist and macabre, to exhibit the *Alcestis*. The fact that the artist was currently in the dock for killing her husband meant, for the first time in the gallery's long history, queues formed outside the entrance.

I stood in line with the other prurient art-lovers, waiting my turn by the neon-red lights of a sex shop next door. One by one, we shuffled inside. Once in the gallery, we were herded toward the painting, like an excitable crowd at a fairground making its way through a haunted house. Eventually, I found myself at the front of the line — and was confronted with the *Alcestis.*

I stared at the painting, staring into Alicia's face, trying to interpret the look in her eyes, trying to understand — but the portrait defied me. Alicia stared back at me — a blank mask — unreadable, impenetrable. I could divine neither innocence nor guilt in her expression.

Other people found her easier to read.

"Pure evil," whispered the woman behind me.

"Isn't she?" her companion agreed. "Cold-blooded bitch."

A little unfair, I thought — considering Alicia's guilt had yet to be proven. But in truth it was a foregone conclusion. The tabloids had cast her as a villain from the start: a femme fatale, a black widow. A monster.

The facts, such as they were, were simple: Alicia was found alone with Gabriel's body; only her fingerprints were on the gun. There was never any doubt she killed Gabriel. *Why* she killed him, on the other hand, remained a mystery.

The murder was debated in the media, and different theories were espoused in print and on the radio and on morning chat shows. Experts were brought in to explain,

23

condemn, justify Alicia's actions. She must have been a victim of domestic abuse, surely, pushed too far, before finally exploding? Another theory proposed a sex game gone wrong — the husband was found tied up, wasn't he? Some suspected it was old-fashioned jealousy that drove Alicia to murder — another woman, probably? But at the trial Gabriel was described by his brother as a devoted husband, deeply in love with his wife. Well, what about money? Alicia didn't stand to gain much by his death; she was the one who had money, inherited from her father.

And so it went on, endless speculation — no answers, only more questions — about Alicia's motives and her subsequent silence. Why did she refuse to speak? What did it mean? Was she hiding something? Protecting someone? If so, who? And why?

At the time, I remember thinking that while everyone was talking, writing, arguing, about Alicia, at the heart of this frantic, noisy activity there was a void — a silence. A sphinx.

During the trial, the judge took a dim view of Alicia's persistent refusal to speak. Innocent people, Mr. Justice Alverstone pointed out, tended to proclaim their innocence loudly — and often. Alicia not only remained silent, but she showed no visible signs of remorse. She didn't cry once throughout the trial — a fact made much of in the press — her face remaining unmoved, cold. Frozen.

The defense had little choice but to enter a plea of diminished responsibility: Alicia had a long history of mental health problems, it was claimed, dating back to her childhood. The judge dismissed a lot of this as hearsay — but in the end he allowed himself to be swayed by Lazarus Diomedes, professor of forensic psychiatry at Imperial College, and clinical director of the Grove, a secure forensic unit in North London. Professor Diomedes argued that Alicia's refusal to speak was in itself evidence of profound psychological distress — and she should be sentenced accordingly.

This was a rather roundabout way of saying something that psychiatrists don't like putting bluntly:

Diomedes was saying Alicia was mad.

It was the only explanation that made any sense: Why else tie up the man you loved to a chair and shoot him in the face at close range? And then express no remorse, give no explanation, not even speak? She must be mad.

She had to be.

25

In the end, Mr. Justice Alverstone accepted the plea of diminished responsibility and advised the jury to follow suit. Alicia was subsequently admitted to the Grove — under the supervision of the same Professor Diomedes whose testimony had been so influential with the judge.

If Alicia wasn't mad — that is, if her silence was merely an act, a performance for the benefit of the jury — then it had worked. She was spared a lengthy prison sentence — and if she made a full recovery, she might well be discharged in a few years. Surely now was the time to begin faking that recovery? To utter a few words here and there, then a few more; to slowly communicate some kind of remorse? But no. Week followed week, month followed month, then the years passed — and still Alicia didn't speak.

There was simply silence.

And so, with no further revelation forthcoming, the disappointed media eventually lost interest in Alicia Berenson. She joined the ranks of other briefly famous murderers; faces we remember, but whose names we forget.

Not all of us. Some people — myself included — continued to be fascinated by the mystery of Alicia Berenson and her enduring silence. As a psychotherapist, I thought it obvious that she had suffered a severe trauma surrounding Gabriel's death; and this silence was a manifestation of that trauma. Unable to come to terms with what she had done, Alicia sputtered and came to a halt, like a broken car. I wanted to help start her up again — help Alicia tell her story, to heal and get well. I wanted to fix her.

Without wishing to sound boastful, I felt uniquely qualified to help Alicia Berenson. I'm a forensic psychotherapist and used to working with some of the most damaged, vulnerable members of society. And something about Alicia's story resonated with me personally — I felt a profound empathy with her right from the start.

Unfortunately, I was still working at Broadmoor in those days, and so treating Alicia would have — should have — remained an idle fantasy, had not fate unexpectedly intervened.

Nearly six years after Alicia was admitted, the position of forensic psychotherapist became available at the Grove. As soon as I saw the advert, I knew I had no choice. I followed my gut — and applied for the job.

CHAPTER THREE

My name is Theo Faber. I'm forty-two years old. And I became a psychotherapist because I was fucked up. That's the truth — though it's not what I said during the job interview, when the question was put to me.

"What drew you to psychotherapy, do you think?" asked Indira Sharma, peering at me over the rims of her owlish glasses.

Indira was consultant psychotherapist at the Grove. She was in her late fifties with an attractive round face and long jet-black hair streaked with gray. She gave me a small smile — as if to reassure me this was an easy question, a warm-up volley, a precursor to trickier shots to follow.

I hesitated. I could feel the other members of the panel looking at me. I remained conscious of maintaining eye contact as I trotted out a rehearsed response, a sympathetic tale about working part-time in a care home as a teenager; and how this inspired an interest in psychology, which led to a postgraduate study of psychotherapy, and so on.

"I wanted to help people, I suppose." I shrugged. "That's it, really."

Which was bullshit.

I mean, of course I wanted to help people. But that was a secondary aim — particularly at the time I started training. The real motivation was purely selfish. I was on a quest to help myself. I believe the same is true for most people who go into mental health. We are drawn to this profession because we are damaged — we study psychology to heal ourselves. Whether we are prepared to admit this or not is another question.

As human beings, in our earliest years we reside in a land before memory. We like to think of ourselves as emerging from this primordial fog with our characters fully formed, like Aphrodite rising perfect from the sea foam. But thanks to increasing research into the development of the brain, we know this is not the case. We are born with a brain half-formed — more like a muddy lump of clay than a divine Olympian. As the psychoanalyst Donald Winnicott put it, "There is no such thing as a baby." The development of our personalities

29

doesn't take place in isolation, but in relationship with others — we are shaped and completed by unseen, unremembered forces; namely, our parents.

This is frightening, for obvious reasons. Who knows what indignities we suffered, what torments and abuses, in this land before memory? Our character was formed without our even knowing it. In my case, I grew up feeling edgy, afraid, anxious. This anxiety seemed to predate my existence and exist independently of me. But I suspect it originated in my relationship with my father, around whom I was never safe.

My father's unpredictable and arbitrary rages made any situation, no matter how benign, into a potential minefield. An innocuous remark or a dissenting voice would trigger his anger and set off a series of explosions from which there was no refuge. The house shook as he shouted, chasing me upstairs into my room. I'd dive and slide under the bed, against the wall. I'd breathe in the feathery air, praying the bricks would swallow me up and I would disappear. But his hand would grab hold of me, drag me out to meet my fate. The belt would be pulled off and whistle in the air before it struck, each successive blow knocking me sideways, burning my flesh. Then the whipping would be over, as abruptly as it had begun. I'd be tossed to the floor, landing in a crumpled heap. A rag doll discarded by an angry toddler.

I was never sure what I had done to trigger this anger, or if I deserved it. I asked my mother why my father was always so angry with me, and she gave a despairing shrug and said, "How should I know? Your father's completely mad."

When she said he was mad, she wasn't joking. If assessed by a psychiatrist today, my father would, I suspect, be diagnosed with a personality disorder — an illness that went untreated for the duration of his life. The result was a childhood and adolescence dominated by hysteria and physical violence: threats, tears, and breaking glass.

There were moments of happiness; usually when my father was away from home. I remember one winter he was in America on a business trip for a month. For thirty days, my mother and I had free rein of the house and garden without his watchful eye. It snowed heavily in London that December, and the whole of our garden was buried beneath a crisp thick white carpet. Mum and I made a snowman. Unconsciously or not, we built him to represent our absent master: I christened him Dad, and with his

31

big belly, two black stones for eyes, and two slanting twigs for stern eyebrows, the resemblance was uncanny. We completed the illusion by giving him my father's gloves, hat, and umbrella. Then we pelted him violently with snowballs, giggling like naughty children.

There was a heavy snowstorm that night. My mother went to bed and I pretended to sleep, then I snuck out to the garden and stood under the falling snow. I held my hands outstretched, catching snowflakes, watching them vanish on my fingertips. It felt joyous and frustrating and spoke to some truth I couldn't express; my vocabulary was too limited, my words too loose a net in which to catch it. Somehow grasping at vanishing snowflakes is like grasping at happiness: an act of possession that instantly gives way to nothing. It reminded me that there was a world outside this house: a world of vastness and unimaginable beauty; a world that, for now, remained out of my reach. That memory has repeatedly returned to me over the years. It's as if the misery that surrounded that brief moment of freedom made it burn even brighter: a tiny light surrounded by darkness.

My only hope of survival, I realized, was to retreat — physically as well as psychically. I had to get away, far away. Only then would I be safe. And eventually, at eighteen, I got the grades I needed to secure a place at university. I left that semi-detached prison in Surrey — and I thought I was free.

I was wrong.

I didn't know it then, but it was too late — I had internalized my father, introjected him, buried him deep in my unconscious. No matter how far I ran, I carried him with me wherever I went. I was pursued by an infernal, relentless chorus of furies, all with his voice — shrieking that I was worthless, shameful, a failure.

During my first term at university, that first cold winter, the voices got so bad, so paralyzing, they controlled me. Immobilized by fear, I was unable to go out, socialize, or make any friends. I might as well have never left home. It was hopeless. I was defeated, trapped. Backed into a corner. No way out.

Only one solution presented itself.

I went from chemist to chemist buying packets of paracetamol. I bought only a few packets at a time to avoid arousing suspicion — but I needn't have worried. No one paid me the least attention; I was clearly as invisible as I felt.

It was cold in my room, and my fingers were numb and clumsy as I tore open the packets. It took an immense effort to swallow all the tablets. But I forced them all down, pill after bitter pill. Then I crawled onto my uncomfortable narrow bed. I shut my eyes and waited for death.

But death didn't come.

Instead a searing, gut-wrenching pain tore through my insides. I doubled up and vomited, throwing up bile and half-digested pills all over myself. I lay in the dark, a fire burning in my stomach, for what seemed like eternity. And then, slowly, in the darkness, I realized something.

I didn't want to die. Not yet; not when I hadn't lived.

This gave me a kind of hope, however murky and ill defined. It propelled me at any rate to acknowledge that I couldn't do this alone: I needed help.

I found it — in the form of Ruth, a psychotherapist referred to me through the university counseling service. Ruth was white-haired and plump and had something grandmotherly about her. She had a sympathetic smile — a smile I wanted to believe in. She didn't say much at first. She just listened while I talked. I talked about my childhood, my home, my parents. As I talked, I found that no matter how distressing the details I related, I could feel nothing. I was disconnected from my emotions, like a hand severed from a wrist. I talked about painful memories and suicidal impulses — but couldn't feel them.

I would, however, occasionally look up at Ruth's face. To my surprise, tears would be collecting in her eyes as she listened. This may seem hard to grasp, but those tears were not hers.

They were mine.

At the time I didn't understand. But that's how therapy works. A patient delegates his unacceptable feelings to his therapist; and she holds everything he is afraid to feel, and she feels it for him. Then, ever so slowly, she feeds his feelings back to him. As Ruth fed mine back to me.

We continued seeing each other for several years, Ruth and I. She remained the one constant in my life. Through her, I internalized a new kind of relationship with another human being: one based on mutual respect, honesty, and kindness — not recrimination, anger, and violence. I slowly started to feel differently inside about myself — less empty, more capable of feeling, less afraid. The hateful internal chorus never entirely left me — but I now had Ruth's voice to counter it, and I paid less attention. As a result, the voices in my head grew quieter and would temporarily vanish. I'd feel peaceful — even happy, sometimes.

Psychotherapy had quite literally saved my life. More important, it had transformed the quality of that life. The talking cure was central to who I became — in a profound sense, it defined me.

It was, I knew, my vocation.

After university, I trained as a psychotherapist in London. Throughout my training, I continued seeing Ruth. She remained supportive and encouraging, although she warned me to be realistic about the path I was undertaking: "It's no walk in the park" was how she put it. She was right. Working with patients, getting my hands dirty — well, it proved far from comfortable.

I remember my first visit to a secure psychiatric unit. Within a few minutes of my arrival, a patient had pulled down his pants, squatted, and defecated in front of me. A stinking pile of shit. And subsequent incidents, less stomach-churning but just as dramatic — messy botched suicides, attempts at self-harm, uncontained hysteria and grief — all felt more than I could bear. But each time, somehow, I drew on hitherto untapped resilience. It got easier.

It's odd how quickly one adapts to the strange new world of a psychiatric unit. You become increasingly comfortable with madness — and not just the madness of others, but your own. We're all crazy, I believe, just in different ways.

Which is why — and how — I related to Alicia Berenson. I was one of the lucky ones. Thanks to a successful therapeutic intervention at a young age, I was able to pull back from the brink of psychic darkness. In my mind, however, the other narrative remained forever a possibility: I might have gone crazy — and ended my days locked in an institution, like Alicia. There but for the grace of God . . .

I couldn't say any of this to Indira Sharma when she asked why I became a psychotherapist. It was an interview panel, after all — and if nothing else, I knew how to play the game.

"In the end," I said, "I believe the training makes you into a psychotherapist. Regardless of your initial intentions."

Indira nodded sagely. "Yes, quite right. Very true."

The interview went well. My experience of working at Broadmoor gave me an edge, Indira said — demonstrating I could cope with extreme psychological distress. I was offered the job on the spot, and I accepted.

One month later, I was on my way to the Grove.

CHAPTER FOUR

I arrived at the Grove pursued by an icy January wind. The bare trees stood like skeletons along the road. The sky was white, heavy with snow that had yet to fall.

I stood outside the entrance and reached for my cigarettes in my pocket. I hadn't smoked in over a week — I'd promised myself that this time I meant it, I'd quit for good. Yet here I was, already giving in. I lit one, feeling annoyed with myself. Psychotherapists tend to view smoking as an unresolved addiction — one that any decent therapist should have worked through and overcome. I didn't want to walk in reeking of cigarettes, so I popped a couple of mints into my mouth and chewed them while I smoked, hopping from foot to foot.

I was shivering — but if I'm honest, it was more with nerves than cold. I was having doubts. My consultant at Broadmoor had made no bones about saying I was making a mistake. He hinted a promising career was being cut short by my departure, and he was sniffy about the Grove, and Professor Diomedes in particular.

"An unorthodox man. Does a lot of work with group relations — worked with Foulkes for a while. Ran some kind of alternative therapeutic community in the eighties in Hertfordshire. Not economically viable, those models of therapy, especially today . . ." He hesitated a second, then went on in a lower voice, "I'm not trying to scare you, Theo. But I've heard rumblings about that place getting axed. You could find yourself out of a job in six months. . . . Are you sure you won't reconsider?"

I hesitated, but only out of politeness. "Quite sure."

He shook his head. "Seems like career suicide to me. But if you've made your decision . . ."

I didn't tell him about Alicia Berenson, about my desire to treat her. I could have put it in terms he might understand: working with her might lead to a book or publication of some kind. But I knew there was little point; he'd still say I was making a mistake. Perhaps he was right. I was about to find out.

I stubbed out my cigarette, banished my

nerves, and went inside.

The Grove was located in the oldest part of Edgware hospital. The original redbrick Victorian building had long since been surrounded and dwarfed by larger, and generally uglier, additions and extensions. The Grove lay in the heart of this complex. The only hint of its dangerous occupants was the line of security cameras perched on the fences like watching birds of prey. In reception, every effort had been made to make it appear friendly — large blue couches, crude, childish artwork by the patients taped to the walls. It looked to me more like a kindergarten than a secure psychiatric unit.

A tall man appeared at my side. He grinned at me and held out his hand. He introduced himself as Yuri, head psychiatric nurse. "Welcome to the Grove. Not much of a welcoming committee, I'm afraid. Just me."

Yuri was good-looking, well built, and in his late thirties. He had dark hair and a tribal tattoo creeping up his neck, above his collar. He smelled of tobacco and too much sweet aftershave.

Although he spoke with an accent, his English was perfect. "I moved here from Latvia seven years ago, and I didn't speak a word of English when I arrived. But in a year I was fluent."

"That's very impressive."

"Not really. English is an easy language. You should try Latvian."

He laughed and reached for the jangling chain of keys around his belt. He pulled off a set and handed it to me. "You'll need these for the individual rooms. And there are codes you need to know for the wards."

"That's a lot. I had fewer keys at Broadmoor."

"Yeah, well. We stepped up security quite a bit recently — since Stephanie joined us."

"Who's Stephanie?"

Yuri didn't reply, but nodded at the woman emerging from the office behind the reception desk.

She was Caribbean, in her midforties, with a sharp, angular bob. "I'm Stephanie Clarke. Manager of the Grove."

Stephanie gave me an unconvincing smile. As I shook her hand, I noticed her grip was firmer and tighter than Yuri's, and rather less welcoming.

"As manager of this unit, safety is my top priority. Both the safety of the patients, and of the staff. If you aren't safe, then neither are your patients." She handed me a small device — a personal attack alarm. "Carry

42

this with you at all times. Don't just leave it in your office."

I resisted the inclination to say, *Yes, ma'am.* Better keep on the right side of her if I wanted an easy life. That had been my tactic with previous bossy ward managers — avoid confrontation and keep under their radar.

"Good to meet you, Stephanie." I smiled.

Stephanie nodded but didn't smile back. "Yuri will show you to your office." She turned and marched off without a second glance.

"Follow me," Yuri said.

I went with him to the ward entrance — a large reinforced steel door. Next to it, a metal detector was manned by a security guard.

"I'm sure you know the drill," Yuri said. "No sharp objects — nothing that could be used as a weapon."

"No lighters," added the security guard as he frisked me, fishing my lighter from my pocket with an accusing look.

"Sorry. I forgot I had it."

Yuri beckoned me to follow him. "I'll show you to your office. Everyone's in the Community meeting, so it's pretty quiet."

"Can I join them?"

"In Community?" Yuri looked surprised.

"You don't want to settle in first?"

"I can settle in later. If it's all the same to you?"

He shrugged. "Whatever you want. This way."

He led me down interconnecting corridors punctuated by locked doors — a rhythm of slams and bolts and keys turning in locks. We made slow progress.

It was obvious not much had been spent on the upkeep of the building in several years: paint was crawling away from the walls, and a faint musty smell of mildew and decay permeated the corridors.

Yuri stopped outside a closed door and nodded. "They're in there. Go ahead."

"Okay, thanks."

I hesitated, preparing myself. Then I opened the door and went inside.

44

CHAPTER FIVE

Community was held in a long room with tall barred windows that overlooked a red-brick wall. The smell of coffee was in the air, mingled with traces of Yuri's aftershave. About thirty people were sitting in a circle. Most were clutching paper cups of tea or coffee, yawning and doing their best to wake up. Some, having drunk their coffees, were fidgeting with the empty cups, crumpling, flattening them, or tearing them to shreds.

Community met once or twice daily; it was something between an administrative meeting and a group therapy session. Items relating to the running of the unit or the patients' care were put on the agenda to be discussed. It was, Professor Diomedes was fond of saying, an attempt to involve the patients in their own treatment and encourage them to take responsibility for their well-being, although this attempt didn't always work. Diomedes's background in group therapy meant he had a fondness for meetings of all kinds, and he encouraged as much group work as possible. You might say he was happiest with an audience. He had the faint air of a theatrical impresario, I thought, as he rose to his feet to greet me, hands outstretched in welcome, and beckoned me over.

"Theo. There you are. Join us, join us."

He spoke with a slight Greek accent, barely detectable — he'd mostly lost it, having lived in England for over thirty years. He was handsome, and although in his sixties, he looked much younger — he had a youthful, mischievous manner, more like an irreverent uncle than a psychiatrist. This isn't to say he wasn't devoted to the patients in his care — he arrived before the cleaners did in the morning and stayed long after the night team had taken over from the day staff, sometimes spending the night on the couch in his office. Twice divorced, Diomedes was fond of saying his third and most successful marriage was to the Grove.

"Sit down here." He gestured to an empty chair by his side. "Sit, sit, sit."

I did as he asked.

Diomedes presented me with a flourish. "Allow me to introduce our new psychotherapist, Theo Faber. I hope you will join

46

me in welcoming Theo to our little family
—"

While Diomedes spoke, I glanced around
the circle, looking for Alicia. But couldn't
see her anywhere. Apart from Professor
Diomedes, impeccably dressed in suit and
tie, the others were mostly in short-sleeved
shirts or T-shirts. It was hard to tell who
was a patient and who was a member of
staff.

A couple of faces were familiar to me —
Christian, for instance. I had known him at
Broadmoor. A rugby-playing psychiatrist
with a broken nose and a dark beard. Good-
looking in a bashed-up kind of way. He'd
left Broadmoor soon after I arrived. I didn't
like Christian much, but to be fair I hadn't
known him well, as we didn't work together
for long.

I remembered Indira, from the interview.
She smiled at me, and I was grateful, for
hers was the only friendly face. The patients
mostly glared at me with surly mistrust. I
didn't blame them. The abuses they had suffered — physical, psychological, sexual —
meant it would be a long time before they
could trust me, if ever. The patients were all
women — and most had coarse features,
lined, scarred. They'd had difficult lives, suf-
fering from horrors that had driven them to

retreat into the no-man's-land of mental illness; their journeys were etched into their faces, impossible to miss.

But Alicia Berenson? Where was she? I looked around the circle again but still couldn't find her. Then I realized — I was looking right at her. Alicia was sitting directly opposite me, across the circle.

I hadn't seen her because she was invisible.

Alicia was slumped forward in the chair. She was obviously highly sedated. She was holding a paper cup, full of tea, and her trembling hand was spilling a steady stream of it onto the floor. I restrained myself from going over and straightening her cup. She was so out of it I doubt she'd have noticed if I had.

I hadn't expected her to be in such bad shape. There were some echoes of the beautiful woman she had once been: deep blue eyes; a face of perfect symmetry. But she was too thin and looked unclean. Her long red hair was hanging in a dirty, tangled mess around her shoulders. Her fingernails were chewed and torn. Faded scars were visible on both her wrists — the same scars I'd seen faithfully rendered in the *Alcestis* portrait. Her fingers didn't stop trembling, doubtless a side effect of the drug cocktail she was on — risperidone and other heavy-weight antipsychotics. And glistening saliva was collecting around her open mouth, uncontrollable drooling being another unfortunate side effect of the medication.

I noticed Diomedes looking at me. I pulled my attention away from Alicia and focused on him.

"I'm sure you can introduce yourself better than I can, Theo," he said. "Won't you say a few words?"

"Thank you." I nodded. "I don't really have anything to add. Just that I'm very happy to be here. Excited, nervous, hopeful. And I'm looking forward to getting to know everyone — particularly the patients. I —"

I was interrupted by a sudden bang as the door was thrown open. At first I thought I was seeing things. A giant charged into the room, holding two jagged wooden spikes, which she raised high above her head and then threw at us like spears. One of the patients covered her eyes and screamed.

I half expected the spears to impale us, but they landed with some force on the floor in the middle of the circle. Then I saw they weren't spears at all. It was a pool cue, snapped in two.

The massive patient, a dark-haired Turkish woman in her forties, shouted, "Pisses me off. Pool cue's been broke a week and you still ain't fucking replaced it."

"Watch your language, Elif," said Diomedes. "I'm not prepared to discuss the matter of the pool cue until we decide whether it's appropriate to allow you to join Community at such a late juncture." He turned his head slyly and threw the question at me. "What do you think, Theo?"

I blinked and took a second to find my voice. "I think it's important to respect time boundaries and arrive on time for Community —"

"Like you did, you mean?" said a man across the circle.

I turned and saw it was Christian who had spoken. He laughed, amused by his own joke.

I forced a smile and turned back to Elif. "He's quite right, I was also late this morning. So maybe it's a lesson we can learn together."

"What you on about?" Elif said. "Who the fuck are you anyway?"

"Elif. Mind your language," said Diomedes. "Don't make me put you on time-out. Sit down."

Elif remained standing. "And what about the pool cue?"

The question was addressed to Diomedes — and he looked at me, waiting for me to answer it.

"Elif, I can see you're angry about the pool cue," I said. "I suspect whoever broke it was also angry. It raises the question of what we do with anger in an institution like this. How about we stick with that and talk about anger for a moment? Won't you sit down?"

Elif rolled her eyes. But she sat down.

Indira nodded, looking pleased. We started talking about anger, Indira and I, trying to draw the patients into a discussion about their angry feelings. We worked well together, I thought. I could sense Diomedes watching, evaluating my performance. He seemed satisfied.

I glanced at Alicia. And to my surprise, she was looking at me — or at least in my direction. There was a dim fogginess in her expression — as if it was a struggle to focus her eyes and see.

If you told me this broken shell had once been the brilliant Alicia Berenson, described by those who knew her as dazzling, fascinating, full of life — I simply wouldn't have believed you. I knew then and there I'd made the right decision in coming to the Grove. All my doubts vanished. I became resolved to stop at nothing until Alicia became my patient.

There was no time to waste: Alicia was lost. She was missing.

And I intended to find her.

CHAPTER SIX

Professor Diomedes's office was in the oldest and most decrepit part of the hospital. There were cobwebs in the corners, and only a couple of the lights in the corridor were working. I knocked at the door, and after a moment's pause I heard his voice from inside.

"Come in."

I turned the handle and the door creaked open. I was immediately struck by the smell inside the room. It smelled different from the rest of the hospital. It didn't smell like antiseptic or bleach; rather bizarrely, it smelled like an orchestra pit. It smelled of wood, strings and bows, polish, and wax. It took a moment for my eyes to become accustomed to the gloom, then I noticed the upright piano against the wall, an incongruous object in a hospital. Twenty-odd metallic music stands gleamed in the shadows, and a stack of sheet music was piled high on a table, an unsteady paper tower reaching for the sky. A violin was on another table, next to an oboe, and a flute. And beside it, a harp — a huge thing with a beautiful wooden frame and a shower of strings.

I stared at it all openmouthed.

Diomedes laughed. "You're wondering about the instruments?" He sat behind his desk, chuckling.

"Are they yours?"

"They are. Music is my hobby. No, I lie — it is my passion." He pointed his finger in the air dramatically. The professor had an animated way of speaking, employing a wide range of hand gestures to accompany and underscore his speech — as if he were conducting an invisible orchestra. "I run an informal musical group, open to whoever wishes to join — staff and patients alike. I find music to be a most effective therapeutic tool." He paused to recite in a lilting, musical tone, " 'Music hath charms to soothe a savage breast.' Do you agree?"

"I'm sure you're right."

"Hmm." Diomedes peered at me for a moment. "Do you play?"

"Play what?"

"Anything. A triangle is a start."

I shook my head. "I'm not very musical. I

played the recorder a bit at school when I was young. That was about it."

"Then you can read music? That is an advantage. Good. Choose any instrument. I will teach you."

I smiled and again shook my head. "I'm afraid I'm not patient enough."

"No? Well, patience is a virtue you would do well to cultivate as a psychotherapist. You know, in my youth, I was undecided whether I should be a musician, a priest, or a doctor." Diomedes laughed. "And now I am all three."

"I suppose that's true."

"You know" — he switched subjects without even a hint of a pause — "I was the deciding voice at your interview. The casting vote, so to speak. I spoke strongly in your favor. You know why? I'll tell you — I saw something in you, Theo. You remind me of myself. . . . Who knows? In a few years, you might be running this place." He left the sentence dangling for a moment, then sighed. "If it's still here, of course."

"You think it won't be?"

"Who knows? Too few patients, too many staff. We are working in close cooperation with the Trust to see if a more 'economically viable' model can be found. Which means we are being endlessly watched,

55

evaluated — spied upon. How can we possibly do therapeutic work under such conditions? you might well ask. As Winnicott said, you can't practice therapy in a burning building." Diomedes shook his head and looked his age suddenly — exhausted and weary. He lowered his voice and spoke in a conspiratorial whisper. "I believe the manager, Stephanie Clarke, is in league with them. The Trust pays her salary, after all. Watch her, and you'll see what I mean."

I thought Diomedes was sounding a little paranoid, but perhaps that was understandable. I didn't want to say the wrong thing, so I remained diplomatically silent for a moment. And then —

"I want to ask you something. About Alicia."

"Alicia Berenson?" Diomedes gave me a strange look. "What about her?"

"I'm curious what kind of therapeutic work is being done with her. Is she in individual therapy?"

"No."

"Is there a reason?"

"It was tried — and abandoned."

"Why was that? Who saw her? Indira?"

"No." Diomedes shook his head. "I saw Alicia myself, as a matter of fact."

"I see. What happened?"

56

He shrugged. "She refused to visit me in my office, so I went to see her in her room. During the sessions, she simply sat on her bed and stared out of the window. She refused to speak, of course. She refused to even look at me." He threw up his hands, exasperated. "I decided the whole thing was a waste of time."

I nodded. "I suppose . . . well, I'm wondering about the transference. . . ."

"Yes?" Diomedes peered at me with curiosity. "Go on."

"It's possible, isn't it, that she experienced you as an authoritarian presence . . . perhaps — potentially punitive? I don't know what her relationship with her father was like, but . . ."

Diomedes listened with a small smile, as if he were being told a joke and anticipating the punch line. "But you think she might find it easier to relate to someone younger? Let me guess. . . . Someone like you? You think you can help her, Theo? You can rescue Alicia? Make her talk?"

"I don't know about rescuing her, but I'd like to help her. I'd like to try."

Diomedes smiled, still with the same sense of amusement. "You are not the first. I believed I would succeed. Alicia is a silent siren, my boy, luring us to the rocks, where

we dash our therapeutic ambition to pieces."
He smiled again. "She taught me a valuable
lesson in failure. Perhaps you need to learn
the same lesson."

I met his gaze defiantly. "Unless, of course,
I succeed."

Diomedes's smile vanished, replaced by
something harder to read. He remained
silent for a moment, then made a decision.

"We'll see, shall we? First, you must meet
Alicia. You've not been introduced to her
yet, have you?"

"Not yet, no."

"Then ask Yuri to arrange it, will you?
Report back to me afterward."

"Good." I tried to conceal my excitement.
"I will."

CHAPTER SEVEN

The therapy room was a small, narrow rectangle; as bare as a prison cell, or barer. The window was closed and barred. A bright pink box of tissues on the small table struck a discordantly cheerful note — presumably it was placed there by Indira: I couldn't imagine Christian offering tissues to his patients.

I sat on one of two battered, faded armchairs. The minutes passed. No sign of Alicia. Perhaps she wasn't coming? Perhaps she had refused to meet me. She would be perfectly within her rights.

Impatient, anxious, nervous, I abandoned sitting and jumped up and walked to the window. I peered out between the bars.

The courtyard was three stories below me. The size of a tennis court, it was surrounded by tall redbrick walls, walls that were too high to climb, though doubtless some had tried. Patients were herded outside for thirty minutes of fresh air every afternoon, whether they wanted it or not, and in this freezing weather I didn't blame them for resisting. Some stood alone, muttering to themselves, or they paced back and forth, like restless zombies, going nowhere. Others huddled in groups, talking, smoking, arguing. Voices and shouts and strange excitable laughter floated up to me.

I couldn't see Alicia at first. Then I located her. She was standing alone at the far end of the courtyard, by the wall. Perfectly still, like a statue. Yuri walked across the courtyard toward her. He spoke to the nurse standing a few feet away. The nurse nodded. Yuri went up to Alicia cautiously, slowly, as you might approach an unpredictable animal.

I had asked him not to go into too much detail, merely to tell Alicia the new psychotherapist at the unit would like to meet her. I requested he phrase it as a request, not a demand. Alicia stood still as he spoke to her. But she neither nodded nor shook her head nor gave any indication of having heard him. After a brief pause, Yuri turned and walked off.

Well, that's it, I thought — she won't come. Fuck it, I should have known. The whole thing has been a waste of time.

60

Then, to my surprise, Alicia took a step forward. Faltering a little, she shuffled after Yuri across the courtyard — until they disappeared from view under my window.

So she was coming. I tried to contain my nerves and prepare myself. I tried to silence the negative voice in my head — my father's voice — telling me I wasn't up to the job, I was useless, a fraud. Shut up, I thought, shut up, shut up —

A couple of minutes later, there was a knock at the door.

"Come in."

The door opened. Alicia was standing with Yuri in the corridor. I looked at her. But she didn't look at me; her gaze remained downcast.

Yuri gave me a proud smile. "She's here."

"Yes. I can see that. Hello, Alicia."

She didn't respond.

"Won't you come in?"

Yuri leaned forward as if to nudge her, but he didn't actually touch her. Instead he whispered, "Go on, honey. Go in and take a seat."

Alicia hesitated. She glanced at him, then made a decision. She walked into the room, slightly unsteadily. She sat on a chair, silent as a cat, her trembling hands in her lap.

I was about to shut the door, but Yuri

didn't leave. I lowered my voice. "I can take it from here, thanks."

Yuri looked worried. "But she's on one-on-one. And the professor said —"

"I'll take full responsibility. It's quite all right." I took my personal attack alarm out of my pocket. "See, I have this — but I won't need it."

I glanced at Alicia. She gave no indication she had even heard me.

Yuri shrugged, obviously unhappy. "I'll be on the other side of the door, just in case you need me."

"That's not necessary, but thanks."

Yuri left, and I closed the door. I placed the alarm on the desk. I sat opposite Alicia. She didn't look up. I studied her for a moment. Her face was expressionless, blank. A medicated mask. I wondered what lay beneath.

"I'm glad you agreed to see me." I waited for a response. I knew there wouldn't be one. "I have the advantage of knowing more about you than you do about me. Your reputation precedes you — your reputation as a painter, I mean. I'm a fan of your work." No reaction. I shifted in my seat slightly. "I asked Professor Diomedes if we might talk, and he kindly arranged this meeting. Thank you for agreeing to it."

I hesitated, hoping for an acknowledgment of some kind — a blink, a nod, a frown. Nothing came. I tried to guess what she was thinking. Perhaps she was too drugged up to think anything at all.

I thought of my old therapist, Ruth. What she would do? She used to say we are made up of different parts, some good, some bad, and that a healthy mind can tolerate this ambivalence and juggle both good and bad at the same time. Mental illness is precisely about a lack of this kind of integration — we end up losing contact with the unacceptable parts of ourselves. If I was to help Alicia, we would have to locate the parts she had hidden from herself, beyond the fringes of consciousness, and connect the various dots in her mental landscape. Only then could we put into context the terrible events of that night she killed her husband. It would be a slow, laborious process.

Normally when beginning with a patient, there is no sense of urgency, no predetermined therapeutic agenda. Normally we start with many months of talking. In an ideal world, Alicia would tell me about herself, her life, her childhood. I would listen, slowly building up a picture until it was complete enough for me to make accurate, helpful interpretations. In this case, there would be no talking. No listening. The information I needed would have to be gathered through nonverbal clues, such as my countertransference — the feelings Alicia engendered in me during the sessions — and whatever information I could gather from other sources.

In other words, I had set into motion a plan to help Alicia without actually knowing how to execute it. Now I had to deliver, not just to prove myself to Diomedes, but, far more important, to do my duty to Alicia: to help her.

Looking at her sitting opposite me, in a medicated haze, drool collecting around her mouth, fingers fluttering like dirty moths, I experienced a sudden and unexpected wrench of sadness. I felt desperately sorry for her, and those like her — for all of us, all the wounded and the lost.

Of course, I said none of this to her. Instead I did what Ruth would have done.

And we simply sat in silence.

CHAPTER EIGHT

I opened Alicia's file on my desk. Diomedes had volunteered it: "You must read my notes. They will help you."

I had no desire to wade through his notes; I already knew what Diomedes thought; I needed to find out what I thought. But nonetheless I accepted it politely.

"Thank you. That will be such a help."

My office was small and sparsely furnished, tucked away at the back of the building, by the fire escape. I looked out the window. A little black bird was pecking at a patch of frozen grass on the ground outside, dispiritedly and without much hope.

I shivered. The room was freezing. The small radiator under the window was broken — Yuri said he'd try to get it fixed, but that my best bet was to talk to Stephanie or, failing that, bring it up in Community. I felt a sudden pang of empathy with Elif and her battle to get the broken pool cue replaced.

I looked through Alicia's file without much expectation. The majority of the information I needed was in the online database. Diomedes, however, like a lot of older staff members, preferred to write his reports by hand and (ignoring Stephanie's nagging requests to the contrary) continued to do so — hence the dog-eared file in front of me.

I flicked through Diomedes's notes, ignoring his somewhat old-fashioned psychoanalytic interpretations, and focused on the nurses' handover reports of Alicia's day-to-day behavior. I read through those reports carefully. I wanted facts, figures, details — I needed to know exactly what I was getting into, what I'd have to deal with, and if any surprises were in store.

The file revealed little. When she was first admitted, Alicia slashed her wrists twice and self-harmed with whatever she could get her hands on. She was kept on two-on-one observation for the first six months — meaning two nurses watched over her at all times — which was eventually relaxed to one-on-one. Alicia made no effort to interact with patients or staff, remaining withdrawn and isolated, and for the most part, the other patients had left her alone. If people don't reply when you speak to them and never initiate conversation, you soon forget they're there. Alicia had quickly melted into the background, becoming invisible.

Only one incident stood out. It took place in the canteen, a few weeks after Alicia's admission. Elif accused Alicia of taking her seat. What exactly had happened was unclear, but the confrontation escalated rapidly. Apparently Alicia became violent — she smashed a plate and tried to slash Elif's throat with the jagged edge. Alicia had to be restrained, sedated, and placed in isolation.

I wasn't sure why this incident drew my attention. But it didn't feel right to me. I decided to approach Elif and ask her about it.

I tore off a sheet of paper from a pad and reached for my pen. An old habit, formed at university — something about putting pen to paper helps me organize my mind. I've always had difficulty formulating an opinion until I've written it down.

I began scribbling ideas, notes, goals — devising a plan of attack. To help Alicia, I needed to understand her, and her relationship with Gabriel. Did she love him? Hate him? Why had she refused to speak about the murder — or anything else? No answers, not yet — just questions.

I wrote down a word and underlined it: <u>ALCESTIS</u>.

The self-portrait — it was important, somehow, I knew that, and understanding why would be central to unlocking this mystery. This painting was Alicia's sole communication, her only testimony. It was saying something I had yet to comprehend. I made a note to revisit the gallery to look at the painting again.

I wrote down another word: <u>CHILD-HOOD</u>. If I was to make sense of Gabriel's murder, I needed to understand not only the events of the night Alicia killed him, but also the events of the distant past. The seeds of what happened in those few minutes when she shot her husband were probably sown years earlier. Murderous rage, homicidal rage, is not born in the present. It originates in the land before memory, in the world of early childhood, with abuse and mistreatment, which builds up a charge over the years, until it explodes — often at the wrong target. I needed to find out how her childhood had shaped her, and if Alicia couldn't or wouldn't tell me, I had to find someone who would. Someone who knew Alicia before the murder, who could help me understand her history, who she was, and how she ended up this way.

In the file, Alicia's next of kin was listed as her aunt — Lydia Rose — who brought her up, following the death of Alicia's mother in a car accident. Alicia had also been in the car crash, but survived. That trauma must have affected the little girl profoundly. I hoped Lydia would be able to tell me about it.

The only other contact was Alicia's lawyer: Max Berenson. Max was Gabriel Berenson's brother. He was perfectly placed to observe their marriage intimately. Whether Max Berenson would confide in me was another matter. An unsolicited approach to Alicia's family by her psychotherapist was unorthodox to say the least. I had a dim feeling Diomedes would not approve. Better not ask his permission, I decided, in case he refused.

As I look back, this was my first professional transgression in dealing with Alicia — setting an unfortunate precedent for what followed. I should have stopped there. But even then it was too late to stop. In many ways my fate was already decided — like in a Greek tragedy.

I reached for the phone. I called Max Berenson at his office, using the contact number listed in Alicia's file. It rang several times before it was answered.

"The offices of Elliot, Barrow, and Berenson," said a receptionist with a bad cold.

"Mr. Berenson, please."

"May I ask who is calling?"

"My name is Theo Faber. I'm a psychotherapist at the Grove. I was wondering if it might be possible to have a word with Mr. Berenson about his sister-in-law."

There was a slight pause before she responded. "Oh. I see. Well, Mr. Berenson is out of the office for the rest of the week. He's in Edinburgh visiting a client. If you leave your number, I'll have him call you on his return."

I gave her my number and hung up.

I dialed the next number in the file — Alicia's aunt, Lydia Rose.

It was answered on the first ring. An elderly woman's voice sounded breathless and rather annoyed. "Yes? What is it?"

"Is that Mrs. Rose?"

"Who are you?"

"I'm calling regarding your niece, Alicia Berenson. I'm a psychotherapist working at the —"

"Fuck off." She hung up.

I frowned to myself.

Not a good start.

CHAPTER NINE

I desperately needed a cigarette. As I left the Grove, I looked for them in my coat pockets, but they weren't there.

"Looking for something?"

I turned around. Yuri was standing right behind me. I hadn't heard him and I was a little startled to find him so close.

"I found them in the nurses' station." He grinned, handing me my pack of cigarettes. "Must have fallen out of your pocket."

"Thanks." I took them and lit one. I offered him the packet.

Yuri shook his head. "I don't smoke. Not cigarettes, anyway." He laughed. "You look like you need a drink. Come on, I'll buy you a pint."

I hesitated. My instinct was to refuse — I had never been one for socializing with work colleagues. And I doubted Yuri and I had much in common. But he probably knew Alicia better than anyone else at the Grove

— and his insights might prove useful.

"Sure," I said. "Why not?"

We went to a pub near the station, the Slaughtered Lamb. Dark and dingy, it had seen better days; so had the old men dozing over their half-finished pints. Yuri got us a couple of beers, and we sat at a table at the back.

Yuri took a long swig of beer and wiped his mouth. "Well? Tell me about Alicia."

"Alicia?"

"How did you find her?"

"I'm not sure I did find her."

Yuri gave me a quizzical look, then smiled. "She doesn't want to be found? Yeah, it's true. She's hiding."

"You're close to her. I can see that."

"I take special care of her. No one knows her like I do, not even Professor Diomedes."

His voice had a boastful note. It annoyed me for some reason — I wondered how well he really knew her, or if he was just bragging.

"What do you make of her silence? What do you think it means?"

Yuri shrugged. "I guess it means she's not ready to talk. She'll talk when she's ready."

"Ready for what?"

"Ready for the truth, my friend."

"And what is that?"

72

Yuri cocked his head to one side slightly, studying me. The question that came out of his mouth surprised me.

"Are you married, Theo?"

I nodded. "I am, yes."

"Yeah, I thought so. I was married once too. We moved here from Latvia. But she didn't fit in like I did. She didn't make an effort, you know, she didn't learn English. Anyway, it wasn't . . . I wasn't happy — but I was in denial, lying to myself . . ." He drained his drink and completed his sentence. "Until I fell in love."

"Presumably you don't mean with your wife?"

Yuri laughed and shook his head. "No. A woman who lived near me. A very beautiful woman. It was love at first sight. I saw her on the street. It took me a long time to get the courage to talk to her. I used to follow her. . . . I'd watch her sometimes, without her knowing. I'd stand outside her house and look, hoping she would appear at the window." He laughed.

This story was starting to make me feel uncomfortable. I finished my beer and glanced at my watch, hoping Yuri would take the hint, but he didn't.

"One day I tried speaking to her. But she wasn't interested in me. I tried a few times,

73

but she told me to stop pestering her."

I didn't blame her, I thought. I was about to make my excuses, but Yuri kept talking.

"It was very hard to accept. I was sure we were meant to be together. She broke my heart. I got very angry with her. Very mad."

"And what happened?" I was curious despite myself.

"Nothing."

"Nothing? You stayed with your wife?"

Yuri shook his head. "No. It was over with her. But it took falling for this woman for me to admit it . . . to face the truth about me and my wife. Sometimes it takes courage, you know, and a long time, to be honest."

"I see. And you think Alicia's not ready to face the truth about her marriage? Is that what you're saying? You may well be right."

Yuri shrugged. "And now I'm engaged to a nice girl from Hungary. She works in a spa. She speaks good English. We're a good match. We have a good time."

I nodded and checked my watch again. I picked up my coat. "I have to go. I'm late to meet my wife."

"Okay, no problem . . . What's her name? Your wife?"

For some reason, I didn't want to tell him. I didn't want Yuri to know anything about her. But that was stupid.

"Kathryn. Her name is Kathryn. But I call her Kathy."

Yuri gave me an odd smile. "Let me give you some advice. Go home to your wife. Go home to Kathy, who loves you. . . . And leave Alicia behind."

CHAPTER TEN

I went to meet Kathy at the National Theatre café on the South Bank, where the performers would often congregate after rehearsal. She was sitting at the back of the café with a couple of fellow actresses, deep in conversation. They looked up at me as I approached.

"Are your ears burning, darling?" Kathy said as she kissed me.

"Should they be?"

"I'm telling the girls all about you."

"Ah. Should I leave?"

"Don't be silly. Sit down — it's perfect timing. I've just got to how we met."

I sat down, and Kathy continued her story. It was a story she enjoyed telling. She occasionally glanced in my direction and smiled, as if to include me — but the gesture was perfunctory, for this was her tale, not mine.

"I was sitting at a bar when he finally

showed up. At last, when I'd given up hope of ever finding him — in he walked, the man of my dreams. Better late than never. I thought I was going to be married by the time I was twenty-five, you know? By thirty, I was going to have two kids, small dog, big mortgage. But here I was, thirty-three-ish, and things hadn't quite gone to plan." Kathy said this with an arch smile and winked at the girls.

"Anyway I was seeing this Australian guy called Daniel. But he didn't want to get married or have kids anytime soon, so I knew I was wasting my time. And we were out one night when suddenly it happened — Mr. Right walked in." Kathy looked at me and smiled and rolled her eyes. "With his *girlfriend*."

This part of the story needed careful handling to retain her audience's sympathy. Kathy and I were both dating other people when we met. Double infidelity isn't the most attractive or auspicious start to a relationship, particularly as we were introduced to each other by our then partners. They knew each other for some reason, I can't remember the precise details — Marianne had once gone out with Daniel's flatmate possibly, or the other way around. I don't remember exactly how we were introduced, but I do remember the first moment I saw Kathy. It was like an electric shock. I remember her long black hair, piercing green eyes, her mouth — she was beautiful, exquisite. An angel.

At this point in telling the tale, Kathy paused and smiled and reached for my hand. "Remember, Theo? How we got talking? You said you were training to be a shrink. And I said I was nuts — so it was a match made in heaven."

This got a big laugh from the girls. Kathy laughed too and glanced at me sincerely, anxiously, her eyes searching mine. "No, but . . . darling . . . seriously, it was love at first sight. Wasn't it?"

This was my cue. I nodded and kissed her cheek. "Of course it was. True love."

This received a look of approval from her friends. But I wasn't performing. She was right, it was love at first sight — well, lust anyway. Even though I was with Marianne that night, I couldn't keep my eyes off Kathy. I watched her from a distance, talking animatedly to Daniel — and then I saw her lips mouth, *Fuck you.* They were arguing. It looked heated. Daniel turned and walked out.

"You're being quiet," Marianne said. "What's wrong?"

"Nothing."

"Let's go home, then. I'm tired."

"Not yet." I was only half listening. "Let's have another drink."

"I want to go now."

"Then go."

Marianne shot me a hurt look, then grabbed her jacket and walked out. I knew there'd be a row the next day, but I didn't care.

I made my way over to Kathy at the bar. "Is Daniel coming back?"

"No. How about Marianne?"

I shook my head. "No. Would you like another drink?"

"Yes, I would."

So we ordered two more drinks. We stood at the bar, talking. We discussed my psycho-therapy training, I remember. And Kathy told me about her stint at drama school — she didn't stay long, as she signed up with an agent at the end of her first year and had been acting professionally ever since. I imagined, without knowing why, that she was probably rather a good actress.

"Studying wasn't for me," she said. "I wanted to get out there and do it — you know?"

"Do what? Act?"

"No. Live." Kathy tilted her head, looking

out from under her dark lashes, her emerald-green eyes peering at me mischievously. "So, Theo. How do you have the patience to keep doing it — studying, I mean?"

"Maybe I don't want to get out there and 'live.' Maybe I'm a coward."

"No. If you were a coward, you'd have gone home with your girlfriend." Kathy laughed, a surprisingly wicked laugh.

I wanted to grab her and kiss her hard. I'd never experienced such overwhelming physical desire before; I wanted to pull her close, feel her lips and the heat of her body against mine.

"I'm sorry," she said. "I shouldn't have said that. I always say whatever pops into my head. I told you, I'm a bit nuts."

Kathy did that a lot, protesting her insanity — "I'm crazy," "I'm nuts," "I'm insane" — but I never believed her. She laughed too easily and too often for me to believe she'd ever suffered the kind of darkness I had experienced. She had a spontaneity, a lightness — she took a delight in living and was endlessly amused by life. Despite her protestations, she seemed the least crazy person I'd ever known. Around her, I felt more sane.

Kathy was American. She was born and

brought up on the Upper West Side of Manhattan. Her English mother gave Kathy dual citizenship, but Kathy didn't seem even remotely English. She was determinedly, distinctly un-English — not just in the way she spoke, but in the way she saw the world and how she approached it. Such confidence, such exuberance. I'd never met anyone like her.

We left the bar, hailed a cab; I gave the address of my flat. We rode the short journey in silence. When we arrived, she gently pressed her lips to mine. I broke through my reserve and pulled her toward me. We kept kissing as I fumbled with the key to the front door. We were scarcely inside before we were undressing, stumbling into the bedroom, falling onto the bed.

That night was the most erotic, blissful night of my life. I spent hours exploring Kathy's body. We made love all night, until dawn. I remember so much white everywhere: white sunlight creeping around the edges of the curtains, white walls, white bedsheets; the whites of her eyes, her teeth, her skin. I'd never known that skin could be so luminous, so translucent: ivory white with occasional blue veins visible just beneath the surface, like threads of color in white marble. She was a statue; a Greek goddess come to life in my hands.

We lay there wrapped in each other's arms. Kathy was facing me, her eyes so close they were out of focus. I gazed into a hazy green sea. "Well?" she said.

"Well?"

"What about Marianne?"

"Marianne?"

A flicker of a smile. "Your girlfriend."

"Oh, yes. Yes." I hesitated, unsure. "I don't know about Marianne. And Daniel?"

Kathy rolled her eyes. "Forget Daniel. I have."

"Have you really?"

Kathy responded by kissing me.

Before Kathy left, she took a shower. While she was showering, I phoned Marianne. I wanted to arrange to see her, to tell her face-to-face. But she was annoyed about the previous night and insisted we have it out then and there, on the phone. Marianne wasn't expecting me to break up with her. But that's what I did, as gently as I could. She started crying and became upset and angry. I hung up on her. Brutal, yes — and unkind. I'm not proud of that phone call. But it seemed like the only honest action to take. I still don't know what I could have done differently.

■ ■ ■ ■

On our first proper date, Kathy and I met at Kew Gardens. It was her idea.

She was astonished I'd never been. "You're kidding. You've never gone to the greenhouses? There's this big one with all the tropical orchids and they keep it so hot, it's like an oven. When I was at drama school, I used to go and hang out there just to warm up. How about we meet there, after you finish work?" Then she hesitated, suddenly unsure. "Or is it too far for you to go?"

"I'd go further than Kew Gardens for you, darling."

"Idiot." She kissed me.

Kathy was waiting at the entrance when I arrived, in her enormous coat and scarf, waving like an excited child. "Come on, come on, follow me."

She led me through the frozen mud to the big glass structure that housed the tropical plants and pushed open the door and charged inside. I followed her and was immediately struck by the sudden rise in temperature, an onslaught of heat. I tore off my scarf and coat.

Kathy smiled. "See? I told you, it's like a

sauna. Ain't it great?"

We walked around along the paths, carrying our coats, holding hands, looking at the exotic flowers.

I felt an unfamiliar happiness just being in her company, as though a secret door had been opened, and Kathy had beckoned me across the threshold — into a magical world of warmth and light and color, and hundreds of orchids in a dazzling confetti of blues and reds and yellows.

I could feel myself thawing in the heat, softening around the edges, like a tortoise emerging into the sun after a long winter's sleep, blinking and waking up. Kathy did that for me — she was my invitation to life, one I grasped with both hands.

So this is it, I remember thinking. This is love.

I recognized it without question and knew clearly that I'd never experienced anything like this before. My previous romantic encounters had been brief, unsatisfactory for all concerned. As a student I had summoned up the nerve, aided by a considerable amount of alcohol, to lose my virginity to a Canadian sociology student called Meredith, who wore sharp metal braces that cut into my lips as we kissed. A string of uninspired relationships followed. I never

84

seemed to find the special connection I longed for. I had believed I was too damaged, too incapable of intimacy. But now every time I heard Kathy's contagious giggle, a wave of excitement ran through me. Through a kind of osmosis, I absorbed her youthful exuberance, her unselfconsciousness and joy. I said yes to her every suggestion and every whim. I didn't recognize myself. I liked this new person, this unafraid man Kathy inspired me to be. We fucked all the time. I was consumed with lust, perpetually, urgently hungry for her. I needed to keep touching her; I couldn't get close enough.

Kathy moved in with me that December, into my one-bedroom apartment in Kentish Town. The dank, thickly carpeted basement flat had windows, but with no view. Our first Christmas together, we were determined to do it properly. We bought a tree from the stall by the tube station and dressed it with a jumble of decorations and lights from the market.

I remember vividly the scent of pine needles and wood and candles burning, and Kathy's eyes staring into mine, sparkling, twinkling like the lights on the tree. I spoke without thinking. The words just came out:

"Will you marry me?"

Kathy stared at me. "What?"

"I love you, Kathy. Will you marry me?"

Kathy laughed. Then, to my joy and amazement, she said, "Yes."

The next day, we went out and she chose a ring. And the reality of the situation dawned on me. We were engaged.

Bizarrely, the first people I thought of were my parents. I wanted to introduce Kathy to them. I wanted them to see how happy I was, that I had finally escaped, that I was free. So we got the train to Surrey. In hindsight, it was a bad idea. Doomed from the start.

My father greeted me with typical hostility. "You look terrible, Theo. You're too thin. Your hair is too short. You look like a convict."

"Thanks, Dad. Good to see you too."

My mother seemed more depressed than usual. Quieter, smaller somehow, as if she weren't there. Dad was a heavier presence, unfriendly, glaring, unsmiling. He didn't take his cold, dark eyes off Kathy the entire time. It was an uncomfortable lunch. They didn't seem to like her, nor did they seem particularly happy for us. I don't know why I was surprised.

After lunch, my father disappeared into his study. He didn't emerge again. When

86

my mother said goodbye, she held on to me for too long, too closely, and was unsteady on her feet. I felt desperately sad. When Kathy and I left the house, part of me hadn't left, I knew, but had remained behind — forever a child, trapped. I felt lost, hopeless, close to tears. Then Kathy surprised me, as always. She threw her arms around me, pulling me into a hug. "I understand now," she whispered in my ear. "I understand it all. I love you so much more now."

She didn't explain further. She didn't need to.

We were married in April, in a small registry office off Euston Square. No parents invited. And no God. Nothing religious, at Kathy's insistence. But I said a secret prayer during the ceremony. I silently thanked Him for giving me such unexpected, undeserved happiness. I saw things clearly now, I understood His greater purpose. God hadn't abandoned me during my childhood, when I had felt so alone and so scared — He had been keeping Kathy hidden up His sleeve, waiting to produce her, like a deft magician.

I felt such humility and gratitude for every second we spent together. I was aware how lucky, how incredibly fortunate I was to have such love, how rare it was, and how others weren't so lucky. Most of my patients weren't loved. Alicia Berenson wasn't.

It's hard to imagine two women more different than Kathy and Alicia. Kathy makes me think of light, warmth, color, and laughter. When I think of Alicia, I think only of depth, of darkness, of sadness.

Of silence.

■ ■ ■ ■

PART TWO

■ ■ ■ ■

Unexpressed emotions will never die.
They are buried alive, and will come forth
    later,
in uglier ways.

— SIGMUND FREUD

Part Two

Unexpressed emotions will never die.
They are buried alive, and will come forth
later,
in uglier ways.

CHAPTER ONE

Alicia Berenson's Diary

July 16

I never thought I'd be longing for rain. We're into our fourth week of the heat wave, and it feels like an endurance test. Each day seems hotter than the last. It doesn't feel like England. More like a foreign country — Greece or somewhere.

I'm writing this on Hampstead Heath. The whole park is strewn with red-faced, semi-naked bodies, like a beach or a battlefield, on blankets or benches or spread out on the grass. I'm sitting under a tree, in the shade. It's six o'clock, and it has started to cool down. The sun is low and red in a golden sky — the park looks different in this light — darker shadows, brighter colors. The grass looks like it's on fire, flickering flames under my feet.

I took off my shoes on my way here and walked barefoot. It reminded me of when I was little and I'd play outside. It reminded me of another summer, hot like this one — the summer Mum died — playing outside with Paul, cycling on our bikes through golden fields dotted with wild daisies, exploring abandoned houses and haunted orchards. In my memory that summer lasts forever. I remember Mum and those colorful tops she'd wear, with the yellow stringy straps, so flimsy and delicate — just like her. She was so thin, like a little bird. She would put on the radio and pick me up and dance me around to pop songs on the radio. I remember how she smelled of shampoo and cigarettes and Nivea hand cream, always with an undertone of vodka. How old was she then? Twenty-eight? Twenty-nine? She was younger then than I am now.

That's an odd thought.

On my way here I saw a small bird on the path, lying by the roots of a tree. I thought it must have fallen from its nest. It wasn't moving and I wondered if it had broken its wings. I stroked its head gently with my finger. It didn't react. I nudged it and turned it over — and the underside of the bird was gone, eaten away, leaving a cavity filled with maggots. Fat, white, slippery maggots . . . twisting, turning, writhing . . . I felt my stomach turn — I thought I was going to be sick. It was so foul, so disgusting — deathly.

I can't get it out of my mind.

July 17
I've started taking refuge from the heat in an air-conditioned café on the high street — Caffe dell'Artista. It's icy cold inside, like climbing into a fridge. There's a table I like by the window, where I sit drinking iced coffee. Sometimes I read or sketch or make notes. Mostly I just let my mind drift, luxuriating in the coldness. The beautiful girl behind the counter stands there looking bored, staring at her phone, checking her watch, and sighing periodically. Yesterday afternoon, her sighs seemed especially long — and I realized she was waiting for me to go so she could close up. I left reluctantly.

Walking in this heat feels like wading through mud. I feel worn down, battered, beaten up by it. We're not equipped for it, not in this country — Gabriel and I don't have air-conditioning at home — who does? But without it, it's impossible to sleep. At night we throw off the covers and lie there in the dark, naked, drenched in sweat. We leave the windows open, but there's no hint of a breeze. Just hot dead air.

I bought an electric fan yesterday. I set it up at the foot of the bed on top of the chest.

Gabriel immediately started complaining. "It makes too much noise. We'll never sleep."

"We can't sleep anyway. At least we won't be lying here in a sauna."

Gabriel grumbled, but he fell asleep before I did. I lay there listening to the fan. I like the sound it makes, a gentle whirring. I can shut my eyes and tune in to it and disappear.

I've been carrying the fan around the house with me, plugging it in and unplugging it as I move around. This afternoon I took it down to the studio at the end of the garden. Having the fan made it just about bearable. But it's still too hot to get much work done. I'm falling behind — but too hot to care.

I did have a bit of a breakthrough — I finally understood what's wrong with the Jesus picture. Why it's not working. The problem isn't with the composition — Jesus on the cross — the problem is it's not a picture of Jesus at all. It doesn't even look like Him — whatever He looked like. Because it's not Jesus.

It's Gabriel.

Incredible that I didn't see it before. Somehow, without intending to, I've put Gabriel up there instead. It's *his* face I've painted, *his* body. Isn't that insane? So I must surrender to that — and do what the painting demands of me.

I know now that when I have an agenda for a picture, a predetermined idea how it should turn out, it never works. It remains stillborn, lifeless. But if I'm really paying attention, really aware, I sometimes hear a whispering voice pointing me in the right direction. And if I give in to it, as an act of faith, it leads me some-where unexpected, not where I intended, but somewhere intensely alive, glorious — and the result is independent of me, with a life force of its own.

I suppose what scares me is giving in to the unknown. I like to know where I'm going. That's why I always make so many sketches — trying to control the outcome — no wonder nothing comes to life — because I'm not really responding to what's going on in front of me. I need to *open my eyes* and *look* — and be aware of life as it is happening, and not simply how I want it to be. Now I know it's a portrait of Gabriel, I can go back to it. I can start again.

I'll ask him to pose for me. He hasn't sat for me in a long time. I hope he likes the idea — and doesn't think it's sacrilegious or anything.

He can be funny like that sometimes.

July 18
I walked down the hill to Camden Market this morning. I've not been there in years, not since Gabriel and I went together one after-noon in search of his lost youth. He used to go when he was a teenager, when he and his friends had been up all night, dancing, drink-ing, talking. They'd turn up at the market in the early morning and watch the traders set up their stalls and try and score some grass from the Rastafarian dealers hanging out on the bridge by Camden Lock. The dealers were no longer there when Gabriel and I went — to Gabriel's dismay. "I don't recognize it here anymore," he said. "It's a sanitized tourist trap."

Walking around today, I wondered if the problem wasn't that the market had changed as the fact Gabriel had changed. It's still populated by sixteen-year-olds, embracing the sunshine, sprawled on either side of the canal, a jumble of bodies — boys in rolled-up shorts with bare chests, girls in bikinis or bras — skin everywhere, burning, reddening flesh. The sexual energy was palpable — their hungry, impatient thirst for life. I felt a sudden desire for Gabriel — for his body and his strong legs, his thick thighs lain over mine. When we have sex, I always feel an insatiable hunger for him — for a kind of union between us — something that's bigger than me, bigger than us, beyond words — something holy.

Suddenly I caught sight of a homeless man, sitting by me on the pavement, staring at me. His trousers were tied up with string, his shoes held together with tape. His skin had sores and a bumpy rash across his face. I felt a sudden sadness and revulsion. He stank of stale sweat and urine. For a second I thought he spoke to me. But he was just swearing to himself under his breath — "fucking" this and "fucking" that. I fished for some change in my bag and gave it to him.

Then I walked home, back up the hill, slowly,

step by step. It seemed much steeper now. It took forever in the sweltering heat. For some reason I couldn't stop thinking about the homeless man. Apart from pity, there was another feeling, unnameable somehow — a kind of fear. I pictured him as a baby in his mother's arms. Did she ever imagine her baby would end up crazy, dirty and stinking, huddled on the pavement, muttering obscenities?

I thought of my mother. Was she crazy? Is that why she did it? Why she strapped me into the passenger seat of her yellow Mini and sped us toward that redbrick wall? I always liked that car, its cheerful canary yellow. The same yellow as in my paint box. Now I hate that color — every time I use it, I think of death.

Why did she do it? I suppose I'll never know. I used to think it was suicide. Now I think it was attempted murder. Because I was in the car too, wasn't I? Sometimes I think I was the intended victim — it was me she was trying to kill, not herself. But that's crazy. Why would she want to kill me?

Tears collected in my eyes as I walked up the hill. I wasn't crying for my mother — or myself — or even that poor homeless man. I was crying for all of us. There's so much pain every-where, and we just close our eyes to it. The truth is we're all scared. We're terrified of each other. I'm terrified of myself — and of my mother in me. Is her madness in my blood? Is it? Am I going to —

No. Stop. Stop —

I'm not writing about that. I'm not.

July 20
Last night Gabriel and I went out for dinner. We usually do on Fridays. "Date night," he calls it, in a silly American accent.

Gabriel always downplays his feelings and makes fun of anything he considers "soppy." He likes to think of himself as cynical and unsentimental. But the truth is he's a deeply romantic man — in his heart if not his speech. Actions speak louder than words, don't they? And Gabriel's actions make me feel totally loved.

"Where do you want to go?" I asked.

"Three guesses."

"Augusto's?"

99

"Got it in one."

Augusto's is our local Italian restaurant, just down the road. It's nothing special, but it's our home away from home, and we've spent many happy evenings there. We went around eight o'clock. The air-conditioning wasn't working, so we sat by the open window in the hot, still, humid air and drank chilled dry white wine. I felt quite drunk by the end, and we laughed a lot, at nothing, really. We kissed outside the restaurant and had sex when we came home.

Thankfully, Gabriel has come around to the portable fan, at least when we're in bed. I positioned it in front of us, and we lay in the cool breeze, wrapped in each other's arms. He stroked my hair and kissed me. "I love you," he whispered. I didn't say anything; I didn't need to. He knows how I feel.

But I ruined the mood, stupidly, clumsily — by asking if he would sit for me.

"I want to paint you," I said.

"Again? You already did."

"That was four years ago. I want to paint you again."

"Uh-huh." He didn't look enthusiastic. "What kind of thing do you have in mind?"

I hesitated — and then said it was for the Jesus picture. Gabriel sat up and gave a kind of strangled laugh.

"Oh, come on, Alicia."

"What?"

"I don't know about that, love. I don't think so."

"Why not?"

"Why do you think? Painting me on the cross? What are people going to say?"

"Since when do you care what people say?"

"I don't, not about most things, but — I mean, they might think that's how you see me."

I laughed. "I don't think you're the son of God, if that's what you mean. It's just an image — something that happened organically while I

101

was painting. I haven't consciously thought about it."

"Well, maybe you should think about it."

"Why? It's not a comment on you, or our marriage."

"Then what is it?"

"How should I know?"

Gabriel laughed at this and rolled his eyes. "All right. Fuck it. If you want. We can try. I suppose you know what you're doing."

That doesn't sound like much of an endorsement. But I know Gabriel believes in me and my talent — I'd never be a painter if it weren't for him. If he hadn't needled and encouraged and bullied me, I'd never have kept going during those first few dead years after college, when I was painting walls with Jean-Felix. Before I met Gabriel, I lost my way, somehow — I lost myself. I don't miss those druggy partyers who passed for friends during my twenties. I only ever saw them at night — they vanished at dawn, like vampires fleeing the light. When I met Gabriel, they faded away into nothing, and I didn't even notice. I didn't need them anymore; I didn't need anyone now that I had him. He saved me — like Jesus. Maybe that's what the painting is about. Gabriel is my whole world — and has been since the day we met. I'll love him no matter what he does, or what happens — no matter how much he upsets me — no matter how untidy or messy he is — how thoughtless, how self-ish. I'll take him just as he is.

Until death do us part.

July 21
Today Gabriel came and sat for me in the studio.

"I'm not doing this for days again," he said. "How long are we talking about?"

"It's going to take more than one session to get it right."

"Is this just a ploy to spend more time together? If so, how about we skip the preamble and go to bed?"

I laughed. "Maybe afterward. If you're good and don't fidget too much."

I positioned him standing in front of the fan.

103

His hair blew in the breeze.

"How should I look?" He struck a pose.

"Not like that. Just be yourself."

"Don't you want me to adopt an anguished expression?"

"I'm not sure Jesus was anguished. I don't see him like that. Don't pull any faces — just stand there. And don't move."

"You're the boss."

He stood for about twenty minutes. Then he broke the pose, saying he was tired.

"Sit down, then. But don't talk. I'm working on the face."

Gabriel sat on a chair and kept quiet while I worked. I enjoyed painting his face. It's a good face. A strong jaw, high cheekbones, elegant nose. Sitting there with the spotlight on him, he looked like a Greek statue. A hero of some kind.

But something was wrong. I don't know what — maybe I was pushing too hard. I just couldn't get the shape of his eyes right, nor the color. The first thing I ever noticed about Gabriel was the sparkle in his eyes — like a tiny diamond in each iris. But now for some reason I couldn't catch it. Maybe I'm just not skilled enough — or maybe Gabriel has something extra that can't be captured in paint. The eyes remained dead, lifeless. I could feel myself getting annoyed.

"Fuck," I said. "It's not going well."

"Time for a break?"

"Yeah. Time for a break."

"Shall we have sex?"

That made me laugh. "Okay."

Gabriel jumped up, took hold of me, and kissed me. We made love in the studio, there on the floor.

The whole time, I kept glancing at the lifeless eyes in Gabriel's portrait. They were staring at me, burning into me. I had to turn away.

But I could still feel them watching.

CHAPTER TWO

I went to find Diomedes to report on my meeting with Alicia. He was in his office, sorting through piles of sheet music.

"Well" — he didn't look up — "how did it go?"

"It didn't, really."

Diomedes gave me a quizzical glance.

I hesitated. "If I'm going to get anywhere with her, I need Alicia to be able to think, and feel."

"Absolutely. And your concern is . . . ?"

"It's impossible to get through to someone when they're so heavily medicated. It's like she's six feet underwater."

Diomedes frowned. "I wouldn't go that far. I'm not familiar with the exact dose she's on —"

"I checked with Yuri. Sixteen milligrams of risperidone. A horse's dose."

Diomedes raised an eyebrow. "That's certainly quite high, yes. It could probably

106

be reduced. You know, Christian is the head of Alicia's care team. You should talk to him about it."

"I think it'll sound better coming from you."

"Hmm." Diomedes gave me a doubtful look. "You and Christian knew each other before, didn't you? At Broadmoor?"

"Very slightly."

Diomedes didn't respond immediately. He reached over to a little dish of sugared almonds on his desk and offered me one.

I shook my head.

He popped an almond in his mouth and crunched it, watching me as he chewed. "Tell me, is everything friendly between you and Christian?"

"That's an odd question. Why do you ask?"

"Because I'm picking up on some hostility."

"Not on my part."

"But on his?"

"You'll have to ask him. I have no problem with Christian."

"Hmm. Perhaps I'm imagining it. But I'm sensing something. . . . Keep an eye on it. Any aggression or competitiveness interferes with the work. You two need to work with each other, not against each other."

"I'm aware of that."

"Well, Christian needs to be included in this discussion. You want Alicia to feel, yes. But remember, with greater feeling comes greater danger."

"Danger for whom?"

"For Alicia, of course." Diomedes wagged his finger at me. "Don't forget she was highly suicidal when we first brought her here. She made numerous attempts to end her life. And the medication keeps her stable. It keeps her alive. If we lower the dose, there's every chance she will be overwhelmed by her feelings and be unable to cope. Are you prepared to take that risk?"

I took what Diomedes said seriously. But I nodded. "It's a risk I believe we need to take, Professor. Otherwise we'll never reach her."

Diomedes shrugged. "Then I shall talk to Christian on your behalf."

"Thank you."

"We'll see how he reacts. Psychiatrists don't often respond well to being told how to medicate their patients. Of course, I can overrule him, but I don't tend to do that — let me broach the subject with him subtly. I'll tell you what he says."

"It might be better not to mention me when you talk to him."

"I see." Diomedes smiled strangely. "Very well, I won't."

He pulled out a little box from his desk, sliding off the cover to reveal a row of cigars. He offered me one. I shook my head.

"You don't smoke?" He seemed surprised. "You look like a smoker to me."

"No, no. Only the occasional cigarette — just now and then . . . I'm trying to quit."

"Good, good for you." He opened the window. "You know that joke, about why you can't be a therapist and smoke? Because it means you're still fucked up." He laughed and popped one of the cigars into his mouth. "I think we're all a bit crazy in this place. You know that sign they used to have in offices? 'You don't need to be mad to work here, but it helps'?"

Diomedes laughed again. He lit the cigar and puffed on it, blowing the smoke outside. I watched him enviously.

CHAPTER THREE

After lunch I prowled the corridors, looking for an exit. I was intending to sneak outside and have a cigarette, but I was discovered by Indira by the fire escape. She assumed I was lost.

"Don't worry, Theo," she said, taking my arm. "It took me months to get my bearings around here. Like a maze with no way out. I still get lost sometimes and I've been here ten years." She laughed. Before I could object, she was guiding me upstairs for a cup of tea in the "goldfish bowl."

"I'll put the kettle on. Bloody miserable weather, isn't it? I wish it would just snow and get it over with. . . . Snow is a very powerful imaginative symbol, don't you think? Wipes everything clean. Have you noticed how the patients keep talking about it? Look out for it. It's interesting."

To my surprise, she reached into her bag and pulled out a thick slice of cake wrapped in cling film. She thrust it into my hand. "Take it. Walnut cake. I made it last night. For you."

"Oh, thank you, I —"

"I know it's unorthodox, but I always get better results with difficult patients if I give them a slice of cake in the session."

I laughed. "I bet you do. Am I a difficult patient?"

Indira laughed. "No, although I find it works just as well on difficult members of staff too — which you're not either, by the way. A little bit of sugar is a great mood enhancer. I used to make cakes for the canteen, but then Stephanie made such a fuss, all this health-and-safety nonsense about food being brought in from the outside. You'd think I was smuggling in a file. But I still bake a little on the sly. My rebellion against the dictator state. Try it."

This was not a question but a command. I took a bite. It was good. Chewy, nutty, sweet. My mouth was full, so I covered it with my hand as I spoke.

"I think this will definitely put your patients in a good mood."

Indira laughed and looked pleased. I realized why I liked her — she radiated a kind of maternal calm. She reminded me of my old therapist, Ruth. It was hard to imagine her ruffled, or upset.

I glanced around the room as she made the tea. The nurses' station is always the hub of a psychiatric unit, its heart: staff flow to and from it, and it is where the ward is run from day to day; at least where all the practical decisions are made. The *goldfish bowl* was the nurses' nickname for the station, as its walls were made of reinforced glass — meaning staff could keep an eye on the patients in the recreation room, in theory at least. In practice, the patients hovered restlessly outside, staring in, watching us, so we were the ones under constant observation. The small space did not have enough chairs, and the ones that were there were generally occupied by nurses typing up notes. So you mostly stood in the middle of the room or leaned awkwardly against a desk, which gave the space a crowded feel, no matter how many people were in it.

"Here you are, love." Indira handed me a mug of tea.

"Thanks."

Christian ambled in and nodded at me. He smelled strongly of the peppermint gum he was always chewing. I remembered he used to smoke heavily when we were at Broadmoor together; it was one of the few things we had in common. Since then

Christian had quit, got married, and had a baby daughter. I wondered what kind of father he made. He didn't strike me as particularly compassionate.

He gave me a cold smile. "Funny seeing you again like this, Theo."

"Small world."

"In mental health terms, it is — yes." Christian said this as if to imply he might be found in other, larger worlds. I tried to imagine what they might be. I could only imagine him in the gym or in a scrum on the rugby field.

Christian stared at me for a few seconds. I'd forgotten his habit of pausing, often lengthily, making you wait while he considered his response. It irritated me here just as much as it had done at Broadmoor.

"You're joining the team at rather an unfortunate moment," he said eventually. "The sword of Damocles is hanging over the Grove."

"You think it's as bad as that?"

"It's only a matter of time. The Trust is bound to shut us down sooner or later. So the question is, what are you doing here?"

"What do you mean?"

"Well, rats desert a sinking ship. They don't clamber on board."

I was startled by Christian's undisguised

aggression. I decided not to rise to the bait. I shrugged. "Possibly. But I'm not a rat."

Before Christian could reply, a massive thud made us jump. Elif was on the other side of the glass, hammering at it with her fists. Her face was pressed up against it, squashing her nose, distorting her features, making her almost monstrous.

"I won't take this shit no more. I hate this — these fucking pills, man —"

Christian opened a small hatch in the glass and spoke through it. "Now is not the time to discuss this, Elif."

"I'm telling you, I'm not taking them no more, they make me fucking sick —"

"I'm not having this conversation now. Make an appointment to see me. Step away, please."

Elif scowled, deliberating for a moment. Then she turned and lumbered off, leaving a faint circle of condensation where her nose had been pressed against the glass.

"Quite a character," I said.

Christian grunted. "Difficult."

Indira nodded. "Poor Elif."

"What's she in for?"

"Double murder," Christian said. "Killed her mother and her sister. Suffocated them while they slept."

I peered through the glass. Elif joined the

114

other patients. She towered over them. One of them slipped some money into her hand, which she pocketed.

Then I noticed Alicia at the far end of the room, sitting by herself, by the window, looking out. I watched her for a moment.

Christian followed my gaze and said, "By the way, I've been talking to Professor Diomedes about Alicia. I want to see how she does on a lower dose of risperidone. I've brought her down to five milligrams."

"I see."

"I thought you might want to know — since I heard you saw her for a session."

"Yes."

"We'll have to monitor her closely to see how she reacts to the change. And, by the way, next time you have a problem with how I medicate my patients, come to me directly. Don't sneak off to Diomedes behind my back." Christian glared at me.

I smiled back at him. "I didn't sneak anywhere. I have no problem talking to you directly, Christian."

There was an uncomfortable pause. Christian nodded to himself, as if he'd made his mind up about something. "You do realize Alicia is borderline? She won't respond to therapy. You're wasting your time."

"How do you know she's borderline if she

can't talk?"

"Won't talk."

"You think she's faking?"

"Yes, as a matter of fact, I do."

"If she's faking, then how can she be borderline?"

Christian looked irritated.

Indira interrupted before he could reply. "With all due respect, I don't feel umbrella terms like *borderline* are particularly helpful. They don't tell us anything very useful at all." She glanced at Christian. "This is a subject Christian and I disagree on frequently."

"And how do you feel about Alicia?" I asked her.

Indira pondered the question for a moment. "I find myself feeling very maternal toward her. That's my countertransference, that's what she brings out in me — I feel she needs someone to take care of her." Indira smiled at me. "And now she has someone. She has you."

Christian laughed that annoying laugh of his. "Forgive me for being so dense, but how can Alicia benefit from therapy if she doesn't talk?"

"Therapy isn't just about talking," Indira said. "It's about providing a safe space — a containing environment. Most communication is nonverbal, as I'm sure you know."

Christian rolled his eyes at me. "Good luck, mate. You'll need it."

tion is nonverbal, as I'm sure you know."

Christian rolled my eyes at this. "Good luck, mate. You'll need it."

CHAPTER FOUR

"Hello, Alicia," I said.

Only a few days had passed since her medication had been lowered, but the difference in Alicia was already apparent. She seemed more fluid in her movements. Her eyes were clearer. The foggy gaze had gone. She seemed like a different person.

She stood at the door with Yuri and hesitated. She stared at me, as if seeing me clearly for the first time, taking me in, sizing me up. I wondered what she was concluding. Evidently she judged it safe to proceed and walked inside. Without being asked, she sat down.

I nodded at Yuri to go. He deliberated for a second, then shut the door behind him.

I sat opposite Alicia. There was silence for a moment. Just the restless sound of the rain outside, raindrops drumming against the window. Eventually I spoke.

"How are you feeling?"

No response. Alicia stared at me. Eyes like lamps, unblinking.

I opened my mouth and closed it again. I was determined to resist the urge to fill the void by talking. Instead, by remaining silent and just sitting there, I hoped to communicate something else, something nonverbal: that it was okay for us to sit together like this, that I wouldn't hurt her, that she could trust me. To have any success at getting Alicia to talk, I needed to win her trust. And this would take time — nothing would be accomplished overnight. It would move slowly, like a glacier, but it would move.

As we sat there in silence, my head started to throb at the temples. The beginnings of a headache. A telltale symptom. I thought of Ruth, who used to say, "In order to be a good therapist, you must be receptive to your patients' feelings — but you must not hold on to them — they are not yours — they do not belong to you." In other words, this thump, thump, thumping in my head wasn't my pain; it belonged to Alicia. And this sudden wave of sadness — this desire to die, die, die — did not belong to me either. It was hers, all hers. I sat there, feeling it for her, my head pounding, my stomach churning, for what seemed like hours. Eventually, the fifty minutes were up.

I looked at my watch. "We have to finish now."

Alicia lowered her head and stared at her lap. I hesitated. I lost control of my reserve. I lowered my voice and spoke from the heart.

"I want to help you, Alicia. I need you to believe that. The truth is, I want to help you see clearly."

At this, Alicia looked up. She stared at me — right through me.

You can't help me, her eyes shouted. *Look at you, you can barely help yourself. You pretend to know so much and be so wise, but you should be sitting here instead of me. Freak. Fraud. Liar. Liar —*

As she stared at me, I became aware of what had been troubling me the whole session. It's hard to put into words, but a psychotherapist quickly becomes attuned to recognizing mental distress, from physical behavior and speech and a glint in the eyes — something haunted, afraid, mad. And that's what bothered me: despite the years of medication, despite everything she had done, and endured, Alicia's blue eyes remained as clear and cloudless as a summer's day. She wasn't mad. So what was she? What was the expression in her eyes? What was the right word? It was —

120

Before I could finish the thought, Alicia leaped from the chair. She threw herself toward me, hands outstretched like claws. I had no time to move or get out of the way. She landed on top of me, knocking me off-balance. We fell to the floor.

The back of my head hit the wall with a thud. She bashed my head against the wall again and again, and started scratching, slapping, clawing — it took all my strength to throw her off.

I scrambled along the floor and reached up to the table. I groped for the attack alarm. Just as my fingers grasped it, Alicia jumped on me and knocked the alarm from my hand.

"Alicia —"

Her fingers were tight around my neck, gripping, choking — I groped for the alarm but couldn't reach it. Her hands dug deeper — I couldn't breathe. I made another lunge — this time I managed to grab hold of the alarm. I pressed it.

A wailing scream instantly filled my ears, deafening me. I could hear the distant sound of a door opening and Yuri calling for backup. Alicia was dragged off me, releasing her choke hold — and I gasped for breath.

It took four nurses to hold Alicia down.

She writhed and kicked and fought like a creature possessed. She didn't seem human, more like a wild animal; something monstrous. Christian appeared and sedated her. She lost consciousness.

At last, there was silence.

CHAPTER FIVE

"This will sting a bit."

Yuri was tending to my bleeding scratches in the goldfish bowl. He opened the bottle of antiseptic and applied it to a swab. The medicinal odor transported me to the sick bay at school, conjuring up memories of playground battle scars, grazed knees and scratched elbows. I remembered the warm, cozy feeling of being taken care of by Matron, bandaged and rewarded for my bravery with a boiled sweet. Then the sting of the antiseptic on my skin brought me back sharply to the present, where the injuries I presented were not so easily remedied. I winced.

"My head feels like she hit me with a fucking hammer."

"It's a nasty bruise. You'll have a lump tomorrow. We'd better keep an eye on it." Yuri shook his head. "I never should have left you alone with her."

"I didn't give you a choice."

He grunted. "That's true enough."

"Thanks for not saying, 'I told you so.' It's noted and appreciated."

Yuri shrugged. "I don't need to, mate. The professor will say it for me. He's asked to see you in his office."

"Ah."

"Rather you than me, by the look of him."

I started getting up.

Yuri watched me carefully. "Don't rush. Take a minute. Make sure you're ready. Any dizziness or headaches, let me know."

"I'm fine. Honestly."

That wasn't strictly true, but I didn't feel as bad as I looked. Bloody scratches, and black bruises around my throat where she'd tried to strangle me — she'd dug so deep with her fingers, she'd drawn blood.

I knocked on the professor's door. Diomedes's eyes widened when he saw me. He tutted. "Po po po. Did you need stitches?"

"No, no, of course not. I'm fine."

Diomedes gave me a disbelieving look and ushered me inside. "Come in, Theo. Sit down."

The others were already there. Christian and Stephanie were standing. Indira was sitting by the window. It felt like a formal reception, and I wondered if I was about to get fired.

Diomedes sat behind his desk. He gestured to me to sit in the remaining empty chair. I sat. He stared at me in silence for a moment, drumming his fingers, deliberating what to say, or how to say it. But before he could make up his mind, he was beaten to it by Stephanie.

"This is an unfortunate incident. Extremely unfortunate." She turned to me. "Obviously we're all relieved you're still in one piece. But that doesn't alter the fact that it raises all kinds of questions. And the first is, what were you doing alone with Alicia?"

"It was my fault. I asked Yuri to leave. I take full responsibility."

"On whose authority did you make that decision? If either of you had been seriously injured —"

Diomedes interrupted. "Please don't let's get dramatic. Thankfully neither was hurt." He gestured at me dismissively. "A few scratches are hardly grounds for a court-martial."

Stephanie pulled a face. "I don't think jokes are really appropriate, Professor. I really don't."

"Who's joking?" Diomedes turned to me. "I'm deadly serious. Tell us, Theo. What happened?"

I felt all their eyes on me; I addressed myself to Diomedes. I chose my words carefully. "Well, she attacked me. That's what happened."

"That much is obvious. But why? I take it it was unprovoked?"

"Yes. At least, consciously."

"And unconsciously?"

"Well, obviously Alicia was reacting to me on some level. I believe it shows us how much she wants to communicate."

Christian laughed. "You call that communication?"

"Yes, I do. Rage is a powerful communication. The other patients — the zombies who just sit there, vacant, empty — they've given up. Alicia hasn't. Her attack tells us something she can't articulate directly — about her pain, her desperation, her anguish. She was telling me not to give up on her. Not yet."

Christian rolled his eyes. "A less poetic interpretation might be that she was off her meds and out of her mind." He turned to Diomedes. "I told you this would happen, Professor. I warned you about lowering the dose."

"Really, Christian?" I said. "I thought it was your idea."

126

Christian dismissed me with a roll of his eyes. He was a psychiatrist through and through, I thought. By that I mean psychiatrists tend to be wary of psychodynamic thinking. They favor a more biological, chemical, and, above all, practical approach — such as the cup of pills Alicia was handed at every meal. Christian's unfriendly, narrow gaze told me that there was nothing I could contribute.

Diomedes, however, eyed me more thoughtfully. "It hasn't put you off, Theo, what happened?"

I shook my head. "On the contrary, I'm encouraged."

Diomedes nodded, looking pleased. "Good. I agree, such an intense reaction to you is certainly worth investigating. I think you should keep going."

At this Stephanie could restrain herself no longer. "That's absolutely out of the question."

Diomedes kept talking as if she hadn't spoken. He kept looking at me. "You think you can get her to talk?"

Before I could reply, a voice said from behind me, "I believe he can, yes."

It was Indira. I'd almost forgotten she was there. I turned around.

"And in a way," Indira said, "Alicia has

begun to talk. She's communicating through Theo — he is her advocate. It's already happening."

Diomedes nodded. He looked pensive for a moment. I knew what was on his mind — Alicia Berenson was a famous patient, and a powerful bargaining tool with the Trust. If we could make demonstrable progress with her, we'd have a much stronger hand in saving the Grove from closure.

"How long to see results?" Diomedes asked.

"I can't answer that," I said. "You know that as well as I do. It takes as long as it takes. Six months. A year. Probably longer — it could be years."

"You have six weeks."

Stephanie drew herself up and crossed her arms. "I am the manager of this unit, and I simply cannot allow —"

"I am clinical director of the Grove. This is my decision, not yours. I take full responsibility for any injuries incurred upon our long-suffering therapist here," Diomedes said, winking at me.

Stephanie didn't say anything further. She glared at Diomedes, then at me. She turned and walked out.

"Oh, dear," Diomedes said. "You appear to have made an enemy of Stephanie. How unfortunate." He shared a smile with Indira, then gave me a serious look. "Six weeks. Under my supervision. Understand?"

I agreed — I had no choice but to agree. "Six weeks."

"Good."

Christian stood up, visibly annoyed. "Alicia won't talk in six weeks, or sixty years. You're wasting your time."

He walked out. I wondered why Christian was so positive I would fail.

But it made me even more determined to succeed.

Chapter Six

I arrived home, feeling exhausted. Force of habit made me flick on the light in the hallway, even though the bulb had gone. We'd been meaning to replace it but kept forgetting.

I knew at once that Kathy wasn't there. It was too quiet; she was incapable of quiet. She wasn't noisy but her world was full of sound — talking on the phone, reciting lines, watching movies, singing, humming, listening to bands I'd never heard of. But now the flat was silent as a tomb. I called her name. Force of habit, again — or a guilty conscience, perhaps, wanting to make sure I was alone before I transgressed?

"Kathy?"

No reply.

I fumbled my way through the dark into the living room. I turned on the light.

The room leaped out at me in the way new furniture always does until you're used to it: new chairs, new cushions; new colors, reds and yellows, where there once had been black and white. A vase of pink lilies — Kathy's favorite flowers — was on the table; their strong musky scent made the air thick and hard to breathe.

What time was it? Eight-thirty. Where was she? Rehearsal? She was in a new production of *Othello* at the RSC, and it wasn't going particularly well. Endless rehearsals had been taking their toll. She seemed visibly tired, pale, thinner than usual, fighting a cold. "I'm so fucking sick all the time," she said. "I'm exhausted."

It was true; she'd come back from rehearsal later and later each night, looking terrible; she'd yawn and stumble straight into bed. So she probably wouldn't be home for a couple of hours at the earliest. I decided to risk it.

I took the jar of weed from its hiding place and started rolling a joint.

I'd been smoking marijuana since university. I first encountered it during my first term, alone and friendless at a fresher party, too paralyzed with fear to initiate a conversation with any of the good-looking and confident young people around me. I was planning my escape when the girl standing next to me offered me something. I thought

131

it was a cigarette until I smelled the spicy, pungent, curling black smoke. Too shy to refuse, I accepted it and brought the joint to my lips. It was badly rolled and coming unstuck, unraveling at the end. The tip was wet and stained red from her lipstick. It tasted different from a cigarette; it was richer, rawer, more exotic. I swallowed down the thick smoke and tried not to cough. Initially all I felt was a little light on my feet. Like sex, clearly more fuss was made over marijuana than it merited. Then — a minute or so later — something happened. Something incredible. It was like being drenched in an enormous wave of well-being. I felt safe, relaxed, totally at ease, silly and unself-conscious.

That was it. Before long I was smoking weed every day. It became my best friend, my inspiration, my solace. An endless ritual of rolling, licking, lighting. I would get stoned just from the rustling of rolling papers and the anticipation of the warm, intoxicating high.

All kinds of theories have been put forward about the origins of addiction. It could be genetic; it could be chemical; it could be psychological. But marijuana was doing something much more than soothing me: crucially, it altered the way I experienced my emotions; it cradled me and held me safe like a well-loved child.

In other words, it contained me.

The psychoanalyst W. R. Bion came up with the term *containment* to describe a mother's ability to manage her baby's pain. Remember, babyhood is not a time of bliss; it's one of terror. As babies we are trapped in a strange, alien world, unable to see properly, constantly surprised at our bodies, alarmed by hunger and wind and bowel movements, overwhelmed by our feelings. We are quite literally under attack. We need our mother to soothe our distress and make sense of our experience. As she does so, we slowly learn how to manage our physical and emotional states on our own. But our ability to contain ourselves directly depends on our mother's ability to contain us — if she had never experienced containment by her own mother, how could she teach us what she did not know? Someone who has never learned to contain himself is plagued by anxious feelings for the rest of his life, feelings that Bion aptly titled *nameless dread.* Such a person endlessly seeks this unquenchable containment from external sources — he needs a drink or a joint to "take the edge off" this endless anxiety. Hence my addiction to marijuana.

I talked a lot about marijuana in therapy. I wrestled with the idea of giving it up and wondered why the prospect scared me so much. Ruth said that enforcement and constraint never produced anything good, and that, rather than force myself to live without weed, a better starting place might be to acknowledge that I was now dependent on it, and unwilling or unable to abandon it. Whatever marijuana did for me was still working, Ruth argued — until the day it would outlive its usefulness, when I would probably relinquish it with ease.

Ruth was right. When I met Kathy and fell in love, marijuana faded into the background. I was naturally high on love, with no need to artificially induce a good mood. It helped that Kathy didn't smoke it. Stoners, in her opinion, were weak willed and lazy and lived in slow motion — you pricked them and six days later they'd say, "Ouch." I stopped smoking weed the day Kathy moved into my flat. And — as Ruth had predicted — once I was secure and happy, the habit fell away from me quite naturally, like dry caked mud from a boot.

I might never have smoked it again if we hadn't gone to a leaving party for Kathy's friend Nicole, who was moving to New York. Kathy was monopolized by all her actor friends, and I found myself alone. A short, stubby man, wearing a pair of neon-pink glasses, nudged me and said, "Want some?" I was about to refuse the joint between his fingers, when something stopped me. I'm not sure what. A momentary whim? Or an unconscious attack on Kathy for forcing me to come to this horrible party and then abandoning me? I looked around, and she was nowhere to be seen. Fuck it, I thought. I brought the joint to my lips and inhaled.

Just like that, I was back where I had started, as if there had been no break. My addiction had been patiently waiting for me all this time, like a faithful dog. I didn't tell Kathy what I had done, and I put it out of my mind. In fact I was waiting for an opportunity, and six weeks later, it presented itself. Kathy went to New York for a week, to visit Nicole. Without Kathy's influence, lonely and bored, I gave in to temptation. I didn't have a dealer anymore, so I did what I had done as a student — and made my way to Camden Town market.

As I left the station, I could smell marijuana in the air, mingled with the scent of incense and food stalls frying onions. I walked over to the bridge by Camden Lock. I stood there awkwardly, pushed and nudged by an endless stream of tourists and teenagers trudging back and forth across the bridge.

I scanned the crowd. There was no sign of any of the dealers who used to line the bridge, calling out to you as you passed. I spotted a couple of police officers, unmissable in their bright yellow jackets, patrolling the crowd. They walked away from the bridge, toward the station. Then I heard a low voice by my side:

"Want some green, mate?"

I looked down and there was a small man. I thought he was a child at first, he was so slight and slender. But his face was a road map of rugged terrain, lined and crossed, like a boy prematurely aged. He was missing his two front teeth, giving his words a slight whistle. "Green?" he repeated.

I nodded.

He jerked his head at me to follow him. He slipped through the crowd and went around the corner and along a backstreet. He entered an old pub and I followed. It was deserted inside, dingy and tattered, and stank of vomit and old cigarette smoke.

"Gissa beer," he said, hovering at the bar. He was scarcely tall enough to see over it. I begrudgingly bought him half a pint. He took it to a table in the corner. I sat op-

136

posite him. He looked around furtively, then reached under the table and slipped me a small package wrapped in cellophane. I gave him some cash.

I went home and I opened the package, half expecting to have been ripped off, but a familiar pungent smell drifted to my nose. I saw the little green buds streaked with gold. My heart raced as though I had encountered a long-lost friend, which I suppose I had.

From then on, I would get high occasionally, whenever I found myself alone in the flat for a few hours, when I was sure Kathy would not be coming back anytime soon.

That night, when I came home, tired and frustrated, and found Kathy out at rehearsal, I quickly rolled a joint. I smoked it out of the bathroom window. But I smoked too much, too fast — it hit me hard, like a punch between the eyes. I was so stoned, even walking felt difficult, like wading through treacle. I went through my usual sanitizing ritual — air freshener, brushing my teeth, taking a shower — and I carefully maneuvered myself to the living room. I sank onto the sofa.

I looked for the TV remote but couldn't see it. Then I located it, peeking out from behind Kathy's open laptop on the coffee table. I reached for it, but was so stoned I knocked over the laptop. I propped the laptop up again — and the screen came to life. It was logged into her email account. For some reason, I kept staring at it. I was transfixed — her in-box stared at me like a gaping hole. I couldn't look away. All kinds of things jumped out before I knew what I was reading: words such as "sexy" and "fuck" in the email headings — and repeated emails from BADBOY22.

If only I'd stopped there. If only I'd got up and walked away — but I didn't.

I clicked on the most recent email and opened it:

Subject: Re: little miss fuck
From: Katerama_1
To: BADBOY22

I'm on the bus. So horny for you. I can smell you on me. I feel like a slut! Kxx
                    Sent from my iPhone

Subject: Re: re: re: little miss fuck
From: BADBOY22
To: Katerama_1

U r a slut! Lol. C u later? After rehearsal?

Subject: Re: re: re: re: little miss fuck
From: Katerama_1
To: BADBOY22

Ok. 830? 9? xx

Sent from my iPhone

Subject: Re: re: re: re: re: little miss fuck
From: BADBOY22
To: Katerama_1

Ok. Will see what time I can get away.
I'll text u.

I pulled the laptop from the table. I sat with it on my lap, staring at it. I don't know how long I sat like that. Ten minutes? Twenty minutes? Half an hour? Maybe longer. Time seemed to slow to a crawl.

I tried to process what I had just seen, but I was still so stoned, I wasn't sure what I *had* seen. Was it real? Or some kind of misunderstanding — some joke I wasn't getting because I was so high?

I forced myself to read another email.

And another.

I ended up going through all of Kathy's emails to BADBOY22. Some were sexual, obscene even. Others were longer, more confessional, emotional, and she sounded

139

drunk — perhaps they were written late at night, after I had gone to bed. I pictured myself in the bedroom, asleep, while Kathy was out here, writing intimate messages to this stranger. This stranger she was fucking.

Time caught up with itself with a jolt. Suddenly I was no longer stoned. I was horribly, painfully sober.

There was a wrenching pain in my stomach. I threw aside the laptop. I ran into the bathroom.

I fell to my knees in front of the toilet and threw up.

CHAPTER SEVEN

"This feels rather different from last time," I said.

No response.

Alicia sat opposite me in the chair, head turned slightly toward the window. She sat perfectly still, her spine rigid and straight. She looked like a cellist. Or a soldier.

"I'm thinking of how the last session ended. When you physically attacked me and had to be restrained."

No response. I hesitated.

"I wonder if you did it as some kind of test? To see what I'm made of? I think it's important that you know I'm not easily intimidated. I can take whatever you throw at me."

Alicia looked out the window at the gray sky beyond the bars. I waited a moment.

"There's something I need to tell you, Alicia. That I'm on your side. Hopefully one day you'll believe that. Of course, it takes time to build trust. My old therapist used to say intimacy requires the repeated experience of being responded to — and that doesn't happen overnight."

Alicia stared at me, unblinking, with an inscrutable gaze. The minutes passed. It felt more like an endurance test than a therapy session.

I wasn't making progress in any direction, it seemed. Perhaps it was all hopeless. Christian had been right to point out that rats desert sinking ships. What the hell was I doing clambering upon this wreck, lashing myself to the mast, preparing to drown?

The answer was sitting in front of me. As Diomedes put it, Alicia was a silent siren, luring me to my doom.

I felt a sudden desperation. I wanted to scream at her, *Say something. Anything. Just talk.*

But I didn't say that. Instead, I broke with therapeutic tradition. I stopped treading softly and got directly to the point:

"I'd like to talk about your silence. About what it means . . . what it feels like. And specifically why you stopped talking."

Alicia didn't look at me. Was she even listening?

"As I sit here with you, a picture keeps coming into my mind — an image of someone biting their fist, holding back a yell, swallowing a scream. I remember when I first started therapy, I found it very hard to cry. I feared I'd be carried away by the flood, overwhelmed. Perhaps that's what it feels like for you. That's why it's important to take your time to feel safe and trust that you won't be alone in this flood — that I'm treading water here with you."

Silence.

"I think of myself as a relational therapist. Do you know what that means?"

Silence.

"It means I think Freud was wrong about a couple of things. I don't believe a therapist can ever really be a blank slate, as he intended. We leak all kinds of information about ourselves unintentionally — by the color of my socks, or how I sit or the way I talk. Just by sitting here with you, I reveal a great deal about myself. Despite my best efforts at invisibility, I'm showing you who I am."

Alicia looked up. She stared at me, her chin slightly tilted — was there a challenge in that look? At last I had her attention. I shifted in my seat.

"The point is, what can we do about this? We can ignore it and deny it and pretend this therapy is all about you. Or we can acknowledge that this is a two-way street and work with that. And then we can really start to get somewhere."

I held up my hand. I nodded at my wedding ring.

"This ring tells you something, doesn't it?"

Alicia's eyes ever so slowly moved in the direction of the ring.

"It tells you I'm a married man. It tells you I have a wife. We've been married for nearly nine years."

No response, yet she kept staring at the ring.

"You were married for about seven years, weren't you?"

No reply.

"I love my wife very much. Did you love your husband?"

Alicia's eyes moved. They darted up to my face. We stared at each other.

"Love includes all kinds of feelings, doesn't it? Good and bad. I love my wife — her name is Kathy — but sometimes I get angry with her. Sometimes . . . *I hate her.*"

Alicia kept staring at me; I felt like a rabbit in the headlights, frozen, unable to look away or move. The attack alarm was on the table, within reach. I made a concerted effort not to look at it.

144

I knew I shouldn't keep talking — that I should shut up — but I couldn't stop myself. I went on compulsively:

"And when I say I hate her, I don't mean *all* of me hates her. Just a part of me hates. It's about holding on to both parts at the same time. Part of you loved Gabriel. Part of you hated him."

Alicia shook her head — no. A brief movement, but definite. Finally — a response. I felt a sudden thrill. I should have stopped there, but I didn't.

"Part of you hated him," I said again more firmly.

Another shake of the head. Her eyes burned through me. She's getting angry, I thought.

"It's true, Alicia. Or you wouldn't have killed him."

Alicia suddenly jumped up. I thought she was about to leap on me. My body tensed in anticipation. But instead she turned and marched to the door. She hammered on it with her fists.

There was the sound of a key turning — and Yuri threw open the door. He looked relieved not to find Alicia strangling me on the floor. She pushed past him and ran into the corridor.

"Steady on, slow down, honey." He

145

glanced back at me. "Everything okay? What happened?"

I didn't reply. Yuri gave me a funny look and left. I was alone.

Idiot, I thought to myself. You idiot. What was I doing? I'd pushed her too far, too hard, too soon. It was horribly unprofessional, not to mention totally fucking inept. It revealed far more about my state of mind than hers.

But that's what Alicia did for you. Her silence was like a mirror — reflecting yourself back at you.

And it was often an ugly sight.

CHAPTER EIGHT

You don't need to be a psychotherapist to suspect that Kathy had left her laptop open because — unconsciously, at least — she wanted me to find out about her infidelity.

Well, now I had found out. Now I knew.

I hadn't spoken to her since the other night, feigning sleep when she got back, and leaving the flat in the morning before she woke up. I was avoiding her — avoiding myself. I was in shock. I knew I had to take a look at myself — or risk losing myself. Get a grip, I muttered under my breath as I rolled a joint. I smoked it out of the window, and then, suitably stoned, I poured a glass of wine in the kitchen.

The glass slipped out of my grasp as I picked it up. I tried to catch it as it fell, but only succeeded in thrusting my hand into a shard of glass as it smashed on the table, slicing a chunk of flesh from my finger.

Suddenly blood was everywhere: blood

trickling down my arm, blood on broken glass, blood mingling with white wine on the table. I struggled to tear off some kitchen paper and bound my finger tight to stem the flow. I held my hand above my head, watching blood stream down my arm in tiny diverging rivulets, mimicking the pattern of veins beneath my skin.

I thought of Kathy.

It was Kathy I would reach for in a moment of crisis — when I needed sympathy or reassurance or someone to kiss it better. I wanted her to look after me. I thought about calling her, but even as I had this thought, I imagined a door closing fast, slamming shut, locking her out of reach. Kathy was gone — I had lost her. I wanted to cry, but couldn't — I was blocked up inside, packed with mud and shit.

"Fuck," I kept repeating to myself, "fuck."

I became conscious of the clock ticking. It seemed louder now somehow. I tried to focus on it and anchor my spinning thoughts: tick, tick, tick — but the chorus of voices in my head grew louder and wouldn't be silenced. She was bound to be unfaithful, I thought, this had to happen, it was inevitable — I was never good enough for her, I was useless, ugly, worthless, nothing — she was bound to tire of me eventually — I didn't deserve her, I didn't deserve anything — it went on and on, one horrible thought after another punching me.

How little I knew her. Those emails demonstrated I'd been living with a stranger. Now I saw the truth. Kathy hadn't saved me — she wasn't capable of saving anyone. She was no heroine to be admired — just a frightened, fucked-up girl, a cheating liar. This whole mythology of *us* that I had built up, our hopes and dreams, likes and dislikes, our plans for the future; a life that had seemed so secure, so sturdy, now collapsed in seconds — like a house of cards in a gust of wind.

My mind went to that cold room at college, all those years ago — tearing open packets of paracetamol with clumsy, numb fingers. The same numbness overtook me now, that same desire to curl up and die. I thought of my mother. Could I call her? Turn to her in my moment of desperation and need? I imagined her answering the phone, her voice shaky; just how shaky depended on my father's mood, and if she'd been drinking. She might listen sympathetically to me, but her mind would be elsewhere, one eye on my dad and his temper. How could she help me? How can one drowning rat save another?

I had to get out. I couldn't breathe in here, in this flat with these stinking lilies. I needed some air. I needed to breathe.

I left the flat. I dug my hands in my pockets and kept my head low. I pounded the streets, walking fast, going nowhere. In my mind I kept going back over our relationship, scene by scene, remembering it, examining it, turning it over, looking for clues. I remembered unresolved fights, unexplained absences, and frequent lateness. But I also remembered small acts of kindness — affectionate notes she'd leave for me in unexpected places, moments of sweetness and apparently genuine love. How was this possible? Had she been acting the whole time? Had she ever loved me?

I remembered the flicker of doubt I'd had upon meeting her friends. They were all actors; loud, narcissistic, preening, endlessly talking about themselves and people I didn't know. Suddenly I was transported back to school, hovering alone on the fringes of the playground, watching the other kids play. I convinced myself Kathy wasn't like them at all — but clearly she was. If I had encountered them that first night at the bar when I met her, would they have put me off her? I doubt it. Nothing could have prevented our union: from the moment I saw Kathy, my fate was written.

What should I do?

Confront her, of course. Tell her everything I had seen. She'd react by denying it — then, seeing it was hopeless, she would admit the truth and prostrate herself, stricken with remorse. She'd beg my forgiveness, wouldn't she?

What if she didn't? What if she scorned me? What if she laughed, turned on her heel, and left? What then?

Between the two of us, I had the most to lose, that was obvious. Kathy would survive — she was fond of saying she was tough as nails. She'd pick herself up, dust herself off, and forget all about me. But I wouldn't forget about her. How could I? Without Kathy, I'd return to that empty, solitary existence I had endured before. I'd never meet anyone like her again, never have that same connection or experience that depth of feeling for another human being. She was the love of my life — she *was* my life — and I wasn't ready to give her up. Not yet. Even though she had betrayed me, I still loved her.

Perhaps I was crazy, after all.

A solitary bird shrieked above my head, startling me. I stopped and looked around. I'd gone much farther than I thought.

Shocked, I saw where my feet had carried me — I had walked to within a couple of streets of Ruth's front door.

Without intending to, I had unconsciously made my way to my old therapist in a time of trouble, as I had done so many times in the past. It was a testament to how upset I was that I considered going up to her door and ringing the bell and asking for help.

And why not? I thought suddenly; yes, it was unprofessional and highly improper conduct, but I was desperate, and I needed help. Before I knew it, I was standing in front of Ruth's green door, watching my hand reach up to the buzzer and press it.

It took her a few moments to answer it. A light went on the hallway, then she opened the door, keeping the chain on.

Ruth peered out through the crack. She looked older. She must be in her eighties now; smaller, frailer than I remembered, and slightly stooped. She was wearing a gray cardigan over a pale pink nightgown.

"Hello?" she said nervously. "Who's there?"

"Hello, Ruth." I stepped into the light.

She recognized me and looked surprised. "Theo? What on earth —" Her eyes went from my face to the clumsy, improvised bandage around my finger, with blood seeping through it. "Are you all right?"

"Not really. May I come in? I — I need to talk to you."

Ruth didn't hesitate, only looked concerned. She nodded. "Of course. Come in." She undid the chain and opened the door.

I stepped inside.

CHAPTER NINE

Ruth showed me into the living room. "Would you like a cup of tea?"

The room was as it had always been, as I'd always remembered it — the rug, the heavy drapes, the silver clock ticking on the mantel, the armchair, the faded blue couch. I felt instantly reassured.

"To be honest, I could do with something stronger."

Ruth shot me a brief, piercing glance, but didn't comment. Nor did she refuse, as I half expected.

She poured me a glass of sherry and handed it to me. I sat on the couch. Force of habit made me sit where I had always done for therapy, on the far left side, resting my arm on the armrest. The fabric underneath my fingertips had been worn thin by the anxious rubbing of many patients, myself included.

I took a sip of sherry. It was warm, sweet,

and a little sickly, but I drank it down, conscious of Ruth watching me the whole time. Her gaze was obvious but not heavy or uncomfortable; in twenty years Ruth had never managed to make me feel uncomfortable. I didn't speak again until I had finished the sherry and the glass was empty.

"It feels odd to be sitting here with a glass in my hand. I know you're not in the habit of offering drinks to your patients."

"You're not my patient anymore. Just a friend — and by the look of you," she added gently, "you need a friend right now."

"Do I look that bad?"

"You do, I'm afraid. And it must be serious, or you wouldn't come over uninvited like this. Certainly not at ten o'clock at night."

"You're right. I felt — I felt I had no choice."

"What is it, Theo? What's the matter?"

"I don't know how to tell you. I don't know where to start."

"How about the beginning?"

I nodded. I took a breath and began. I told her about everything that had happened; I told her about starting marijuana again, and how I had been smoking it secretly — and how it had led to my discovering Kathy's emails and her affair. I spoke

155

quickly, breathlessly, wanting to get it off my chest. I felt as if I were at confession.

Ruth listened without interruption until I had finished. It was hard to read her expression. Finally she said, "I am very sorry this happened, Theo. I know how much Kathy means to you. How much you love her."

"Yes. I love —" I stopped, unable to say her name. There was a tremor in my voice. Ruth picked up on it and edged the box of tissues toward me. I used to get angry when she would do that in our sessions; I'd accuse her of trying to make me cry. She would generally succeed. But not tonight. Tonight my tears were frozen. A reservoir of ice.

I had been seeing Ruth for a long time before I met Kathy, and I continued therapy for the first three years of our relationship. I remember the advice Ruth gave me when Kathy and I first got together: "Choosing a lover is a lot like choosing a therapist. We need to ask ourselves, is this someone who will be honest with me, listen to criticism, admit making mistakes, and not promise the impossible?"

I told all this to Kathy at the time, and she suggested we make a pact. We swore never to lie to each other. Never pretend. Always be truthful.

156

"What happened?" I said. "What went wrong?"

Ruth hesitated before she spoke. What she said surprised me.

"I suspect you know the answer to that. If you would just admit it to yourself."

"I don't know." I shook my head. "I don't."

I fell into indignant silence — yet I had a sudden image of Kathy writing all those emails, and how passionate they were, how charged, as if she was getting high from writing them, from the clandestine nature of her relationship with this man. She enjoyed lying and sneaking around: it was like acting, but offstage.

"I think she's bored," I said eventually.

"What makes you say that?"

"Because she needs excitement. Drama. She always has. She's been complaining — for a while, I suppose — that we don't have any fun anymore, that I'm always stressed, that I work too hard. We fought about it recently. She kept using the word *fireworks*."

"Fireworks?"

"As in there aren't any. Between us."

"Ah. I see." Ruth nodded. "We've talked about this before. Haven't we?"

"About fireworks?"

"About love. About how we often mistake

love for fireworks — for drama and dysfunction. But real love is very quiet, very still. It's boring, if seen from the perspective of high drama. Love is deep and calm — and constant. I imagine you do give Kathy love — in the true sense of the word. Whether or not she is capable of giving it back to you is another question."

I stared at the box of tissues on the table in front of me. I didn't like where Ruth was going. I tried to deflect her.

"There are faults on both sides. I lied to her too. About the weed."

Ruth smiled sadly. "I don't know if persistent sexual and emotional betrayal with another human being is on the same level as getting stoned every now and then. I think it points to a very different kind of individual — someone who is able to lie repeatedly and lie well, who can betray their partner without feeling any remorse —"

"You don't know that." I sounded as pathetic as I felt. "She might feel terrible."

But even as I said that, I didn't believe it.

Neither did Ruth. "I don't think so. I think her behavior suggests she is quite damaged — lacking in empathy and integrity and just plain kindness — all the qualities you brim with."

I shook my head. "That's not true."

"It is true, Theo." Ruth hesitated. "Don't you think perhaps you've been here before?"

"With Kathy?"

Ruth shook her head. "I don't mean that. I mean with your parents. When you were younger. If there's a childhood dynamic here you might be replaying."

"No." I suddenly felt irritated. "What's happening with Kathy has got nothing to do with my childhood."

"Oh, really?" Ruth sounded disbelieving. "Trying to please someone unpredictable, someone emotionally unavailable, uncaring, unkind — trying to keep them happy, win their love — is this not an old story, Theo? A familiar story?"

I clenched my fist and didn't speak.

Ruth went on hesitantly, "I know how sad you feel. But I want you to consider the possibility that you felt this sadness long before you met Kathy. It's a sadness you've been carrying around for many years. You know, Theo, one of the hardest things to admit is that we weren't loved when we needed it most. It's a terrible feeling, the pain of not being loved."

She was right. I had been groping for the right words to express that murky feeling of betrayal inside, the horrible hollow ache, and to hear Ruth say it — "the pain of not

159

being loved" — I saw how it pervaded my entire consciousness and was at once the story of my past, present, and future. This wasn't just about Kathy: it was about my father, and my childhood feelings of abandonment; my grief for everything I never had and, in my heart, still believed I never would have. Ruth was saying that was why I chose Kathy. What better way for me to prove that my father was correct — that I'm worthless and unlovable — than by pursuing someone who will never love me?

I buried my head in my hands. "So all this was inevitable? That's what you're saying — I set myself up for this? It's fucking hopeless?"

"It's not hopeless. You're not a boy at the mercy of your father anymore. You're a grown man now — and you have a choice. Use this as another confirmation of how unworthy you are — or break with the past. Free yourself from endlessly repeating it."

"How do I do that? You think I should leave her?"

"I think it's a very difficult situation."

"But you think I should leave, don't you?"

"You've come too far and worked too hard to return to a life of dishonesty and denial and emotional abuse. You deserve someone who treats you better, *much* better —"

"Just say it, Ruth. Say it. You think I should leave."

Ruth looked me in the eyes. She held my gaze. "I think you *must* leave. And I'm not saying this as your old therapist — but as your old friend. I don't think you could go back, even if you wanted to. It might last a little while perhaps, but in a few months something else will happen and you'll end up back here on this couch. Be honest with yourself, Theo — about Kathy and this situation — and everything built on lies and untruths will fall away from you. Remember, love that doesn't include honesty doesn't deserve to be called love."

I sighed, deflated, depressed, and tired.

"Thank you, Ruth — for your honesty. It means a lot."

Ruth gave me a hug at the door as I left. She'd never done that before. She was fragile in my arms, her bones so delicate; I breathed in her faint flowery scent and the wool of her cardigan and again I felt like crying. But I didn't, or couldn't, cry.

Instead I walked away and didn't look back.

I caught a bus back home. I sat by the window, staring out, thinking of Kathy, of her white skin, and those beautiful green eyes. I was filled with such a longing — for

161

the sweet taste of her lips, her softness. But Ruth was right. Love that doesn't include honesty doesn't deserve to be called love.

I had to go home and confront Kathy.

I had to leave her.

CHAPTER TEN

Kathy was there when I got home. She was sitting on the couch, texting.

"Where were you?" she asked without looking up.

"Just a walk. How was rehearsal?"

"All right. Tiring."

I watched her texting, wondering who she was writing to. I knew this was my moment to speak. *I know you're having an affair — I want a divorce.* I opened my mouth to say it. But I found I was mute. Before I could recover my voice, Kathy beat me to it. She stopped texting and put down her phone.

"Theo, we need to talk."

"What about?"

"Don't you have something to tell me?" Her voice had a stern note.

I avoided looking at her, in case she could read my thoughts. I felt ashamed and furtive — as if I were the one with the guilty secret.

163

And I was, as far as she was concerned. Kathy reached behind the sofa and picked something up. At once my heart sank. She was holding the small jar where I kept the grass. I'd forgotten to hide it back in the spare room after I'd cut my finger.

"What's this?" She held it up.

"It's weed."

"I'm aware of that. What's it doing here?"

"I bought some. I fancied it."

"Fancied what? Getting high? Are you — serious?"

I shrugged, evading her eye, like a naughty child.

"What the fuck? I mean, Jesus —" Kathy shook her head, outraged. "Sometimes I think I don't know you at all."

I wanted to hit her. I wanted to leap on her and beat her with my fists. I wanted to smash up the room, break the furniture against the walls. I wanted to weep and howl and bury myself in her arms.

I did none of this.

"Let's go to bed," I said, and walked out.

We went to bed in silence. I lay in the dark next to her. I lay awake for hours, feeling the heat from her body, staring at her while she slept.

Why didn't you come to me? I wanted to say. Why didn't you talk to me? I was your best friend. If you had said just one word, we could have worked through it. Why didn't you talk to me? I'm here. *I'm right here.*

I wanted to reach out and pull her close. I wanted to hold her. But I couldn't. Kathy had gone — the person I loved so much had disappeared forever, leaving this stranger in her place.

A sob rose at the back of my throat. Finally, the tears came, streaming down my cheeks.

Silently, in the darkness, I wept.

The next morning, we got up and performed the usual routine — she went into the bathroom while I made coffee. I handed her a cup when she came into the kitchen.

"You were making strange sounds in the night," she said. "You were talking in your sleep."

"What did I say?"

"I don't know. Nothing. Didn't make sense. Probably because you were so *stoned.*" She gave me a withering look and glanced at her watch. "I have to go. I'll be late."

Kathy finished her coffee and placed the cup in the sink. She gave me a quick kiss on the cheek. The touch of her lips almost made me flinch.

After she left, I showered. I turned up the temperature until it was almost scalding. The hot water lashed against my face as I wept, burning away messy, babyish tears. As I dried myself afterward, I caught a glimpse of my reflection in the mirror. I was shocked — I was ashen, shrunken, had aged thirty years overnight. I was old, exhausted, my youth evaporated.

I made a decision, there and then.

Leaving Kathy would be like tearing off a limb. I simply wasn't prepared to mutilate myself like that. No matter what Ruth said. Ruth wasn't infallible. Kathy was not my father; I wasn't condemned to repeat the past. I could change the future. Kathy and I were happy before; we could be again. One day she might confess it all to me, tell me about it, and I would forgive her. We would work through this.

I would not let Kathy go. Instead I would say nothing. I would pretend I had never read those emails. Somehow, I'd forget. I'd bury it. I had no choice but to go on. I refused to give in to this; I refused to break down and fall apart.

After all, I wasn't just responsible for myself. What about the patients in my care?

**Certain people depended on me.
I couldn't let them down.**

CHAPTER ELEVEN

"I'm looking for Elif. Any idea where I can find her?"

Yuri gave me a curious look. "Any reason you want her?"

"Just to say a quick hello. I want to meet all the patients — let them know who I am, that I'm here."

Yuri looked doubtful. "Right. Well, don't take it personally if she's not very receptive." He glanced at the clock on the wall. "It's after half past, so she's just out of art therapy. Your best bet is the recreation room."

"Thanks."

The recreation area was a large circular room furnished with battered couches, low tables, a bookcase full of tattered books no one wanted to read. It smelled of stale tea and old cigarette smoke that had stained the furnishings. A couple of patients were playing backgammon in a corner. Elif was alone at the pool table. I approached with a smile.

"Hello, Elif."

She looked up with scared, mistrustful eyes. "What?"

"Don't worry, there's nothing wrong. I just want a quick word."

"You ain't my doctor. I already got one."

"I'm not a doctor. I'm a psychotherapist."

Elif grunted contemptuously. "I got one of them too."

I smiled, secretly relieved she was Indira's patient and not mine. Up close Elif was even more intimidating. It wasn't just her massive size, but also the rage etched deep into her face — a permanent scowl and angry black eyes, eyes that were quite clearly disturbed. She stank of sweat and the hand-rolled cigarettes she was always smoking that had left her fingertips stained black and her nails and teeth a dark yellow.

"I just wanted to ask you a couple of questions, if that's okay — about Alicia."

Elif scowled and banged the cue on the table. She starting setting up the balls for another game. Then she stopped. She just stood there, looking distracted, in silence.

"Elif?"

She didn't respond. I could tell from her expression what was wrong. "Are you hearing voices, Elif?"

A suspicious glance. A shrug.

"What are they saying?"

"You ain't safe. Telling me to watch out."

"I see. Quite right. You don't know me —
so it's sensible not to trust me. Not yet.
Perhaps, over time, that will change."

Elif gave me a look that suggested she
doubted it.

I nodded at the pool table. "Fancy a
game?"

"Nope."

"Why not?"

She shrugged. "Other cue's broke. They
ain't replaced it yet."

"But I can share your cue, can't I?"

The cue was resting on the table. I went
to touch it — and she yanked it out of
reach. "It's my fuckin' cue! Get your own!"

I stepped back, unnerved by the ferocity
of her reaction. She played a shot with
considerable force. I watched her play for a
moment. Then I tried again.

"I was wondering if you could tell me
about something that happened when Alicia
was first admitted to the Grove. Do you
remember?"

Elif shook her head.

"I read in her file that you had an altera-
tion in the canteen. You were on the receiv-

170

ing end of an attack?"

"Oh, yeah, yeah, she tried to kill me, innit? Tried to cut my fucking throat."

"According to the handover notes, a nurse saw you whisper something to Alicia before the attack. I was wondering what it was?"

"No." Elif shook her head furiously. "I didn't say nothing."

"I'm not trying to suggest you provoked her. I'm just curious. What was it?"

"I asked her something, so fucking what?"

"What did you ask?"

"I asked if he deserved it."

"Who?"

"Him. Her bloke." Elif smiled, although it wasn't really a smile, more a misshapen grimace.

"You mean her husband?" I hesitated, unsure if I understood. "You asked Alicia if her husband deserved to be killed?"

Elif nodded and played a shot. "And I asked what he looked like. When she shot him and his skull was broke, and his brains all spilled out." Elif laughed.

I felt a sudden wave of disgust — similar to the feelings I imagined Elif had provoked in Alicia. Elif made you feel repulsion and hatred — that was her pathology, that was how her mother had made her feel as a small child. Hateful and repulsive. So Elif

171

unconsciously provoked you to hate her — and mostly she succeeded.

"And how are things now? Are you and Alicia on good terms?"

"Oh, yeah, mate. We're real tight. Best mates." Elif laughed again.

Before I could respond, I felt my phone vibrating in my pocket. I checked it. I didn't recognize the number.

"I should answer this. Thank you. You've been very helpful."

Elif muttered something unintelligible and went back to her game.

I walked into the corridor and answered the phone. "Hello?"

"Is that Theo Faber?"

"Speaking. Who's this?"

"Max Berenson here, returning your call."

"Oh, yes. Hi. Thanks for calling me back. I was wondering if we could have a conversation about Alicia?"

"Why? What's happened? Is something wrong?"

"No. I mean, not exactly — I'm treating her, and I wanted to ask you a couple of questions about her. Whenever's convenient."

"I don't suppose we could do it on the phone? I'm rather busy."

"I'd rather talk in person, if possible."

Max Berenson sighed and mumbled as he spoke to someone off the phone. And then: "Tomorrow evening, seven o'clock, my office."

I was about to ask for the address — but he hung up.

CHAPTER TWELVE

Max Berenson's receptionist had a bad cold. She reached for a tissue, blew her nose, and gestured at me to wait.

"He's on the phone. He'll be out in a minute."

I nodded and took a seat in the waiting area. A few uncomfortable upright chairs, a coffee table with a stack of out-of-date magazines. All waiting rooms looked alike, I thought; I could just as easily have been waiting to see a doctor or funeral director as a lawyer.

The door across the hallway opened. Max Berenson appeared and beckoned me over. He disappeared back into his office. I got up and followed him inside.

I expected the worst, given his gruff manner on the phone. But to my surprise, he began with an apology.

"I'm sorry if I was abrupt when we spoke. It's been a long week and I'm a bit under the weather. Won't you sit down?"

I sat on the chair on the other side of the desk. "Thanks. And thank you for agreeing to see me."

"Well, I wasn't sure I should at first. I thought you were a journalist, trying to get me to talk about Alicia. But then I called the Grove and checked you worked there."

"I see. Does that happen a lot? Journalists, I mean?"

"Not recently. It used to. I learned to be on my guard —" He was about to say something else, but a sneeze overtook him. He reached for a box of tissues. "Sorry — I have the family cold."

He blew his nose. I glanced at him more closely. Unlike his younger brother, Max Berenson was not attractive. Max was imposing, balding, and his face was speckled with deep acne scars. He was wearing an old-fashioned spicy men's cologne, the kind my father used to wear. His office was similarly traditional and had the reassuring smell of leather furniture, wood, books. It couldn't be more different from the world inhabited by Gabriel — a world of color and beauty for beauty's sake. He and Max were obviously nothing alike.

A framed photograph of Gabriel was on the desk. A candid shot — possibly taken

175

by Max? Gabriel was sitting on a fence in a country field, his hair blowing in the breeze, a camera slung around his neck. He looked more like an actor than a photographer. Or an actor playing a photographer.

Max caught me looking at the picture and nodded as if reading my mind. "My brother got the hair and the looks. I got the brains." Max laughed. "I'm joking. Actually, I was adopted. We weren't blood related."

"I didn't know that. Were you both adopted?"

"No, just me. Our parents thought they couldn't have children. But after they adopted me, they conceived a child of their own soon after. It's quite common apparently. Something to do with relieving stress."

"Were you and Gabriel close?"

"Closer than most. Though he took center stage, of course. I was rather overshadowed by him."

"Why was that?"

"Well, it was difficult not to be. Gabriel was special, even as a child." Max had a habit of playing with his wedding ring. He kept turning it around his finger as he talked. "Gabriel used to carry his camera everywhere, you know, taking pictures. My father thought he was mad. Turns out he was a bit of a genius, my brother. Do you know his work?"

I smiled diplomatically. I had no desire to get into a discussion of Gabriel's merits as a photographer.

Instead I steered the conversation back to Alicia. "You must have known her quite well?"

"Alicia? Must I?" Something in Max changed at the mention of her name. His warmth evaporated. His tone was cold. "I don't know if I can help you. I didn't represent Alicia in court. I can put you in touch with my colleague Patrick Doherty if you want details about the trial."

"That's not the kind of information I'm after."

"No?" Max gave me a curious look. "As a psychotherapist, it can't be common practice to meet your patient's lawyer?"

"Not if my patient can speak for herself, no."

Max seemed to mull this over. "I see. Well, as I said, I don't know how I can help, so —"

"I just have a couple of questions."

"Very well. Fire away."

"I remember reading in the press at the time that you saw Gabriel and Alicia the night before the murder?"

"Yes, we had dinner together."

"How did they seem?"

Max's eyes glazed over. Presumably he'd been asked this question hundreds of times, and his response was automatic, without thinking. "Normal. Totally normal."

"And Alicia?"

"Normal." He shrugged. "Maybe a bit more jumpy than usual, but . . ."

"But?"

"Nothing."

I sensed there was more. I waited.

And after a moment, Max went on, "I don't know how much you know about their relationship."

"Only what I read in the papers."

"And what did you read?"

"That they were happy."

"Happy?" Max smiled coldly. "Oh, they were happy. Gabriel did everything he could to make her happy."

"I see." But I didn't see. I didn't know where Max was going.

I must have looked puzzled because he shrugged. "I'm not going to elaborate. If it's gossip you're after, talk to Jean-Felix, not me."

"Jean-Felix?"

"Jean-Felix Martin. Alicia's gallerist. They'd known each other for years. As thick as thieves. Never liked him much, if I'm

178

honest."

"I'm not interested in gossip." I made a mental note to talk to Jean-Felix as soon as possible. "I'm more interested in your personal opinion. May I ask you a direct question?"

"I thought you just did."

"Did you like Alicia?"

Max looked at me expressionlessly as he spoke. "Of course I did."

I didn't believe him. "I sense you're wearing two different hats. The lawyer's hat, which is understandably discreet. And the brother's hat. It's the brother I came to see."

There was a pause. I wondered if Max was about to ask me to leave. He seemed about to say something but changed his mind. Then he suddenly left the desk and went to the window. He opened it. There was a blast of cold air. Max breathed in deeply, as if the room had been stifling him.

Finally he said in a low voice, "The truth is . . . I hated her . . . I loathed her."

I didn't say anything. I waited for him to go on.

He kept looking out the window and said slowly, "Gabriel wasn't just my brother, he was my best friend. He was the kindest man you ever met. Too kind. And all his talent, his goodness, his passion for life — wiped

179

out, because of *that bitch.* It wasn't just his life she destroyed — it was mine too. Thank God my parents didn't live to see it." Max choked up, suddenly emotional.

It was hard not to sense his pain, and I felt sorry for him. "It must have been extremely difficult for you to organize Alicia's defense."

Max shut the window and returned to the desk. He had regained control of himself. He was wearing the lawyer's hat again. Neutral, balanced, emotionless.

He shrugged. "It's what Gabriel would have wanted. He wanted the best for Alicia, always. He was mad about her. She was just mad."

"You think she was insane?"

"You tell me — you're her shrink."

"What do you think?"

"I know what I observed."

"And what was that?"

"Mood swings. Rages. Violent fits. She'd break things, smash stuff up. Gabriel told me she threatened to murder him on several occasions. I should have listened, done something — after she tried to kill herself, I should have intervened, insisted she got some help. But I didn't. Gabriel was determined to protect her, and like an idiot, I let him."

Max sighed and checked his watch — a cue for me to wrap up the conversation.

But I just stared at him blankly. "Alicia tried to kill herself? What do you mean? When? You mean after the murder?"

Max shook his head. "No, several years before that. You don't know? I assumed you knew."

"When was this?"

"After her father died. She took an overdose . . . pills or something. I can't remember exactly. She had a kind of breakdown."

I was about to press him further when the door opened. The receptionist appeared and spoke in a sniffly voice. "Darling, we should go. We'll be late."

"Right. Coming, dear."

The door shut. Max stood up, giving me an apologetic glance. "We have theater tickets." I must have looked startled, because he laughed. "We — Tanya and I — were married last year."

"Oh. I see."

"Gabriel's death brought us together. I couldn't have gotten through it without her."

Max's phone rang, distracting him.

I nodded at him to take the call. "Thank you, you've been a great help."

I slipped out of the office. I took a closer

look at Tanya in reception — she was blond, pretty, rather petite. She blew her nose, and I noticed the large diamond on her wedding finger.

To my surprise, she got up and walked toward me, frowning. She spoke urgently in a low voice. "If you want to know about Alicia, talk to her cousin, Paul — he knows her better than anyone."

"I tried calling her aunt, Lydia Rose. She wasn't particularly forthcoming."

"Forget Lydia. Go to Cambridge. Talk to Paul. Ask him about Alicia and the night after the accident, and —"

The office door opened. Tanya immediately fell silent. Max emerged and she hurried over to him, smiling broadly.

"Ready, darling?" she asked.

Tanya was smiling, but she sounded nervous. She's afraid of Max, I thought. I wondered why.

CHAPTER THIRTEEN

Alicia Berenson's Diary

July 22

I hate the fact there's a gun in the house.

We had another argument about it last night. At least I thought that's what we were fighting about — I'm not so sure now.

Gabriel said it was my fault we argued. I suppose it was. I hated seeing him so upset, looking at me with hurt eyes. I hate causing him pain — and yet sometimes I desperately want to hurt him, and I don't know why.

He said I came home in a horrible mood. That I marched upstairs and started screaming at him. Perhaps I did. I suppose I was upset. I'm not altogether sure what happened. I had just gotten back from the park. I don't remember much of the walk — I was daydreaming, thinking about work, about the Jesus picture. I remember walking past a house on my way home. Two boys were playing with a hose. They couldn't have been older than seven or eight. The older boy was spraying the younger with a jet of water, a rainbow of color sparkling in the light. A perfect rainbow. The younger boy stretched out his hands, laughing. I walked past and I realized my cheeks were wet with tears.

I dismissed it then, but thinking about it now, it seems obvious. I don't want to admit the truth to myself — that a huge part of my life is missing. That I've denied I want children, pretending I have no interest in them, that all I care about is my art. And it's not true. It's just an excuse — the truth is I'm scared to have kids. I am not to be trusted with them.

Not with my mother's blood running through my veins.

That's what was on my mind, consciously or unconsciously, when I got home. Gabriel was right, I was in a bad state.

But I never would have exploded if I hadn't found him cleaning the gun. It upsets me so much that he has it. And it hurts me he won't

184

get rid of it, no matter how many times I beg him. He always says the same thing — that it was one of his father's old rifles from their farm and he gave it to him when he was sixteen, that it has sentimental value and blah blah blah. I don't believe him. I think there's another reason he's keeping it. I said so. And Gabriel said there was nothing wrong with wanting to be safe — wanting to protect his house and wife. What if someone broke in?

"Then we call the police," I said. "We don't fucking shoot them!"

I had raised my voice, but he raised his louder, and before I knew it, we were yelling at each other. Maybe I was a bit out of control. But I was only reacting to him — there's an aggressive side to Gabriel, a part of him I only glimpse occasionally, and when I do, it scares me. For those brief moments it's like living with a stranger. And that's terrifying.

We didn't speak for the rest of the evening. We went to bed in silence.

This morning we had sex and made up. We always seem to resolve our problems in bed. It's easier, somehow — when you're naked and half-asleep under the covers — to whisper, "I'm sorry," and mean it. All defenses and bullshit justifications are discarded, lying in a heap on the floor with our clothes.

"Maybe we should make it a rule to always conduct arguments in bed." He kissed me. "I love you. I'll get rid of the rifle, I promise."

"No," I said. "It doesn't matter, forget it. It's okay. Really."

Gabriel kissed me again and pulled me close. I held on to him, laying my naked body on his. I closed my eyes and stretched out on a friendly rock that was molded to my shape. And I felt at peace at last.

July 23
I'm writing this in Caffe dell'Artista. I come here most days now. I keep feeling the need to get out of the house. When I'm around other people, even if it's only the bored waitress in here, I feel connected to the world somehow, like a human being.

Otherwise I'm in danger of ceasing to exist. Like I might disappear.

Sometimes I wish I could disappear — like tonight. Gabriel has invited his brother over

186

for dinner. He sprung it on me this morning.

"We've not seen Max in ages," he said. "Not since Joel's housewarming. I'll do a barbecue." Gabriel looked at me strangely. "You don't mind, do you?"

"Why would I mind?"

Gabriel laughed. "You're such a bad liar, you know that? I can read your face like a very short book."

"And what does it say?"

"That you don't like Max. You never have."

"That's not true." I could feel myself going red. I shrugged and looked away. "Of course I like Max. It'll be nice to see him. When are you going to sit for me again? I need to finish the picture."

Gabriel smiled. "How about this weekend? And about the painting — do me a favor. Don't show Max, all right? I don't want him to see me as Jesus — I'll never live it down."

"Max won't see it. It's not ready yet."

And even if it were, Max is the last person I want in my studio. I thought that but didn't say it.

I'm dreading going home now. I want to stay here in this air-conditioned café and hide until Max has left. But the waitress is already making little impatient noises and emphatically checking her watch. I'll be kicked out soon. And that means short of wandering the streets all night like a mad person, I have no choice but to go home and face the music. And face Max.

July 24
I'm back in the café. Someone was sitting at my table, and the waitress gave me a sympathetic look — at least I think that's what she was communicating, a sense of solidarity, but I could be wrong. I took another table, facing in, not out, by the air-conditioning unit. There's not much light — it's cold and dark, which suits my mood.

Last night was awful. Worse than I thought it would be.

I didn't recognize Max when he arrived — I don't think I've ever seen him out of a suit before. He looked a bit silly in shorts. He was sweating profusely after the walk from the station — his bald head was red and shiny, and dark patches were spreading out from under his armpits. He wouldn't meet my eyes at first. Or was it me, not looking at him?

He made a big thing of the house, saying how different it looked, how long it was since we'd invited him that he was starting to think we'd never ask again. Gabriel kept apologizing, saying how busy we'd been, me with the upcoming exhibition and him with work, and we'd not seen anyone. Gabriel was smiling, but I could tell he felt annoyed that Max had made such a point of it.

I kept up a pretty good front at first. I was waiting for the right moment. And then I found it. Max and Gabriel went into the garden and got the barbecue going. I hung around in the kitchen on the pretext of making a salad. I knew Max would make an excuse to come and find me. And I was right. After about five minutes, I heard his heavy, thudding footsteps. He doesn't walk at all like Gabriel — Gabriel is so silent, he's like a cat, I never hear him moving around the house at all.

"Alicia," Max said.

I realized my hands were shaking as I chopped the tomatoes. I put down the knife. I turned around to face him.

Max held up his empty beer bottle and smiled. He still wouldn't look at me. "I've come for another."

I nodded. I didn't say anything. He opened the fridge and took out another beer. He looked around for the opener. I pointed at it on the counter.

He gave me a funny smile as he opened the beer, like he was going to say something. But I beat him to it:

"I'm going to tell Gabriel what happened. I thought you should know."

Max stopped smiling. He looked at me for the first time, with snakelike eyes. "What?"

"I'm telling Gabriel. About what happened at Joel's."

"I don't know what you're talking about."

"Don't you?"

"I don't remember. I was rather drunk, I'm afraid."

"Bullshit."

"It's true."

"You don't remember kissing me? You don't remember grabbing me?"

"Alicia, don't."

"Don't what? Make a big deal out of it? You assaulted me."

I could feel myself getting angry. It was an effort to control my voice and not start shouting. I glanced out the window. Gabriel was at the end of the garden, standing over the barbecue. The smoke and the hot air distorted my view of him, and he was all bent out of shape.

"He looks up to you," I said. "You're his older brother. He's going to be so hurt when I tell him."

"Then don't. There's nothing to tell him."

"He needs to know the truth. He needs to know what his brother is really like. You —"

191

Before I could finish, Max grabbed my arm hard and pulled me toward him. I lost my balance and fell onto him. He raised his fist and I thought he was going to punch me. "I love you," he said, "I love you, I love you, I love —"

Before I could react, he kissed me. I tried to pull away but he wouldn't let me. I felt his rough lips all over mine, and his tongue pushing its way into my mouth. Instinct took over.

I bit his tongue as hard as I could.

Max cried out and shoved me away. When he looked up, his mouth was full of blood.

"Fucking bitch!" His voice was garbled, his teeth red. He glared at me like a wounded animal.

I can't believe Max is Gabriel's brother. He has none of Gabriel's fine qualities, none of his decency, none of his kindness. Max disgusts me — and I said so.

"Alicia, don't say anything to Gabriel," he said. "I mean it. I'm warning you."

I didn't say another word. I could taste his blood on my tongue, so I turned on the tap and rinsed my mouth until it was gone. Then I walked out into the garden.

Occasionally I sensed Max staring at me over dinner. I'd look up and catch his eye and he'd look away. I didn't eat anything. The thought of eating made me sick. I kept tasting his blood in my mouth.

I don't know what to do. I don't want to lie to Gabriel. Nor do I want to keep it a secret. But if I tell Gabriel, he'll never speak to Max again. It would devastate him to know he'd misplaced his trust in his brother. Because he does trust Max. He idolizes him. And he shouldn't.

I don't believe that Max is in love with me. I believe he hates Gabriel, that's all. I think he's madly jealous of him — and he wants to take everything that belongs to Gabriel, which includes me. But now that I've stood up to him, I don't think he'll bother me again — at least I hope not. Not for a while, anyway.

So, for the moment, I'm going to remain silent.

Of course, Gabriel can read me like a book. Or maybe I'm just not a very good actress. Last night, as we were getting ready for bed, he said I'd been weird the whole time Max was there.

"I was just tired."

"No, it was more than that. You were so distant. You might have made more of an effort. We barely ever see him. I don't know why you have such a problem with him."

"I don't. It was nothing to do with Max. I was distracted, I was thinking about work. I'm behind with the exhibition — it's all I can think about." I said this with as much conviction as I could muster.

Gabriel gave me a disbelieving look but he let it go, for the moment. I'll have to face it again next time we see Max — but something tells me that won't be for a while.

I feel better for having written this down. I feel safer, somehow, having it on paper. It means I have some evidence — some proof.

If it ever comes to that.

July 26
It's my birthday today. I'm thirty-three years old.

194

It's strange — it's older than I ever saw myself as being; my imagination only ever extended this far. I've outlived my mother now — it's an unsteady feeling, being older than she was. She got to thirty-two, and then she stopped. Now I've outlived her, and won't stop. I will grow older and older — but she won't.

Gabriel was so sweet this morning — he kissed me awake and presented me with thirty-three red roses. They were beautiful. He pricked his finger on one of the thorns. A bloodred teardrop. It was perfect.

Then he took me for a picnic in the park for breakfast. The sun was barely up, so the heat wasn't unbearable. A cool breeze was coming off the water and the air smelled of cut grass. We lay by the pond under a weeping willow, on the blue blanket we bought in Mexico. The willow branches formed a canopy over us, and the sun burned hazily through the leaves. We drank champagne and ate small sweet toma-toes with smoked salmon and slivers of bread. Somewhere, in the back of my mind, was a vague feeling of familiarity, a nagging sense of déjà vu I couldn't quite place. Perhaps it was simply a recollection of childhood stories, fairy tales, and magical trees being gateways to other worlds. Perhaps it was something more prosaic. And then the memory came back to me:

I saw myself when very young, sitting under the branches of the willow tree in our garden in Cambridge. I'd spend hours hiding there. I may not have been a happy child, but during the time I spent under the willow tree, I felt a similar contentment to lying here with Gabriel. And now it was as if the past and the present were coexisting simultaneously in one perfect moment. I wanted that moment to last forever. Gabriel fell asleep, and I sketched him, trying to capture the dappled sunlight on his face. I did a better job with his eyes this time. It was easier because they were closed — but at least I got their shape right. He looked like a little boy, curled up asleep and breathing gently, crumbs around his mouth.

We finished the picnic, went home, and had sex. And Gabriel held me in his arms and said something astonishing:

"Alicia, darling, listen. There's something on my mind I want to talk to you about."

The way he said it made me instantly nervous. I braced myself, fearing the worst. "Go on."

"I want us to have a baby."

It took me a moment to speak. I was so taken aback I didn't know what to say.

"But — you didn't want any children. You said —"

"Forget that. I changed my mind. I want us to have a child together. Well? What do you say?"

Gabriel looked at me hopefully, expectantly, waiting for my response. I felt my eyes welling up with tears. "Yes," I said, "yes, yes, yes . . ."

We hugged each other and cried and laughed.

He's in bed now, asleep. I had to sneak away and write all this down — I want to remember this day for the rest of my life. Every single second of it.

I feel joyous. I feel full of hope.

CHAPTER FOURTEEN

I kept thinking about what Max Berenson had said — about Alicia's suicide attempt, following her father's death. There was no mention of it in her file, and I wondered why.

I rang Max the next day, catching him just as he was leaving the office.

"I just want to ask you a couple more questions if you don't mind."

"I'm literally walking out the door."

"This won't take long."

Max sighed and lowered the phone to say something unintelligible to Tanya.

"Five minutes," he said. "That's all you get."

"Thanks, I appreciate it. You mentioned Alicia's suicide attempt. I was wondering, which hospital treated her?"

"She wasn't admitted to hospital."

"She wasn't?"

"No. She recovered at home. My brother

looked after her."

"But — surely she saw a doctor? It was an overdose, you said?"

"Yes. And of course Gabriel got a doctor over. And he . . . the doctor — agreed to keep it quiet."

"Who was the doctor? Do you remember his name?"

There was a pause as Max thought for a moment. "I'm sorry, I can't tell you. . . . I can't recall."

"Was it their GP?"

"No, I'm sure it wasn't. My brother and I shared a GP. I remember Gabriel made a point of asking me not to mention it to him."

"And you're sure you can't remember a name?"

"I'm sorry. Is that all? I have to go."

"Just one more thing . . . I was curious about the terms of Gabriel's will."

A slight intake of breath, and Max's tone instantly sharpened. "His will? I really don't see the relevance —"

"Was Alicia the main beneficiary?"

"I must say, I find that rather an odd question."

"Well, I'm trying to understand —"

"Understand what?" Max went on without waiting for a reply, sounding annoyed. "I was the main beneficiary. Alicia had inherited a great deal of money from her father, so Gabriel felt she was well provided for. And so he left the bulk of his estate to me. Of course, he had no idea his estate would become so valuable after his death. Is that it?"

"And what about Alicia's will? When she dies, who inherits?"

"That," Max said firmly, "is more than I can tell you. And I sincerely hope this will be our last conversation."

There was a click as he hung up. But something in his tone told me this wouldn't be the last I'd hear from Max Berenson.

I didn't have to wait long.

Diomedes called me into his office after lunch. He looked up when I walked in but didn't smile. "What is the matter with you?"

"With me?"

"Don't play the idiot. You know who I had a call from this morning? Max Berenson. He says you contacted him twice and asked a lot of personal questions."

"I asked him for some information about Alicia. He seemed fine with it."

"Well, he's not fine now. He's calling it harassment."

"Oh, come on —"

200

"The last thing we need is a lawyer making a fuss. Everything you do must be within the confines of the unit, and under my supervision. Understood?"

I was angry, but I nodded. I stared at the floor like a sullen teenager.

Diomedes responded appropriately, giving me a paternal pat on the shoulder. "Theo. Let me give you some advice. You're going about this the wrong way. You're asking questions, searching for clues, like it's a detective story." He laughed and shook his head. "You won't get to it like that."

"Get to what?"

"The truth. Remember Bion: 'No memory — no desire.' No agenda — as a therapist, your only goal is to be present and receptive to your feelings as you sit with her. That's all you need to do. The rest will take care of itself."

"I know. You're right."

"Yes, I am. And don't let me hear you've been making any more visits to Alicia's relations, understood?"

"You have my word."

CHAPTER FIFTEEN

That afternoon I went to Cambridge, to visit Alicia's cousin, Paul Rose.

As the train approached the station, the landscape flattened out and the fields let in an expanse of cold blue light. I felt glad to be out of London — the sky was less oppressive, and I could breathe more easily.

I left the train along with a trickle of students and tourists, using the map on my phone to guide me. The streets were quiet; I could hear my footsteps on the pavement echoing. Abruptly the road stopped. A wasteland lay ahead, muddy earth and grass leading to the river.

Only one house stood alone by the river. Obstinate and imposing, like a large red brick thrust into the mud. It was ugly, a Victorian monster. The walls were overgrown with ivy, and the garden had been overtaken by plants, weeds mostly. I got the sense of nature encroaching, reclaiming territory that had once been hers. This was the house where Alicia had been born. It was where she spent the first eighteen years of her life. Within these walls her personality had been formed: the roots of her adult life, all causes and subsequent choices, were buried here. Sometimes it's hard to grasp why the answers to the present lie in the past. A simple analogy might be helpful: a leading psychiatrist in the field of sexual abuse once told me she had, in thirty years of extensive work with pedophiles, never met one who hadn't himself been abused as a child. This doesn't mean that all abused children go on to become abusers, but it is impossible for someone who was not abused to become an abuser. No one is born evil. As Winnicott put it, "A baby cannot hate the mother, without the mother first hating the baby." As babies, we are innocent sponges, blank slates, with only the most basic needs present: to eat, shit, love, and be loved. But something goes wrong, depending on the circumstances into which we are born, and the house in which we grow up. A tormented, abused child can never take revenge in reality, as she is powerless and defenseless, but she can — and must — harbor vengeful fantasies in her imagination. Rage, like fear, is reactive.

Something bad happened to Alicia, probably early in her childhood, to provoke the murderous impulses that emerged all those years later. Whatever the provocation, not everyone in this world would have picked up the gun and fired it point-blank into Gabriel's face — most people could not. That Alicia did so points to something disordered in her internal world. That's why it was crucial for me to understand what life had been like for her in this house, to find out what happened to shape her, make her into the person she became — a person capable of murder.

I wandered farther into the overgrown garden, through the weeds and waving wildflowers, and made my way along the side of the house. At the back was a large willow tree — a beautiful tree, majestic, with long bare branches sweeping to the ground. I pictured Alicia as a child playing around it and in the secret, magical world beneath its branches. I smiled.

Then I felt uneasy suddenly. I could sense someone's eyes on me.

I looked up at the house. A face appeared at an upstairs window. An ugly face, an old woman's face, pressed against the glass — staring straight at me. I felt a strange, inexplicable shiver of fear.

I didn't hear the footsteps behind me until too late. There was a bang — a heavy thud — and a stab of pain at the back of my head. Everything went black.

CHAPTER SIXTEEN

I woke up on the hard, cold ground, on my back. My first sensation was pain. My head was throbbing, stabbing, as if my skull had been cracked open. I reached up and gingerly touched the back of my head.

"No blood," said a voice. "But you'll have a nasty bruise tomorrow. Not to mention a cracking headache."

I looked up and saw Paul Rose for the first time. He was standing above me, holding a baseball bat. He was about my age, but taller, and broad with it. He had a boyish face and a shock of red hair, the same color as Alicia's. He reeked of whiskey.

I tried to sit up but couldn't quite manage it.

"Better stay there. Recover for a sec."

"I think I've got a concussion."

"Possibly."

"What the fuck did you do that for?"

"What did you expect, mate? I thought

you were a burglar."

"Well, I'm not."

"I know that now. I went through your wallet. You're a psychotherapist."

He reached into his back pocket and pulled out my wallet. He tossed it at me. It landed on my chest. I reached for it.

"I saw your ID. You're at that hospital — the Grove?"

I nodded and the movement made my head throb. "Yes."

"Then you know who I am."

"Alicia's cousin?"

"Paul Rose." He held out his hand. "Here. Let me help you up."

He pulled me to my feet with surprising ease. He was strong. I was unsteady on my feet. "You could have killed me," I muttered.

Paul shrugged. "You could have been armed. You were trespassing. What did you expect? Why are you here?"

"I came to see you." I grimaced in pain. "I wish I hadn't."

"Come in, sit down for a second."

I was in too much pain to do anything other than go where he led me. My head was throbbing with every step. We went inside the back door.

The inside of the house was just as dilapidated as the outside. The kitchen walls were covered with an orange geometric design that looked forty years out-of-date. The wallpaper was coming away from the wall in patches, curling, twisting, and blackening as if it were catching fire. Mummified insects were hanging suspended from cobwebs in the corners of the ceiling. The dust was so thick on the floor, it looked like a dirty carpet. And an underlying odor of cat piss made me feel sick. I counted at least five cats around the kitchen, sleeping on chairs and surfaces. On the floor, open plastic bags overflowed with stinking tins of cat food.

"Sit down. I'll make some tea." Paul leaned the baseball bat against the wall, by the door. I kept my eye on it. I didn't feel safe around him.

Paul handed me a cracked mug full of tea. "Drink this."

"You have any painkillers?"

"I've got some aspirin somewhere, I'll have a look. Here." He showed me a bottle of whiskey. "This'll help."

He poured some of the whiskey into the mug. I sipped it. It was hot, sweet, and strong. There was a pause as Paul drank his tea, staring at me — I was reminded of Alicia and that piercing gaze of hers.

"How is she?" he asked eventually. He continued before I could reply, "I've not been to see her. It's not easy getting away. . . . Mum's not well — I don't like to leave her alone."

"I see. When was the last time you saw Alicia?"

"Oh, years. Not for a long while. We lost touch. I was at their wedding, and I saw her a couple of times after that, but . . . Gabriel was quite possessive, I think. She stopped calling, anyway, once they got married. Stopped visiting. Mum was pretty hurt, to be honest."

I didn't speak. I could hardly think, with the throbbing in my head. I could feel him watching me.

"So what did you want to see me for?"

"Just some questions . . . I wanted to ask you about Alicia. About . . . her childhood."

Paul nodded and poured some whiskey into his mug. He seemed to be relaxing now; the whiskey was having an effect on me too, taking the edge off my pain, and I was thinking better. Stay on track, I told myself. Get some facts. Then get the hell out of here.

"You grew up together?"

Paul nodded. "Mum and I moved in when my dad died. I was about eight or nine. It was only meant to be temporary, I think — but then Alicia's mother was killed in the accident. So Mum stayed on — to take care of Alicia and Uncle Vernon."

"Vernon Rose — Alicia's father?"

"Right."

"And Vernon died here a few years ago?"

"Yes. Several years ago." Paul frowned. "He killed himself. Hanged himself. Upstairs, in the attic. I found the body."

"That must have been terrible."

"Yeah, it was tough — on Alicia mostly. Come to think of it, that's the last time I saw her. Uncle Vernon's funeral. She was in a bad way." Paul stood up. "You want another drink?"

I tried to refuse but he kept talking as he poured more whiskey. "I never believed it, you know. That she killed Gabriel — it didn't make any sense to me."

"Why not?"

"Well, she wasn't like that at all. She wasn't a violent person."

She is now, I thought. But I didn't say anything. Paul sipped his whiskey. "She's still not talking?"

"No. She's still not talking."

"It doesn't make sense. None of it. You know, I think she was —"

We were interrupted by a thumping, a

banging on the floor above. There was a muffled voice, a woman's voice; her words were unintelligible.

Paul leapt to his feet. "Just a sec." He walked out. He hurried to the foot of the stairs. He raised his voice. "Everything all right, Mum?"

A mumbled response that I couldn't understand came from upstairs.

"What? Oh, all right. Just — just a minute." He sounded uneasy.

Paul glanced at me across the hallway, frowning. He nodded at me. "She wants you to go up."

CHAPTER SEVENTEEN

Steadier on my feet, but still feeling faint, I followed Paul as he thudded up the dusty staircase.

Lydia Rose was waiting at the top. I recognized her scowling face from the window. She had long white hair, spreading across her shoulders like a spider's web. She was enormously overweight — a swollen neck, fleshy forearms, massive legs like tree trunks. She was leaning heavily on her walking stick, which was buckling under her weight and looked like it might give way at any moment.

"Who is he? Who is he?"

Her shrill question was directed to Paul, even though she was staring at me. She didn't take her eyes off me. Again, the same intense gaze I recognized from Alicia.

Paul spoke in a low voice. "Mum. Don't get upset. He's Alicia's therapist, that's all. From the hospital. He's here to talk to me."

"You? What does he want to talk to you for? What have you done?"

"He just wants to find out a bit about Alicia."

"He's a journalist, you fucking idiot." Her voice approached a shriek. "Get him out!"

"He's not a journalist. I've seen his ID, all right? Now, come on, Mum, please. Let's get you back to bed."

Grumbling, she allowed herself to be guided back into her bedroom. Paul nodded at me to follow.

Lydia flopped back with a deep thud. The bed quivered as it absorbed her weight. Paul adjusted her pillows. An ancient cat lay asleep by her feet, the ugliest cat I'd ever seen — battle scarred, bald in places, one ear bitten off. It was growling in its sleep.

I glanced around the room. It was full of junk — stacks of old magazines and yellowing newspapers, piles of old clothes. An oxygen canister stood by the wall, and a cake tin full of medications was on the bedside table.

I could feel Lydia's hostile eyes on me the whole time. There was madness in her gaze; I felt quite sure of that.

"What does he want?" Her eyes darted up and down feverishly as she sized me up. "Who is he?"

213

"I just told you, Mum. He wants to know some background on Alicia, to help him treat her. He's her psychotherapist."

Lydia left no doubt about her opinion of psychotherapists. She turned her head, cleared her throat — and spat onto the floor in front of me.

Paul groaned. "Mum, please —"

"Shut up." Lydia glared at me. "Alicia doesn't deserve to be in hospital."

"No?" I said. "Where should she be?"

"Where do you think? Prison." Lydia eyed me scornfully. "You want to hear about Alicia? I'll tell you about her. She's a little bitch. She always was, even as a child."

I listened, my head throbbing, as Lydia went on, with mounting anger:

"My poor brother, Vernon. He never recovered from Eva's death. I took care of him. I took care of Alicia. And was she grateful?"

Obviously, no response was required. Not that Lydia waited for one.

"You know how Alicia repaid me? All my kindness? Do you know what she did to me?"

"Mum, please —"

"Shut up, Paul!" Lydia turned to me. I was surprised how much anger was in her voice. "The bitch *painted* me. She painted

214

me, without my knowledge or permission. I went to her exhibition — and there it was, hanging there. Vile, disgusting — an obscene mockery."

Lydia was trembling with anger, and Paul looked concerned. He gave me an unhappy glance. "Maybe it's better if you go now, mate. It's not good for Mum to get upset."

I nodded. Lydia Rose was not well, no doubt about that. I was more than happy to escape.

I left the house and made my way back to the train station, with a swollen head and a splitting headache. What a fucking waste of time. I'd found out nothing — except it was obvious why Alicia had gotten out of that house as soon as she could. It reminded me of my own escape from home at the age of eighteen, fleeing my father. It was all too obvious who Alicia was running away from — Lydia Rose.

I thought about the painting Alicia had done of Lydia. "An obscene mockery," she called it. Well, time to pay a visit to Alicia's gallery and find out why the picture had upset her aunt so much.

As I left Cambridge, my last thoughts were of Paul. I felt sorry for him, having to live with that monstrous woman — be her unpaid slave. It was a lonely life — I didn't

215

imagine he had many friends. Or a girl-friend. I wouldn't be surprised if he was still a virgin. Something about him remained stunted, despite his size; something thwarted.

I had taken an instant and violent dislike to Lydia — probably because she reminded me of my father. I would have ended up like Paul if I had stayed in that house, if I had stayed with my parents in Surrey, at the beck and call of a madman.

I felt depressed all the way back to London. Sad, tired, close to tears. I couldn't tell if I was feeling Paul's sadness — or my own.

CHAPTER EIGHTEEN

Kathy was out when I got home.

I opened her laptop and tried to access her email — but with no luck. She was logged out.

I had to accept that she might never repeat her mistake. Would I keep checking ad nauseam, give in to obsession, driving myself mad? I had enough self-awareness to appreciate the cliché I had become — the jealous husband — and the irony that Kathy was currently rehearsing Desdemona in *Othello* hadn't escaped me.

I should have forwarded the emails to myself that first night, as soon as I'd read them. Then I'd have some actual physical evidence. That was my mistake. As it was, I had begun questioning what I had seen. Was my recollection to be trusted? I'd been stoned out of my mind, after all — had I misunderstood what I had read? I found myself concocting outlandish theories to

217

prove Kathy's innocence. Maybe it was just an acting exercise — she was writing in character, in preparation for *Othello*. She had spent six weeks speaking in a regional American accent when preparing for *All My Sons*. It was possible something similar was going on here. Except the emails were signed by Kathy — not Desdemona.

If only I had imagined it all, then I could forget it, the way you forget a dream — I could wake up and it would fade away. Instead I was trapped in this endless nightmare of mistrust, suspicion, paranoia. Although on the surface, little had changed. We still went for a walk together on Sunday. We looked like every other couple strolling in the park. Perhaps our silences were longer than usual, but they seemed comfortable enough. Under the silence, however, a fevered one-sided conversation was taking place in my mind. I rehearsed a million questions. Why did she do it? How could she? Why say she loved me and marry me, fuck me, and share my bed — then lie to my face, and keep lying, year after year? How long had it been going on? Did she love this man? Was she going to leave me for him?

I looked through her phone a couple of times when she was in the shower, searching for text messages, but found nothing. If she'd received any incriminating texts, she had deleted them. She wasn't stupid, apparently, just occasionally careless.

It was possible I'd never know the truth. I might never find out.

In a way, I hoped I wouldn't.

Kathy peered at me as we sat on the couch after the walk. "Are you all right?"

"What do you mean?"

"I don't know. You seem a bit flat."

"Today?"

"Not just today. Recently."

I evaded her eyes. "Just work. I've got a lot on my mind."

Kathy nodded. A sympathetic squeeze of my hand. She was a good actress. I could almost believe she cared.

"How are rehearsals going?"

"Better. Tony came up with some good ideas. We're going to work late next week to go over them."

"Right."

I no longer believed a word she said. I analyzed every sentence, the way I would with a patient. I was looking for subtext, reading between the lines for nonverbal clues — subtle inflections, evasions, omissions. Lies.

"How is Tony?"

"Fine." She shrugged, as if to indicate she couldn't care less. I didn't believe that. She idolized Tony, her director, and was forever talking about him — at least she used to; she hadn't mentioned him quite so much recently. They talked about plays and acting and the theater — a world beyond my knowledge. I'd heard a lot about Tony, but only glimpsed him once, briefly, when I went to meet Kathy after a rehearsal. I thought it odd that Kathy didn't introduce us. He was married, and his wife was an actress; I got the sense Kathy didn't like her much. Perhaps his wife was jealous of their relationship, as I was. I suggested the four of us go out for dinner, but Kathy hadn't been particularly keen on the idea. Sometimes I wondered if she was trying to keep us apart.

I watched Kathy open her laptop. She angled the screen away from me as she typed. I could hear her fingers tapping. Who was she writing to? Tony?

"What are you doing?" I yawned.

"Just emailing my cousin . . . She's in Sydney now."

"Is she? Send her my love."

"I will."

Kathy typed for a moment longer, then stopped typing and put down the laptop.

"I'm going to have a bath."

I nodded. "Okay."

She gave me an amused look. "Cheer up, darling. Are you sure you're okay?"

I smiled and nodded. She stood up and walked out. I waited until I heard the bathroom door close, and the sound of running water. I slid over to where she had been sitting. I reached for her laptop. My fingers were trembling as I opened it. I re-opened her browser — and went to her email login.

But she'd logged out.

I pushed away the laptop with disgust. This must stop, I thought. This way madness lies. Or was I mad already?

I was getting into bed, pulling back the covers, when Kathy walked into the bedroom, brushing her teeth.

"I forgot to tell you. Nicole is back in London next week."

"Nicole?"

"You remember Nicole. We went to her going-away party."

"Oh, yeah. I thought she moved to New York."

"She did. And now she's back." A pause. "She wants me to meet her on Thursday . . . Thursday night after rehearsal."

I don't know what aroused my suspicion.

221

Was it the way Kathy was looking in my direction but not making eye contact? I sensed she was lying. I didn't say anything. Neither did she. She disappeared from the door. I could hear her in the bathroom, spitting out the toothpaste and rinsing her mouth.

Perhaps there was nothing to it. Perhaps it was entirely innocent and Kathy really was going to meet Nicole on Thursday.

Perhaps.

Only one way to find out.

CHAPTER NINETEEN

There were no queues outside Alicia's gallery this time, as there had been that day, six years ago, when I had gone to see the *Alcestis*. A different artist was hanging in the window now, and despite his possible talent, he lacked Alicia's notoriety and subsequent ability to draw in the crowds.

As I entered the gallery, I shivered; it was even colder in here than on the street. There was something chilly about the atmosphere as well as the temperature; it smelled of exposed steel beams and bare concrete floors. It was soulless, I thought. Empty.

The gallerist was sitting behind his desk. He stood up as I approached.

Jean-Felix Martin was in his early forties, a handsome man with black eyes and hair, and a tight T-shirt with a red skull on it. I told him who I was and why I had come. To my surprise, he seemed perfectly happy to talk about Alicia. He spoke with an accent.

I asked if he was French.

"Originally — from Paris. But I've been here since I was a student — oh, twenty years at least. I think of myself more as British these days." He smiled and gestured to a back room. "Come in, we can have a coffee."

"Thanks."

Jean-Felix led me into an office that was essentially a storeroom, crowded with stacks of paintings.

"How is Alicia?" he asked, using a complicated-looking coffee machine. "Is she still not talking?"

I shook my head. "No."

He nodded and sighed. "So sad. Won't you sit down? What do you want to know? I'll do my best to answer truthfully." Jean-Felix gave me a wry smile, tinged with curiosity. "Although I'm not entirely sure why you've come to me."

"You and Alicia were close, weren't you? Apart from your professional relationship —"

"Who told you that?"

"Gabriel's brother, Max Berenson. He suggested I talk to you."

Jean-Felix rolled his eyes. "Oh, so you saw Max, did you? What a *bore.*"

He said it with such contempt I couldn't

224

help laughing. "You know Max Berenson?"

"Well enough. Better than I'd like." He handed me a small cup of coffee. "Alicia and I were close. Very close. We knew each other for years — long before she met Gabriel."

"I didn't realize that."

"Oh, yes. We were at art school together. And after we graduated, we painted together."

"You mean you collaborated?"

"Well, not really." Jean-Felix laughed. "I mean we painted walls together. As housepainters."

I smiled. "Oh, I see."

"It turned out I was better at painting walls than paintings. So I gave up, about the same time as Alicia's art started to really take off. And when I started running this place, it made sense for me to show Alicia's work. It was a very natural, organic process."

"Yes, it sounds like it. And what about Gabriel?"

"What about him?"

I sensed a prickliness here, a defensive reaction that told me this was an avenue worth exploring. "Well, I wonder how he fit into this dynamic. Presumably you knew him quite well?"

"Not really."

225

"No?"

"No." Jean-Felix hesitated a second. "Gabriel didn't take time to know me. He was very . . . caught up in himself."

"Sounds like you didn't like him."

"I didn't particularly. I don't think he liked me. In fact, I know he didn't."

"Why was that?"

"I have no idea."

"Do you think perhaps he was jealous? Of your relationship with Alicia?"

Jean-Felix sipped his coffee and nodded. "Yeah, yes. Possibly."

"He saw you as a threat, perhaps?"

"You tell me. Sounds like you have all the answers."

I took the hint. I didn't push it any further. Instead I tried a different approach. "You saw Alicia a few days before the murder, I believe?"

"Yes. I went to the house to see her."

"Can you tell me a little about that?"

"Well, she had an exhibition coming up, and she was behind with her work. She was rightfully concerned."

"You hadn't seen any of the new work?"

"No. She'd been putting me off for ages. I thought I'd better check on her. I expected she'd be in the studio at the end of the garden. But she wasn't."

"No?"

"No, I found her in the house."

"How did you get in?"

Jean-Felix looked surprised by the question. "What?" I could tell he was making some quick mental evaluation. Then he nodded. "Oh, I see what you mean. Well, there was a gate that led from the street to the back garden. It was usually unlocked. And from the garden I went into the kitchen through the back door. Which was also unlocked." He smiled. "You know, you sound more like a detective than a psychiatrist."

"I'm a psychotherapist."

"Is there a difference?"

"I'm just trying to understand Alicia's mental state. How did you experience her mood?"

Jean-Felix shrugged. "She seemed fine. A little stressed about work."

"Is that all?"

"She didn't look like she was going to shoot her husband in a few days, if that's what you mean. She seemed — fine." He drained his coffee and hesitated as a thought struck him. "Would you like to see some of her paintings?" Without waiting for a reply, Jean-Felix got up and walked to the door,

227

beckoning me to follow.

"Come on."

CHAPTER TWENTY

I followed Jean-Felix into a storage room. He went over to a large case, pulled out a hinged rack, and lifted out three paintings wrapped in blankets. He propped them up. He carefully unwrapped each one. Then he stood back and presented the first to me with a flourish.

"Voilà."

I looked at it. The painting had the same photo-realistic quality as the rest of Alicia's work. It represented the car accident that killed her mother. A woman's body was sitting in the wreck, slumped at the wheel. She was bloodied and obviously dead. Her spirit, her soul, was rising from the corpse, like a large bird with yellow wings, soaring to the heavens.

"Isn't it glorious?" Jean-Felix gazed at it. "All those yellows and reds and greens — I can quite get lost in it. It's joyous."

Joyous wasn't the word I would have

chosen. *Unsettling,* perhaps. I wasn't sure how I felt about it.

I moved on to the next picture. A painting of Jesus on the cross. Or was it?

"It's Gabriel," Jean-Felix said. "It's a good likeness."

It was Gabriel — but Gabriel portrayed as Jesus, crucified, hanging from the cross, blood trickling from his wounds, a crown of thorns on his head. His eyes were not downcast but staring out — unblinking, tortured, unashamedly reproachful. They seemed to burn right through me. I peered at the picture more closely — at the incongruous item strapped to Gabriel's torso. A rifle.

"That's the gun that killed him?"

Jean-Felix nodded. "Yes. It belonged to him, I think."

"And this was painted before his murder?"

"A month or so before. It shows you what was on Alicia's mind, doesn't it?" Jean-Felix moved on to the third picture. It was a larger canvas than the others. "This one's the best. Stand back to get a better look."

I did as he said and took a few paces back. Then I turned and looked. The moment I saw the painting, I let out an involuntary laugh.

The subject was Alicia's aunt, Lydia Rose.

It was obvious why she had been so upset by it. Lydia was nude, reclining on a tiny bed. The bed was buckling under her weight. She was enormously, monstrously fat — an explosion of flesh spilling over the bed and hitting the floor and spreading across the room, rippling and folding like waves of gray custard.

"Jesus. That's cruel."

"I think it's quite lovely." Jean-Felix looked at me with interest. "You know Lydia?"

"Yes, I went to visit her."

"I see." He smiled. "You have been doing your homework. I never met Lydia. Alicia hated her, you know."

"Yes." I stared at the painting. "Yes, I can see that."

Jean-Felix began carefully wrapping up the pictures again.

"And the *Alcestis*?" I said. "Can I see it?"

"Of course. Follow me."

Jean-Felix led me along the narrow passage to the end of the gallery. There the *Alcestis* occupied a wall to itself. It was just as beautiful and mysterious as I remembered it. Alicia naked in the studio, in front of a blank canvas, painting with a bloodred paintbrush. I studied Alicia's expression. Again it defied interpretation. I frowned.

231

"She's impossible to read."

"That's the point — it is a refusal to comment. It's a painting about silence."

"I'm not sure I understand what you mean."

"Well, at the heart of all art lies a mystery. Alicia's silence is her secret — her mystery, in the religious sense. That's why she named it *Alcestis*. Have you read it? By Euripides." He gave me a curious look. "Read it. Then you'll understand."

I nodded — and then I noticed something in the painting I hadn't before. I leaned forward to look closely. A bowl of fruit sat on the table in the background of the picture — a collection of apples and pears. On the red apples were some small white blobs — slippery white blobs creeping in and around the fruit.

I pointed at them. "Are they . . . ?"

"Maggots?" Jean-Felix nodded. "Yes."

"Fascinating. I wonder what that means."

"It's wonderful. A masterpiece. It really is." Jean-Felix sighed and glanced at me across the portrait. He lowered his voice as if Alicia were able to hear us. "It's a shame you didn't know her then. She was the most interesting person I've ever met. Most people aren't alive, you know, not really — sleepwalking their way through life. But

Alicia was so intensely alive. . . . It was hard to take your eyes off her." Jean-Felix turned his head back to the painting and gazed at Alicia's naked body. "So beautiful."

I looked back at Alicia's body. But where Jean-Felix saw beauty, I saw only pain; I saw self-inflicted wounds, and scars of self-harm.

"Did she ever talk to you about her suicide attempt?"

I was fishing, but Jean-Felix took the bait. "Oh, you know about that? Yes, of course."

"After her father died?"

"She went to pieces." Jean-Felix nodded. "The truth is Alicia was hugely fucked up. Not as an artist, but as a person she was extremely vulnerable. When her father hanged himself, it was too much. She couldn't cope."

"She must have loved him a great deal."

Jean-Felix gave a kind of strangled laugh. He looked at me as if I were mad. "What are you talking about?"

"What do you mean?"

"Alicia didn't love him. She hated her father. She despised him."

I was taken aback by this. "Alicia told you that?"

"Of course she did. She hated him ever

since she was a kid — ever since her mother died."

"But — then why try to commit suicide after his death? If it wasn't grief, what was it?"

Jean-Felix shrugged. "Guilt, perhaps? Who knows?"

There was something he wasn't telling me, I thought. Something didn't fit. Something was wrong.

His phone rang. "Excuse me a moment." He turned away from me to answer it. A woman's voice was on the other end. They talked for a moment, arranging a time to meet. "I'll call you back, baby," he said, and hung up.

Jean-Felix turned back to me. "Sorry about that."

"That's all right. Your girlfriend?"

He smiled. "Just a friend . . . I have a lot of friends."

I'll bet you do, I thought. I felt a flicker of dislike; I wasn't sure why.

As he showed me out, I asked a final question. "Just one more thing. Did Alicia ever mention a doctor to you?"

"A doctor?"

"Apparently she saw a doctor, around the time of her suicide attempt. I'm trying to locate him."

"Hmm." Jean-Felix frowned. "Possibly — there was someone . . ."

"Can you remember his name?"

He thought for a second and shook his head. "I'm sorry. No, I honestly can't."

"Well, if it comes to you, perhaps you can let me know?"

"Sure. But I doubt it." He glanced at me and hesitated. "You want some advice?"

"I'd welcome some."

"If you really want to get Alicia to talk . . . give her some paint and brushes. Let her paint. That's the only way she'll talk to you. Through her art."

"That's an interesting idea. . . . You've been very helpful. Thank you, Mr. Martin."

"Call me Jean-Felix. And when you see Alicia, tell her I love her."

He smiled, and again I felt a slight repulsion: I found something about Jean-Felix hard to stomach. I could tell he had been genuinely close to Alicia; they had known each other a long time, and he was obviously attracted to her. Was he in love with her? I wasn't so sure. I thought of Jean-Felix's face when he was looking at the *Alcestis*. Yes, love was in his eyes — but love for the painting, not necessarily the painter. Jean-Felix coveted *the art*. Otherwise he would have visited Alicia at the Grove. He would have stuck by her — I knew that for a fact. A man never abandons a woman like that.

Not if he loves her.

CHAPTER TWENTY-ONE

I went into Waterstones on my way to work and bought a copy of *Alcestis.* The introduction said it was Euripides's earliest extant tragedy, and one of his least-performed works.

I started reading it on the Tube. Not exactly a page-turner. An odd play. The hero, Admetus, is condemned to death by the Fates. But thanks to Apollo's negotiating, he is offered a loophole — Admetus can escape death if he can persuade someone else to die for him. He asks his mother and father to die in his place, and they refuse in no uncertain terms. It's hard to know what to make of Admetus. Not exactly heroic behavior, and the ancient Greeks must have thought him a bit of a twit. Alcestis is made of stronger stuff — she steps forward and volunteers to die for her husband. Perhaps she doesn't expect Admetus to accept her offer — but he does, and Alcestis dies and departs for Hades.

It doesn't end there, though. There is a happy ending, of sorts, a deus ex machina. Heracles seizes Alcestis from Hades and brings her triumphantly back to the land of the living. She comes alive again. Admetus is moved to tears by the reunion with his wife. Alcestis's emotions are harder to read — she remains silent. She doesn't speak.

I sat up with a jolt as I read this. I couldn't believe it.

I read the final page of the play again slowly, carefully:

Alcestis returns from death, alive again. And she remains silent — unable or unwilling to speak of her experience. Admetus appeals to Heracles in desperation:

"My wife stands here, but why does she not speak?"

No answer is forthcoming. The tragedy ends with Alcestis being led back into the house by Admetus — in silence.

Why? Why does she not speak?

CHAPTER TWENTY-TWO

Alicia Berenson's Diary

August 2
It's even hotter today. It's hotter in London than in Athens, apparently. But at least Athens has a beach.

Paul called me today from Cambridge. I was surprised to hear his voice. We've not spoken in months. My first thought was Auntie Lydia must be dead — I'm not ashamed to say I felt a flicker of relief.

But that's not why Paul was calling. In fact I'm still not sure why he did call me. He was pretty evasive. I kept waiting for him to get to the point, but he didn't. He kept asking if I was okay, if Gabriel was okay, and muttered something about Lydia being the same as always.

"I'll come for a visit," I said. "I haven't been for ages, I've been meaning to."

The truth is, I have many complicated feelings around going home, and being at the house, with Lydia and Paul. So I avoid going back — and I end up feeling guilty, so I can't win either way.

"It would be nice to catch up," I said. "I'll come see you soon. I'm just about to go out, so —"

Then Paul spoke so quietly I couldn't hear him.

"Sorry? Can you repeat that?"

"I said I'm in trouble, Alicia. I need your help."

"What's the matter?"

"I can't talk about it on the phone. I need to see you."

"It's just — I'm not sure I can make it up to Cambridge at the minute."

"I'll come to you. This afternoon. Okay?"

Something in Paul's voice made me agree

240

without thinking about it. He sounded desperate.

"Okay. Are you sure you can't tell me about it now?"

"I'll see you later." Paul hung up.

I kept thinking about it for the rest of the morning. What could be serious enough that Paul would turn to me, of all people? Was it about Lydia? Or the house, perhaps? It didn't make sense.

I wasn't able to get any work done after lunch. I blamed the heat, but in truth my mind was elsewhere. I hung around in the kitchen, glancing out the windows, until I saw Paul on the street.

He waved at me. "Alicia, hi."

The first thing that struck me was how terrible he looked. He'd lost a lot of weight, particularly around his face, the temples and jaw. He looked skeletal, unwell. Exhausted. Scared.

We sat in the kitchen with the portable fan on. I offered him a beer but he said he'd rather have something stronger, which surprised me

241

because I don't remember him being much of a drinker. I poured him a whiskey — a small one — and he topped it up when he thought I wasn't looking.

He didn't say anything at first. We sat there in silence for a moment. Then he repeated what he had said on the phone. The same words:

"I'm in trouble."

I asked him what he meant. Was it about the house?

Paul looked at me blankly. No, it wasn't the house.

"Then what?"

"It's me." He hesitated, then came out with it. "I've been gambling. And losing a lot, I'm afraid."

He'd been gambling regularly for years. He said it started as a way of getting out of the house — somewhere to go, something to do, a bit of fun — and I can't say I blame him. Living with Lydia, fun must be in short supply. But he's been losing more and more, and now it had gotten out of hand. He's been dipping into the savings account. And not much was there to start with.

"How much do you need?"

"Twenty grand."

I couldn't believe my ears. "You lost twenty grand?"

"Not all at once. And I borrowed from some people — and now they want it back."

"What people?"

"If I don't pay them back, I'm going to be in trouble."

"Have you told your mother?" I already knew the answer. Paul may be a mess but he's not stupid.

"Of course not. Mum would kill me. I need your help, Alicia. That's why I'm here."

"I haven't got that kind of money, Paul."

"I'll pay it back. I don't need it all at once. Just something."

I didn't say anything and he kept pleading. They wanted something tonight. He didn't dare go back empty-handed. Whatever I could give him, anything. I didn't know what to do. I wanted to help him, but I suspected giving him money wasn't the way to deal with this. I also knew his debts were going to be a tough secret to keep from Auntie Lydia. I didn't know what I'd do if I were Paul. Facing up to Lydia was probably scarier than the loan sharks.

"I'll write you a check," I said finally.

Paul seemed pathetically grateful and kept muttering, "Thank you, thank you."

I wrote him a check for two thousand pounds, payable to cash. I know that's not what he wanted, but the whole thing was uncharted territory for me. And I'm not sure I believed everything he said. Something about it didn't ring true.

"Maybe I can give you more once I've talked to Gabriel," I said. "But it's better if we work out another way to handle this. You know, Gabriel's brother is a lawyer. Maybe he could —"

Paul jumped up, terrified, shaking his head. "No, no, no. Don't tell Gabriel. Don't involve

244

him. Please. I'll work out how to handle it. I'll work it out."

"What about Lydia? I think maybe you should —"

Paul shook his head fiercely and took the check. He looked disappointed at the amount but didn't say anything. He left soon afterward.

I have the feeling I let him down. It's a feeling I've always had about Paul, since we were kids. I've always failed to live up to his expectations of me — that I should be a mothering figure to him. He should know me better than that. I'm not the mothering type.

I told Gabriel about it when he got back. He was annoyed with me. He said I shouldn't have given Paul any money, that I don't owe him anything, he's not my responsibility.

I know Gabriel is right, but I can't help feeling guilty. I escaped from that house, and from Lydia — Paul didn't. He's still trapped there. He's still eight years old. I want to help him.

But I don't know how.

August 6

I spent all day painting, experimenting with the background of the Jesus picture. I've been making sketches from the photos we took in Mexico — red, cracked earth, dark, spiny shrubs — thinking about how to capture that heat, that intense dryness — and then I heard Jean-Felix calling my name.

I thought for a second about ignoring him, pretending I wasn't there. But then I heard the clink of the gate, and it was too late. I stuck my head outside and he was walking across the garden.

He waved at me. "Hey, babes. Am I disturbing you? Are you working?"

"I am, actually."

"Good, good. Keep at it. Only six weeks until the exhibition, you know. You're horribly behind." He laughed that annoying laugh of his. My expression must have given me away because he added quickly, "Only joking. I'm not here to check up on you."

I didn't say anything. I just went back into the studio, and he followed. He pulled up a chair in front of the fan. He lit a cigarette, and the smoke whirled about him in the breeze. I went back to the easel and picked up my brush. Jean-Felix talked as I worked. He complained about the heat, saying London wasn't designed to cope with this kind of weather. He compared it unfavorably with Paris and other cities. I stopped listening after a while. He went on complaining, self-justifying, self-pitying, boring me to death. He never asks me anything. He doesn't have any actual interest in me. Even after all these years, I'm just a means to an end — an audience of the Jean-Felix Show.

Maybe that's unkind. He's an old friend — and he's always been there for me. He's lonely, that's all. So am I. Well, I'd rather be lonely than be with the wrong person. That's why I never had any serious relationships before Gabriel. I was waiting for Gabriel, for someone real, as solid and true as the others were false. Jean-Felix was always jealous of our relationship. He tried to hide it — and still does — but it's obvious to me he hates Gabriel. He's always bitching about him, implying Gabriel's not as talented as I am, that he's vain and egocentric. I think Jean-Felix believes that one day he will win me over to his side, and I'll fall at his feet. But what he doesn't realize is that with every snide comment and bitchy remark, he drives me further into Gabriel's arms.

Jean-Felix is always alluding to our long, long friendship — it's the hold he has on me — the intensity of those early years, when it was just "us against the world." But I don't think Jean-Felix realizes he's holding on to a part of my life when I wasn't happy. And any affection I have for Jean-Felix is for that time. We're like a married couple who have fallen out of love. Today I realized just how much I dislike him.

"I'm working," I said. "I need to get on with this, so if you don't mind . . ."

Jean-Felix pulled a face. "Are you asking me to leave? I've been watching you paint since you first picked up a brush. If I've been a distraction all these years, you might have said something sooner."

"I'm saying something now."

My face was feeling hot and I was getting angry. I couldn't control it. I tried to paint but my hand was shaking. I could feel Jean-Felix watching me — I could practically hear his mind working — ticking, whirring, spinning. "I've upset you," he said at last. "Why?"

"I just told you. You can't keep popping over like this. You need to text me or call first."

"I didn't realize I needed a written invitation to see my best friend."

There was a pause. He'd taken it badly. I guess there was no other way to take it. I hadn't planned on telling him like this — I'd intended to break it to him more gently. But somehow I was unable to stop myself. And the funny thing is, I *wanted* to hurt him. I wanted to be brutal.

"Jean-Felix, listen."

"I'm listening."

"There's no easy way to say this. But after the show, it's time for a change."

"Change of what?"

"Change of gallery. For me."

Jean-Felix looked at me, astonished. He looked like a little boy, I thought, about to burst into tears, and I found myself feeling nothing but irritation.

"It's time for a fresh start. For both of us."

"I see." He lit another cigarette. "And I suppose this is Gabriel's idea?"

"Gabriel's got nothing to do with it."

"He hates my guts."

"Don't be stupid."

"He poisoned you against me. I've seen it happening. He's been doing it for years."

"That's not true."

"What other explanation is there? What other reason could you have for stabbing me in the back?"

"Don't be so dramatic. This is only about the gallery. It's not about you and me. We'll still be friends. We can still hang out."

"If I text or call first?" He laughed and started talking fast, as if he was trying to get it out before I could stop him. "Wow, wow, wow. All this time I really believed in something, you know, in you and me — and now you've decided it was nothing. Just like that. No one

250

cares about you like I do, you know. No one."

"Jean-Felix, please —"

"I can't believe you just decided like that."

"I've been wanting to tell you for a while."

This was clearly the wrong thing to say. Jean-Felix looked stunned. "What do you mean, a while? How long?"

"I don't know. A while."

"And you've been acting for me? Is that it? Christ, Alicia. Don't end it like this. Don't discard me like this."

"I'm not discarding you. Don't be so dramatic. We'll always be friends."

"Let's just slow down here. You know why I came over? To ask you to the theater on Friday." He pulled two tickets from inside his jacket and showed them to me — they were for a tragedy by Euripides, at the National. "I'd like you to come with me. It's a more civilized way to say goodbye, don't you think? For old times' sake. Don't say no."

251

I hesitated. It was the last thing I wanted to do. But I didn't want to upset him further. I think I would have agreed to anything — just to get him out of there. So I said yes.

10:30 P.M.
When Gabriel got home, I talked to him about what happened with Jean-Felix. He said he never understood our friendship anyway. He said Jean-Felix is creepy and he doesn't like the way he looks at me.

"And how is that?"

"Like he owns you or something. I think you should leave the gallery now — before the show."

"I can't do that — it's too late. I don't want him to hate me. You don't know how vindictive he can be."

"It sounds like you're afraid of him."

"I'm not. It's just easier this way — to pull away gradually."

"The sooner the better. He's in love with you. You know that, don't you?"

I didn't argue — but Gabriel is wrong. Jean-Felix isn't in love with me. He's more attached to my paintings than he is to me. Which is another reason to get away from him. Jean-Felix doesn't care about me at all. Gabriel was right about one thing, though.

I am afraid of him.

CHAPTER TWENTY-THREE

I found Diomedes in his office. He was sitting on a stool, in front of his harp. It had a
large and ornate wooden frame, with a
shower of golden strings.

"That's a beautiful object," I said.

Diomedes nodded. "And very difficult to
play." He demonstrated, sweeping his fingers
lovingly along the strings. A cascading scale
resounded through the room. "Would you
like to try?"

I smiled — and shook my head.

He laughed. "I keep asking, you see, in
the hope you will change your mind. I'm
nothing if not persistent."

"I'm not very musical. I was told so in no
uncertain terms by my music teacher at
school."

"Like therapy, music is about a relationship, entirely dependent on the teacher you
choose."

"No doubt that's true."

He glanced out the window and nodded at the darkening sky. "Those clouds, they have snow in them."

"It looks like rain clouds to me."

"No, it's snow. Trust me, I come from a long line of Greek shepherds. It will be snowing tonight."

Diomedes gave the clouds a last hopeful look, then turned back to me. "What can I do for you, Theo?"

"It's this."

I slid the copy of the play across the desk. He peered at it.

"What is it?"

"A tragedy by Euripides."

"I can see that. Why are you showing it to me?"

"Well, it's the *Alcestis* — the title Alicia gave her self-portrait, painted after Gabriel's murder."

"Oh, yes, yes, of course." Diomedes looked at it with more interest. "Casting herself as a tragic heroine."

"Possibly. I must admit, I'm rather stumped. I thought you might have a better handle on it than me."

"Because I'm Greek?" He laughed. "You assume I will have an intimate knowledge of every Greek tragedy?"

"Well, better than me, at any rate."

"I don't see why. It's like assuming every Englishman is familiar with the works of Shakespeare." He gave me a pitying smile. "Fortunately for you, that is the difference between our countries. Every Greek knows his tragedies. The tragedies are our myths, our history — our blood."

"Then you'll be able to help me with this one."

Diomedes picked it up and flicked through it. "And what is your difficulty?"

"My difficulty is the fact she doesn't speak. Alcestis dies for her husband. And at the end, she comes back to life — but remains silent."

"Ah. Like Alicia."

"Yes."

"Again, I pose the question — what is your difficulty?"

"Well, obviously there's a link — but I don't understand it. Why doesn't Alcestis speak at the end?"

"Well, why do you think?"

"I don't know. She's overcome with emotion, possibly?"

"Possibly. What kind of emotion?"

"Joy?"

"Joy?" He laughed. "Theo, think. How would you feel? The person you love most in the world has condemned you to die,

256

through their own cowardice. That's quite a betrayal."

"You're saying she was upset?"

"Have you never been betrayed?"

The question cut through me like a knife. I felt my face go red. My lips moved but no sound came out.

Diomedes smiled. "I can see that you have. So . . . tell me. How does Alcestis feel?"

I knew the answer this time. "Angry. She's . . . angry."

"Yes." Diomedes nodded. "More than angry. She's murderous — with rage." He chuckled. "One can't help but wonder what their relationship will be like in the future, Alcestis and Admetus. Trust, once lost, is hard to recover."

It took a few seconds before I trusted myself to speak. "And Alicia?"

"What about her?"

"Alcestis was condemned to die by her husband's cowardice. And Alicia —"

"No, Alicia didn't die . . . not physically." He left the word hanging. "*Psychically,* on the other hand . . ."

"You mean something happened — to kill her spirit . . . to kill her sense of being alive?"

"Possibly."

I felt dissatisfied. I picked up the play and

looked at it. On the cover was a classical statue — a beautiful woman immortalized in marble. I stared at it, thinking of what Jean-Felix had said to me. "If Alicia is dead . . . like Alcestis, then we need to bring her back to life."

"Correct."

"It occurs to me that if Alicia's art is her means of expression, how about we provide her with a voice?"

"And how do we do that?"

"How about we let her paint?"

Diomedes gave me a surprised look, followed by a dismissive wave of his hand. "She already has art therapy."

"I'm not talking about art therapy. I'm talking about Alicia working on her own terms — alone, with her own space to create. Let her express herself, free up her emotions. It might work wonders."

Diomedes didn't reply for a moment. He mulled it over. "You'll have to square it with her art therapist. Have you come across her yet? Rowena Hart? She's no pushover."

"I'll talk to her. But I have your blessing?"

Diomedes shrugged. "If you can persuade Rowena, go ahead. I can tell you now — she won't like the idea. She won't like it one bit."

CHAPTER TWENTY-FOUR

"I think it's a great idea," said Rowena.

"You do?" I tried not to look surprised. "Really?"

"Oh, yes. Only problem is, Alicia won't go for it."

"What makes you so sure?"

Rowena gave a derisive snort. "Because Alicia's the least responsive, most uncommunicative bitch I've ever worked with."

"Ah."

I followed Rowena into the art room. The floor was splashed with paint like an abstract mosaic, and the walls were covered with artwork — some of it good, most just weird. Rowena had short blond hair, a deep-etched frown, and a weary put-upon manner, doubtless due to her endless sea of uncooperative patients. Alicia was clearly one such disappointment.

"She doesn't participate in art therapy?" I said.

"She does not." Rowena continued stacking artwork on a shelf as she spoke. "I had high hopes when she joined the group — I did everything I could to make her feel welcome — but she just sits there, staring at the blank page. Nothing will induce her to paint or even pick up a pencil and draw. Terrible example to the others."

I nodded sympathetically. The purpose of art therapy is to get the patients drawing and painting and, more important, talking about their artwork, linking it to their emotional state. It's a great way to literally get their unconscious onto the page, where it can be thought about and talked about. As always, it comes down to the individual skill of the therapist. Ruth used to say that too few therapists were skilled or intuitive — most were just plumbers. Rowena was, in my opinion, very much a plumber. She obviously felt snubbed by Alicia. I tried to be as placating as possible. "Perhaps it's painful for her," I suggested gently.

"Painful?"

"Well, it can't be easy for an artist of her ability to sit and paint with the other patients."

"Why not? Because she's above it? I've seen her work. I don't rate her highly at all." Rowena sucked in her mouth as if she had tasted something unpleasant.

So that was why Rowena disliked Alicia — jealousy.

"Anyone can paint like that," Rowena said. "It's not difficult to represent something photo-realistically — what's harder is to have point of view about it."

I didn't want to get into a debate about Alicia's art. "So what you're saying is you'll be relieved if I take her off your hands?"

Rowena shot me a sharp look. "You're welcome to her."

"Thank you. I'm grateful."

Rowena sniffed contemptuously. "You'll need to supply the art materials. My budget doesn't stretch to oils."

CHAPTER TWENTY-FIVE

"I have a confession to make."

Alicia didn't look at me.

I went on, watching her carefully, "I happened to pass your old gallery the other day when I was in Soho. So I went inside. The manager was kind enough to show me some of your work. He's an old friend of yours? Jean-Felix Martin?"

I waited for a response. None came.

"I hope you don't think it was an invasion of your privacy. Perhaps I should have consulted you first. I hope you don't mind."

No response.

"I saw a couple of paintings I'd not seen before. The one of your mother . . . And the one of your aunt, Lydia Rose."

Alicia slowly raised her head and looked at me. An expression was in her eyes I'd not seen before. I couldn't quite place it. Was it . . . amusement?

"Quite apart from the obvious interest for

me — as your therapist, I mean — I found the paintings affecting on a personal level. They're extremely powerful pieces."

Alicia eyes lowered. She was losing interest.

I persevered quickly. "A couple of things struck me. In the painting of your mother's car accident, there's something missing from the picture. You. You didn't paint yourself in the car, even though you were there."

No reaction.

"I wondered if that means you're only able to think of it as her tragedy? Because she died? But in fact there was also a little girl in that car. A girl whose feelings of loss were I suspect neither validated nor fully experienced."

Alicia's head moved. She glanced at me. It was a challenging look. I was on to something. I kept going.

"I asked Jean-Felix about your self-portrait, *Alcestis.* About its meaning. And he suggested I have a look at this."

I pulled out the copy of the play, *Alcestis.* I slid it across the coffee table. Alicia glanced at it.

" 'Why does she not speak?' That's what Admetus asks. And I'm asking you the same question, Alicia. What is it that you can't

263

say? Why do you have to keep silent?"

Alicia closed her eyes — making me disappear. Conversation over. I glanced at the clock on the wall behind her. The session was nearly finished. A couple of minutes remained.

I had been saving my trump card until now. And I played it, with a feeling of nervousness that I hoped wasn't apparent.

"Jean-Felix made a suggestion. I thought it was rather a good one. He thought you should be allowed to paint. Would you like that? We could provide you with a private space, with canvases and brushes and paints."

Alicia blinked. Her eyes opened. It was as if a light had been switched on inside them. They were the eyes of a child, wide and innocent, free of scorn or suspicion. Color seemed to come into her face. Suddenly she seemed wonderfully alive.

"I had a word with Professor Diomedes — he's agreed to it, and so has Rowena. . . . So it's up to you, really, Alicia. What do you think?"

I waited. She stared at me.

And then, finally, I got what I wanted — a definite reaction — a sign that told me I was on the right track.

It was a small movement. Tiny, really.

264

Nonetheless, it spoke volumes.

Alicia smiled.

CHAPTER TWENTY-SIX

The canteen was the warmest room at the Grove. Piping-hot radiators lined the walls, and the benches closest to them were always filled first. Lunch was the busiest meal, with staff and patients eating side by side. The raised voices of the diners created a cacophony of noise, born from an uncomfortable excitement when all the patients were in the same space.

A couple of jolly Caribbean dinner ladies laughed and chatted as they served up bangers and mash, fish-and-chips, chicken curry, all of which smelled better than they tasted. I selected fish-and-chips as the lesser of three evils. On my way to sit down, I passed Elif. She was surrounded by her gang, a surly-looking crew of the toughest patients. She was complaining about the food as I walked by her table.

"I'm not eating this shit." She pushed away her tray.

The patient to her right pulled the tray toward her, preparing to take it off Elif's hands, but Elif whacked her across the head.

"Greedy bitch!" Elif shouted. "Give that back."

This prompted a guffaw of laughter around the table. Elif pulled back her plate and tucked into her meal with renewed relish.

Alicia was sitting alone, I noticed, at the back of the room. She was picking at a meager bit of fish like an anorexic bird, moving it around the plate but not bringing it to her mouth. I was half tempted to sit with her but decided against it. Perhaps if she had looked up and made eye contact, I would have walked over. But she kept her gaze lowered, as if attempting to block out her surroundings and those around her. It felt like an invasion of privacy to intrude, so I sat at the end of another table, a few spaces away from any patients, and started eating my fish-and-chips. I ate just a mouthful of the soggy fish, which was tasteless, reheated but still cold in the center. I concurred with Elif's appraisal. I was about to throw it in the bin when someone sat down opposite me.

To my surprise, it was Christian.

"All right?" he said with a nod.

"Yeah, you?"

Christian didn't reply. He hacked with determination through the rock-solid rice and curry. "I heard about your plan to get Alicia painting," he said between mouthfuls.

"I see news travels fast."

"It does in this place. Your idea?"

I hesitated. "It was, yes. I think it'll be good for her."

Christian gave me a doubtful look. "Be careful, mate."

"Thanks for the warning. But it's rather unnecessary."

"I'm just saying. Borderlines are seductive. That's what's going on here. I don't think you fully get that."

"She's not going to seduce me, Christian."

He laughed. "I think she already has. You're giving her just what she wants."

"I'm giving her what she needs. There's a difference."

"How do you know what she needs? You're overidentifying with her. It's obvious. She's the patient, you know — not you."

I looked at my watch in an attempt to disguise my anger. "I have to go."

I stood and picked up my tray. I started walking away, but Christian called after me,

"She'll turn on you, Theo. Just wait. Don't say I didn't warn you."

I felt annoyed. And the annoyance stayed with me for the rest of the day.

After work, I left the Grove and went to the small shop at the end of the road and bought a pack of cigarettes. I put a cigarette in my mouth, lit it, and inhaled deeply, barely conscious of my actions. I was thinking about what Christian had said, going over it in my mind while the cars sped past. *Borderlines are seductive,* I heard him saying.

Was it true? Was that why I was so annoyed? Had Alicia emotionally seduced me? Christian clearly thought so, and I had no doubt Diomedes suspected it. Were they right?

Searching my conscience, I felt confident the answer was no. I wanted to help Alicia, yes — but I was also perfectly able to remain objective about her, stay vigilant, tread carefully, and keep firm boundaries.

I was wrong. It was already too late, though I wouldn't admit this, even to myself.

I called Jean-Felix at the gallery. I asked what had happened to Alicia's art materials

269

— her paints, brushes, and canvases. "Is it all in storage?"

After a slight pause he answered, "Well, no, actually . . . I have all her stuff."

"You do?"

"Yes. I cleared out her studio after the trial — and got hold of everything worth keeping — all her preliminary sketches, notebooks, her easel, her oils. I'm storing it all for her."

"How nice of you."

"So you're following my advice? Letting Alicia paint?"

"Yes. Whether anything will come of it remains to be seen."

"Oh, something will come of it. You'll see. All I ask is you let me have a look at the finished paintings."

A strange note of hunger was in his voice. I had a sudden image of Alicia's pictures swaddled like babies in blankets in that storage room. Was he really keeping them safe for her? Or because he couldn't bear to let go of them?

"Would you mind dropping off the materials to the Grove?" I said. "Would that be convenient?"

"Oh, I —" There was a moment's hesitation. I felt his anxiety.

I found myself coming to his rescue. "Or I

270

can pick them up from you if that's easier?"

"Yes, yes, perhaps that would be better."

Jean-Felix was scared of coming here, scared of seeing Alicia. Why? What was there between them?

What was it that he didn't want to face?

CHAPTER TWENTY-SEVEN

"What time are you meeting your friend?" I asked.

"Seven o'clock. After rehearsal." Kathy handed me her coffee cup. "If you can't remember her name, Theo, it's Nicole."

"Right." I yawned.

Kathy gave me a stern look. "You know, it's a little insulting that you don't remember — she's one of my best friends. You went to her going-away party for fuck's sake."

"Of course I remember Nicole. I just forgot her name, that's all."

Kathy rolled her eyes. "Whatever. Pothead. I'm having a shower." She walked out of the kitchen.

I smiled to myself.

Seven o'clock.

At a quarter to seven I walked along the river toward Kathy's rehearsal space on the

South Bank.

I sat on a bench across the way from the rehearsal room, facing away from the entrance so Kathy wouldn't immediately see me if she left early. Every so often I turned my head and glanced over my shoulder. But the door remained obstinately shut.

Then, at five minutes past seven, it opened. There was the sound of animated conversation and laughter as the actors left the building. They wandered out in groups of two or three. No sign of Kathy.

I waited five minutes. Ten minutes. The trickle of people stopped, and no one else came out. I must have missed her. She must have left before I arrived. Unless she hadn't been here at all?

Had she been lying about the rehearsal?

I got up and made my way toward the entrance. I needed to be sure. If she was still inside and she saw me, what then? What excuse could I have for being here? I'd come to surprise her? Yes — I'd say I was here to take her and "Nicole" out for dinner. Kathy would squirm and lie her way out of it with some bullshit excuse — "Nicole is sick, Nicole has canceled" — so Kathy and I would end up spending an uncomfortable evening alone together. Another evening of long silences.

I reached the entrance. I hesitated, grabbed the rusted green handle, and pushed open the door. I went inside.

The bare concrete interior smelled damp. Kathy's rehearsal space was on the fourth floor — she had moaned about having to climb the stairs every day — so I went up the main central staircase. I reached the first floor and was starting for the second when I heard a voice on the stairs, coming from the floor above. It was Kathy. She was on the phone:

"I know, I'm sorry. I'll see you soon. I won't be long. . . . Okay, okay, bye."

I froze — we were seconds away from colliding with each other. I dashed down the steps, hiding around the corner. Kathy walked past without seeing me. She went out the door. It slammed shut.

I hurried after her and left the building. Kathy was walking away, moving fast, toward the bridge. I followed, weaving between commuters and tourists, trying to keep a distance without losing sight of her.

She crossed the bridge and went down the steps into the Embankment Tube station. I went after her, wondering which line she would take.

But she didn't get on the tube. Instead she walked straight through the station and out the other side. She continued walking toward Charing Cross Road. I followed. I stood a few steps behind her at the traffic lights. We crossed Charing Cross Road and headed into Soho. I followed her along the narrow streets. She took a right turn, a left, another right. Then she abruptly stopped. She stood on the corner of Lexington Street. And waited.

So this was the meeting place. A good spot — central, busy, anonymous. I hesitated and slipped into a pub on the corner. I positioned myself at the bar. It offered a clear view through the window of Kathy across the road. The barman, bored, with an unruly beard, glanced at me. "Yeah?"

"A pint. Guinness."

He yawned and went to the other side of the bar to pour the pint. I kept my eyes on Kathy. I was pretty sure she wouldn't be able to see me through the window even if she looked in this direction. At one point Kathy did look over — straight at me. My heart stopped for a second — I was sure she had noticed me — but no, her gaze drifted on.

The minutes passed, and still Kathy waited. So did I. I sipped my pint slowly, watching. He was taking his time, whoever he was. She wouldn't like that. Kathy didn't like to be kept waiting — even though she was perpetually late. I could see she was getting annoyed, frowning and checking her watch.

A man crossed the road toward her. In the few seconds he took to cross the street, I had already assessed him. He was well built. He had shoulder-length fair hair, which surprised me, as Kathy always said she only went for men with dark hair and eyes like mine — unless that was another lie.

But the man walked right by her. She didn't even look at him. Soon he was out of sight. So it wasn't him. I wondered if Kathy and I were both thinking the same thing — had she been stood up?

Then her eyes widened. She smiled. She waved across the street — at someone out of sight. At last, I thought. It's him. I craned my neck to see —

To my surprise, a tarty-looking blonde, about thirty, wearing an impossibly short skirt and improbably high heels, tottered over to Kathy. I recognized her at once. Nicole. They greeted each other with hugs and kisses. They walked off, talking and laughing, arm in arm. So Kathy hadn't been lying about meeting Nicole.

I registered my emotions with shock — I

ought to have been hugely relieved that Kathy had been telling the truth. I ought to have been grateful. But I wasn't.

I was disappointed.

CHAPTER TWENTY-EIGHT

"Well, what do you think, Alicia? Lots of
light, eh? Do you like it?"

Yuri showed off the new studio proudly. It
had been his idea to commandeer the
unused room next to the goldfish bowl, and
I agreed — it seemed a better idea than
sharing Rowena's art-therapy room, which,
given her obvious hostility, would have created difficulties. Now Alicia could have a
room of her own, where she'd be free to
paint whenever she wished and without interruption.

Alicia looked around. Her easel had been
unpacked and set up by the window, where
there was the most light. Her box of oils
was open on a table. Yuri winked at me as
Alicia approached the table. He was enthusiastic about this painting scheme, and I
was grateful for his support — Yuri was a
useful ally, as he was by far the most popular
member of the staff; with the patients,

anyway. He gave me a nod, saying, "Good luck, you're on your own now." Then he left. The door closed after him with a bang. But Alicia didn't seem to hear it.

She was in her own world, bent over the table, examining her paints with a small smile. She picked up the sable brushes and stroked them as if they were delicate flowers. She unpacked three tubes of oils — Prussian blue, Indian yellow, cadmium red — and lined them up. She turned to the blank canvas on the easel. She considered it. She stood there for a long time. She seemed to enter a trance, a reverie — her mind was elsewhere, having escaped somehow, traveled far beyond this cell — until finally she came out of it and turned back to the table. She squeezed some white paint onto the palette and combined it with a small amount of red. She had to mix the paints with a paintbrush: her palette knives had immediately been confiscated upon their arrival at the Grove by Stephanie, for obvious reasons.

Alicia lifted the brush to the canvas — and made a mark. A single red stroke of paint in the middle of the white space.

She considered it for a moment. Then made another mark. Another. Soon she was painting without pause or hesitation, with total fluidity of movement. It was a kind of dance between Alicia and the canvas. I stood there, watching the shapes she was creating.

I remained silent, scarcely daring to breathe. I felt as if I was present at an intimate moment, watching a wild animal give birth. Although Alicia was aware of my presence, she didn't seem to mind. She occasionally looked up, while painting, and glanced at me.

Almost as if she was studying me.

Over the next few days the painting slowly took shape, roughly at first, sketchily, but with increasing clarity — then it emerged from the canvas with a burst of pristine photo-realistic brilliance.

Alicia had painted a redbrick building, a hospital — unmistakably the Grove. It was on fire, burning to the ground. Two figures were discernible on the fire escape. A man and a woman escaping the fire. The woman was unmistakably Alicia, her red hair the same color as the flames. I recognized the man as myself. I was carrying Alicia in my arms, holding her aloft while the fire licked at my ankles.

I couldn't tell if I was depicted as rescu-

ing Alicia — or about to throw her in the
flames.

CHAPTER TWENTY-NINE

"This is ridiculous. I've been coming here for years and nobody ever told me to call ahead before. I can't stand around waiting all day. I'm an extremely busy person."

An American woman was standing by the reception desk, complaining loudly to Stephanie Clarke. I recognized Barbie Hellmann from the newspapers and TV coverage of the murder. She was Alicia's neighbor in Hampstead, who heard the gunshots the night of Gabriel's murder and phoned the police.

Barbie was a Californian blonde in her mid-sixties, possibly older. She was drenched in Chanel No. 5, and she'd had considerable plastic surgery. Her name suited her — she looked like a startled Barbie doll. She was obviously used to getting what she wanted — hence her loud protestations at the reception desk when she discovered she needed to make an appointment to visit a patient.

"Let me talk to the manager," she said with a grand gesture, as if this were a restaurant, instead of a psychiatric unit. "This is absurd. Where is he?"

"I am the manager, Mrs. Hellmann," said Stephanie. "We've met before."

This was the first time I'd felt even vaguely sympathetic to Stephanie; it was hard not to pity her for being on the receiving end of Barbie's onslaught. Barbie talked a lot and talked fast, leaving no pauses, giving her opponent no time to respond.

"Well, you never mentioned anything about making appointments before." Barbie laughed loudly. "For Christ's sake, it's easier to get a table at the Ivy."

I joined them and smiled at Stephanie innocently. "Can I help?"

Stephanie shot me an irritated look. "No, thanks. I can manage."

Barbie looked me up and down with some interest. "Who are you?"

"I'm Theo Faber. Alicia's therapist."

"Oh, really?" Barbie said. "How interesting." Therapists were obviously something she could relate to, unlike ward managers. From then on, she deferred solely to me, treating Stephanie as if she were nothing more than a receptionist, which I must

283

admit rather wickedly amused me.

"You must be new, if we've not met?" I opened my mouth to reply, but Barbie got there first. "I usually come every couple of months or so. I left it a bit longer this time, as I've been in the States seeing my family, but as soon as I got back, I thought I must visit my Alicia — I miss her so much. Alicia was my best friend, you know."

"No, I didn't know."

"Oh, yeah. When they moved in next door, I was a great help in getting Alicia and Gabriel settled into the neighborhood. Alicia and I became extremely close. We'd confide in each other about *everything*."

"I see."

Yuri appeared in the reception, and I beckoned him over.

"Mrs. Hellmann is here to see Alicia," I said.

"Call me Barbie, honey. Yuri and I are old friends." She winked at Yuri. "We go way back. He's not the problem. It's this lady here —"

Barbie gestured dismissively at Stephanie, who finally found an opportunity to speak. "I'm sorry, Mrs. Hellmann, but hospital policy has changed since you were here last year. We've tightened our security. From now on you'll have to call before —"

"Oh God, do we have to go through this *again*? I'll scream if I have to hear it one more time. As if life weren't complicated enough."

Stephanie gave up, and Yuri led off Barbie. I followed.

We entered the visitors' room and waited for Alicia. The bare room had a table and two chairs, no windows, and a sickly yellow fluorescent light. I stood at the back and watched Alicia appear at the other door, accompanied by two nurses. Alicia didn't betray any obvious reaction to seeing Barbie. She walked over to the table and sat down without looking up.

Barbie seemed much more emotional. "Alicia, darling, I've missed you. You're so thin, there's nothing left of you. I'm so jealous. How are you? That awful woman nearly didn't let me see you. It's been a *nightmare* —"

So it went, an endless stream of inane chatter from Barbie, details of her trip to San Diego to visit her mother and brother. Alicia just sat there, silent, her face a mask, betraying nothing, showing nothing. After about twenty minutes, the monologue mercifully ended. Alicia was led away by Yuri, as uninterested as she was when she had entered.

I approached Barbie as she was leaving the Grove. "Can I have a word?"

Barbie nodded, as if she had been expecting this. "You want to talk to me about Alicia? It's about time somebody asked me some goddamn questions. The police didn't want to hear anything — which was crazy, because Alicia confided in me all the time, you know? About everything. She told me things you wouldn't *believe*." Barbie said this with a definite emphasis and gave me a coy smile. She knew she had piqued my interest.

"Such as?"

Barbie smiled cryptically and pulled on her fur coat. "Well, I can't go into it here. I'm late enough as it is. Come over this evening — say six p.m.?"

I didn't relish the prospect of visiting Barbie at her house — I sincerely hoped Diomedes wouldn't find out. But I had no choice — I wanted to find out what she knew. I forced a smile. "What's your address?"

CHAPTER THIRTY

Barbie's house was one of several across the road from Hampstead Heath, overlooking one of the ponds. It was large and, given its location, probably fantastically overpriced.

Barbie had lived in Hampstead for several years before Gabriel and Alicia moved in next door. Her ex-husband was an investment banker and had commuted between London and New York until they divorced. He found himself a younger, blonder version of his wife — and Barbie got the house. "So everyone was happy," she said with a laugh. "Particularly me."

Barbie's house was painted pale blue, in contrast to the other houses on the street, which were white. Her front garden was decorated with little trees and potted plants.

Barbie greeted me at the door. "Hi, honey. I'm glad you're on time. That's a good sign. This way."

She led me through the hallway to the living room, talking the entire time. I only partially listened and took in my surroundings. The house smelled like a greenhouse; it was full of plants and flowers — roses, lilies, orchids, everywhere you looked. Paintings, mirrors, and framed photographs were crammed together on the walls; little statues, vases, and other objets d'art competed for space on tables and dressers. All expensive items, but crammed together like this, they looked like junk. Taken as a representation of Barbie's mind, it suggested a disordered inner world, to say the least. It made me think of chaos, clutter, greed — insatiable hunger. I wondered what her childhood had been like.

I shifted a couple of tasseled cushions to make room and sat on the uncomfortable large sofa. Barbie opened a drinks cabinet and pulled out a couple of glasses.

"Now, what do you want to drink? You look like a whiskey drinker to me. My ex-husband drank a gallon of whiskey a day. He said he needed it to put up with me." She laughed. "I'm a wine connoisseur, actually. I went on a course in the Bordeaux region in France. I have an excellent nose."

She paused for breath and I took the opportunity to speak while I had the chance. "I don't like whiskey. I'm not much of a drinker . . . just the odd beer, really."

"Oh." Barbie looked rather annoyed. "I don't have any beer."

"Well, that's fine, I don't need a drink —"

"Well, I do, honey. It's been one of those days."

Barbie poured herself a large glass of red wine and curled up in the armchair as if she were settling in for a good chat. "I'm all yours." She smiled flirtatiously. "What do you want to know?"

"I have couple of questions, if that's all right."

"Well, fire away."

"Did Alicia ever mention seeing a doctor?"

"A doctor?" Barbie seemed surprised by the question. "You mean a shrink?"

"No, I mean a medical doctor."

"Oh, well, I don't . . ." Barbie hesitated. "Actually, now that you mention it, yes, there was someone she was seeing. . . ."

"Do you know the name?"

"No, I don't — but I remember I told her about my doctor, Dr. Monks, who's just incredible. He only has to look at you to see what's wrong with you straightaway, and he tells you exactly what to eat. It's amazing." A long and complicated explanation of the dietary demands by Barbie's doctor followed, and an insistence I pay him a visit soon. I was starting to lose patience. It took some effort to get her back on track.

"You saw Alicia on the day of the murder?"

"Yes, just a few hours before it happened." Barbie paused to gulp some more wine. "I went over to see her. I used to pop over all the time, for coffee — well, she drank coffee, I usually took a bottle of something. We'd talk for hours. We were so close, you know."

So you keep saying, I thought. But I had already diagnosed Barbie as almost entirely narcissistic; I doubted she was able to relate to others except as a function of her own needs. I imagined Alicia didn't do much talking during these visits.

"How would you describe her mental state that afternoon?"

Barbie shrugged. "She seemed fine. She had a bad headache, that was all."

"She wasn't on edge at all?"

"Should she be?"

"Well, given the circumstances . . ."

Barbie gave me an astonished look. "You don't think she was guilty, do you?" She laughed. "Oh, honey — I thought you were smarter than that."

"I'm afraid I don't —"

"Alicia was *no way* tough enough to kill anyone. She wasn't a killer. Take it from me. She's innocent. I'm a hundred percent sure."

"I'm curious how you can be so positive, given the evidence —"

"I don't give a shit about that. I've got my own evidence."

"You do?"

"You bet. But first . . . I need to know if I can trust you." Barbie's eyes searched mine hungrily.

I met her gaze steadily.

Then she came out with it, just like that: "You see, there was a *man.*"

"A man?"

"Yes. Watching."

I was a little taken aback and immediately alert. "What do you mean, watching?"

"Just what I said. Watching. I told the police, but they didn't seem interested. They made up their minds the moment they found Alicia with Gabriel's body and the gun. They didn't want to listen to any other story."

"What story — exactly?"

"I'll tell you. And you'll see why I wanted you to come over tonight. It's worth hearing."

Just get on with it, I thought. But I said

291

nothing and smiled encouragingly.

She refilled her glass. "It started a couple of weeks before the murder. I went over to see Alicia, and we had a drink, and I noticed she was quieter than usual — I said, 'Are you okay?' And she started crying. I'd never seen her like that before. She was crying her eyes out. She was normally so reserved, you know . . . but that day she just let go. She was a mess, honey, a real mess."

"What did she say?"

"She asked me if I'd noticed anyone hanging around in the neighborhood. She'd seen a man on the street, watching her." Barbie hesitated. "I'll show you. She texted this to me."

Barbie's manicured hands stretched for her phone, and she searched through her photos on it. She thrust the phone at my face.

I stared at it. It took me a second to make sense of what I was seeing. A blurred photograph of a tree.

"What is it?"

"What does it look like?"

"A tree?"

"Behind the tree."

Behind the tree was a gray blob — it could have been anything from a lamppost to a large dog.

"It's a *man.* You can see his outline quite distinctly."

I wasn't convinced but didn't argue. I didn't want Barbie to get distracted. "Keep going."

"That's it."

"But what happened?"

Barbie shrugged. "Nothing. I told Alicia to tell the cops — and that was when I found out she hadn't even told her husband about it."

"She hadn't told Gabriel? Why not?"

"I don't know. I got the feeling he wasn't all that sympathetic a person. Anyway. I insisted she tell the police. I mean, what about *me*? What about my safety? A prowler's outside — and I'm a woman living alone, you know? I want to feel safe when I go to bed at night."

"Did Alicia follow your advice?"

Barbie shook her head. "No, she did not. A few days later, she told me she'd talked it over with her husband and decided she was imagining it all. She told me to forget it — and asked me not to mention it to Gabriel if I saw him. I don't know, the whole thing stank to me. And she asked me to delete the photo. I didn't — I showed it to the police when she was arrested. But they weren't interested. They'd already made up

293

their minds. But I'm positive there's more to it. Can I tell you . . . ?" She lowered her voice to a dramatic whisper. "Alicia was *scared.*"

Barbie left a dramatic pause, finishing her wine. She reached for the bottle. "Sure you don't want a drink?"

I refused again, thanked her, made my excuses, and left. There was no point in staying further; she had nothing else to tell me. I had more than enough to think about.

It was dark when I left her house. I paused a moment outside the house next door — Alicia's old house. It had been sold soon after the trial, and a Japanese couple lived there. They were — according to Barbie — most unfriendly. She had made several advances, which they had resisted. I wondered how I'd feel if Barbie lived next door to me, endlessly popping over. I wondered how Alicia felt about her.

I lit a cigarette and thought about what I had just heard. So Alicia told Barbie she was being watched. The police had presumably thought Barbie was attention-seeking and making it up, which was why they had ignored her story. I wasn't surprised; Barbie was hard to take seriously.

It meant that Alicia had been scared enough to appeal to Barbie for help — and afterward to Gabriel. What then? Did Alicia confide in someone else? I needed to know.

I had a sudden image of myself as a child. A little boy close to bursting with anxiety, holding in all my terrors, all my pain; pacing endlessly, restless, scared; alone with the fears of my crazy father. No one to tell. No one who'd listen. Alicia must have felt similarly desperate, or she'd never have confided in Barbie.

I shivered — and sensed a pair of eyes on the back of my head.

I spun around — but no one was there. I was alone. The street was empty, shadowy, and silent.

CHAPTER THIRTY-ONE

I arrived at the Grove the next morning, intending to talk to Alicia about what Barbie had told me. But as soon as I entered reception, I heard a woman screaming. Howls of agony echoing along the corridors.

"What is it? What's going on?"

The security guard ignored my questions. He ran past me into the ward. I followed him. The screams grew louder as I approached. I hoped Alicia was okay, that she wasn't involved — but somehow I had a bad feeling.

I turned the corner. A crowd of nurses, patients, and security staff were gathered outside the goldfish bowl. Diomedes was on the phone, calling for paramedics. His shirt was spattered with blood — but not his blood. Two nurses were kneeling on the floor, assisting a screaming woman. The woman was not Alicia.

It was Elif.

Elif was writhing, screaming in agony, clutching at her bloody face. Her eye was gushing blood. Something stuck out of her eye socket, plunged into the eyeball. It looked like a stick. But it wasn't a stick. I knew at once what it was. It was a paint-brush.

Alicia was standing by the wall, being restrained by Yuri and another nurse. But no physical restraint was necessary. She was totally calm, perfectly still, like a statue. Her expression reminded me sharply of the painting — the *Alcestis*. Blank, expression-less. Empty. She stared straight at me.

For the first time, I felt afraid.

CHAPTER THIRTY-TWO

"How is Elif?" I was waiting in the goldfish bowl and caught Yuri once he returned from the emergency ward.

"Stable." He sighed heavily. "Which is about the best we can hope for."

"I'd like to see her."

"Elif? Or Alicia?"

"Elif first."

Yuri nodded. "They want her to rest tonight, but in the morning I'll take you to her."

"What happened? Were you there? I presume Alicia was provoked?"

Yuri sighed again and shrugged. "I don't know. Elif was hanging around outside Alicia's studio. There must have been a confrontation of some kind. I've no idea what they were fighting about."

"Have you got the key? Let's go and have a look. See if we can find any clues."

We left the goldfish bowl and walked to

Alicia's studio. Yuri unlocked the door and opened it. He flicked on the light.

And there, on the easel, was the answer we were looking for.

Alicia's painting — the picture of the Grove going up in flames — had been defaced. The word slut was crudely daubed across it in red paint.

I nodded. "Well, that explains it."

"You think Elif did it?"

"Who else?"

I found Elif in the emergency ward. She was propped up in bed, attached to a drip. Padded bandages were wrapped around her head, covering one eye. She was upset, angry, and in pain.

"Fuck off," she said when she saw me.

I pulled up a chair by the bed and sat down. I spoke gently, respectfully. "I'm sorry, Elif. Truly sorry. This is an awful thing to happen. A tragedy."

"Too fucking right. Now, piss off and leave me alone."

"Tell me what happened."

"That bitch took out my fucking eye. That's what happened."

"Why did she do that? Did you have a fight?"

"You trying to blame me? I didn't do

299

nothing!"

"I'm not trying to blame you. I just want to understand why she did it."

" 'Cause she's got a fucking screw loose, that's why."

"It had nothing to do with the painting? I saw what you did. You defaced it, didn't you?"

Elif narrowed her remaining eye, then firmly closed it.

"That was a bad thing to do, Elif. It doesn't justify her response, but still —"

"That ain't why she did it." Elif opened her eye and stared at me scornfully.

I hesitated. "No? Then why did she attack you?"

Elif's lips twisted into a kind of smile. She didn't speak. We sat like that for a few moments. I was about to give up, then she spoke.

"I told her the truth."

"What truth?"

"That you're soft on her."

I was startled by this.

Before I could respond, Elif went on, speaking with cold contempt. "You're in love with her, mate. I told her so. 'He *loves* you,' I said. 'He *loves* you — Theo and Alicia sitting in a tree. Theo and Alicia K I S S I N G —' " Elif started laughing, a hor-

300

rible shrieking laugh. I could picture the rest — Alicia goaded into a frenzy, spinning round, raising her paintbrush . . . and plunging it into Elif's eye.

"She's a fucking nutter." Elif sounded close to tears, anguished, exhausted. "She's a psycho."

Looking at Elif's bandaged wound, I couldn't help but wonder if she was right.

301

CHAPTER THIRTY-THREE

The meeting took place in Diomedes's office, but Stephanie Clarke assumed control from the start. Now that we had left the abstract world of psychology and entered the concrete realm of health and safety, we were under her jurisdiction and she knew it. Judging by Diomedes's sullen silence, it was obvious so did he.

Stephanie was standing with her arms crossed; her excitement was palpable. She's getting off on this, I thought — being in charge, and having the last word. How she must have resented us all, overruling her, teaming up against her. Now she was relishing her revenge. "The incident yesterday morning was totally unacceptable," she said. "I warned against Alicia being allowed to paint, but I was overruled. Individual privileges always stir up jealousies and resentments. I knew something like this would

302

happen. From now on, safety must come first."

"Is that why Alicia has been put in seclusion?" I said. "In the interest of safety?"

"She is a threat to herself, and others. She attacked Elif — she could have killed her."

"She was provoked."

Diomedes shook his head and spoke wearily. "I don't think any level of provocation justifies that kind of attack."

Stephanie nodded. *"Precisely."*

"It was an isolated incident," I said. "Putting Alicia in seclusion isn't just cruel — it's barbaric." I had seen patients subjected to seclusion in Broadmoor, locked in a tiny, windowless room, barely enough space for a bed, let alone other furniture. Hours or days in seclusion was enough to drive anyone mad, let alone someone who was already unstable.

Stephanie shrugged. "As manager of the clinic, I have the authority to take any action I deem necessary. I asked Christian for his guidance, and he agreed with me."

"I bet he did."

Across the room, Christian smiled smugly at me. I could also feel Diomedes watching me. I knew what they were thinking — I was letting it get personal, and letting my feelings show; but I didn't care.

303

"Locking her up is not the answer. We need to keep talking to her. We need to understand."

"I understand perfectly," Christian said with a heavy, patronizing tone, as if he were talking to a backward child. "It's you, Theo."

"Me?"

"Who else? You're the one who's been stirring things up."

"In what sense, stirring?"

"It's true, isn't it? You campaigned to lower her medication —"

I laughed. "It was hardly a campaign. It was an intervention. She was drugged up to the eyeballs. A zombie."

"Bullshit."

I turned to Diomedes. "You're not seriously trying to pin this on me? Is that what's happening here?"

Diomedes shook his head but evaded my eye. "Of course not. Nonetheless, it's obvious that her therapy has destabilized her. It's challenged her too much, too soon. I suspect that's why this unfortunate event took place."

"I don't accept that."

"You're possibly too close to see it clearly." Diomedes threw up his hands and sighed, a man defeated. "We can't afford any more mistakes, not at such a critical juncture —

as you know, the future of the unit is at stake. Every mistake we make gives the Trust another excuse to close us down."

I felt intensely irritated at his defeatism, his weary acceptance. "The answer is not to drug her up and throw away the key. We're not jailers."

"I agree." Indira gave me a supportive smile and went on, "The problem is we've become so risk averse, we'd rather overmedicate than take any chances. We need to be brave enough to sit with the madness, to hold it — instead of trying to lock it up."

Christian rolled his eyes and was about to object, but Diomedes spoke first, shaking his head. "It's too late for that. This is my fault. Alicia isn't a suitable candidate for psychotherapy. I should never have allowed it."

Diomedes said he blamed himself, but I knew he was really blaming me. All eyes were on me: Diomedes's disappointed frown; Christian's gaze, mocking, triumphant; Stephanie's hostile stare; Indira's look of concern.

I tried not to sound as if I was pleading. "Stop Alicia painting if you must. But don't stop her therapy — it's the only way to reach her."

Diomedes shook his head. "I'm beginning

to suspect she's unreachable."

"Just give me some more time —"

"No." The note of finality in Diomedes's voice told me that arguing further was pointless. It was over.

CHAPTER THIRTY-FOUR

Diomedes was wrong about it snowing. It didn't snow; instead it started raining heavily that afternoon. A storm with angry drumbeats of thunder and lightning flashes.

I waited for Alicia in the therapy room, watching the rain batter the window.

I felt weary and depressed. The whole thing had been a waste of time. I had lost Alicia before I could help her; now I never would.

A knock at the door. Yuri escorted Alicia into the therapy room. She looked worse than I expected. She was pale, ashen, ghostlike. She moved clumsily, and her right leg trembled nonstop. Fucking Christian, I thought — she was drugged out of her mind.

There was a long pause after Yuri left. Alicia didn't look at me. Eventually I spoke. Loudly and clearly, to make sure she understood.

"Alicia. I'm sorry you were put in seclusion. I'm sorry you had to go through that."

No reaction.

I hesitated. "I'm afraid that because of what you did to Elif, our therapy has been terminated. This wasn't my decision — far from it — but there's nothing I can do about it. I'd like to offer you this opportunity to talk about what happened, to explain your attack on Elif. And express the remorse I'm sure you're feeling."

Alicia said nothing. I wasn't sure my words were penetrating her medicated haze.

"I'll tell you how I feel. I feel angry, to be honest. I feel angry that our work is ending before we've even properly begun — and I feel angry that you didn't try harder."

Alicia's head moved. Her eyes stared into mine.

"You're afraid, I know that. I've been trying to help you — but you won't let me. And now I don't know what to do."

I fell silent, defeated.

Then Alicia did something I will never forget.

She held out her trembling hand toward me. She was clutching something — a small leatherbound notebook.

"What's that?"

No reply. She kept holding it out.

I peered at it, curious. "Do you want me to take it?"

No response. I hesitated and gently took the notebook from her fluttering fingers. I opened it and thumbed through the pages. It was a handwritten diary, a journal.

Alicia's journal.

Judging by the handwriting, it was written in a chaotic state of mind, particularly the last pages, where the writing was barely legible — arrows connecting different paragraphs written in different angles across the page, doodles and drawings taking over some pages, flowers growing into vines, covering what had been written and making it almost indecipherable.

I looked at Alicia, burning with curiosity. "What do you want me to do with this?"

The question was quite unnecessary. It was obvious what Alicia wanted.

She wanted me to read it.

■ ■ ■ ■

PART THREE

■ ■ ■ ■

I mustn't put strangeness where there's nothing. I think that is the danger of keeping a diary: you exaggerate everything, you are on the lookout, and you continually stretch the truth.

— JEAN-PAUL SARTRE

Though I am not naturally honest, I am sometimes so by chance.

— WILLIAM SHAKESPEARE,
The Winter's Tale

Alicia Berenson's Diary

August 8
Something odd happened today.

I was in the kitchen, making coffee, looking out the window — looking without seeing — daydreaming — and then I noticed something, or rather someone — outside. A man. I noticed him because he was standing so still — like a statue — and facing the house. He was on the other side of the road, by the entrance to the park. He was standing in the shadow of a tree. He was tall, well built. I couldn't make out his features, as he was wearing sunglasses and a cap.

I couldn't tell if he could see me or not, through the window, but it felt as if he was staring right at me. I thought it was weird — I'm used to people waiting across the street at

313

the bus stop, but he wasn't waiting for a bus. He was staring at the house.

I realized that I had been standing there for several minutes, so I made myself leave the window. I went to the studio. I tried to paint but couldn't concentrate. My mind kept going back to the man. I decided to give myself another twenty minutes, then I'd go back to the kitchen and look. If he was still there, then what? He wasn't doing anything wrong. He might be a burglar, studying the house — I suppose that was my first thought — but why just stand there like that, so conspicuously? Maybe he was thinking of moving here? Maybe he's buying the house for sale at the end of the street? That could explain it.

But when I went back to the kitchen and peered out of the window, he had gone. The street was empty.

I guess I'll never know what he was doing. How strange.

August 10
I went to the play with Jean-Felix last night. Gabriel didn't want me to, but I went anyway. I was dreading it, but I thought if I gave Jean-Felix what he wanted and went with him,

maybe that would be an end to this. I hoped so, anyway.

We arranged to meet early, to have a drink — his idea — and when I got there, it was still light. The sun was low in the sky, coloring the river bloodred. Jean-Felix was waiting for me outside the National. I saw him before he saw me. He was scanning the crowds, scowling. If I had any doubt I was doing the right thing, seeing his angry face dispelled it. I was filled with a horrible kind of dread — and nearly turned and bolted. But he turned and saw me before I could. He waved, and I went over to him. I pretended to smile, and so did he.

"I'm so glad you came," Jean-Felix said. "I was worried you wouldn't show up. Shall we go in and have a drink?"

We had a drink in the foyer. It was awkward, to say the least. Neither of us mentioned the other day. We talked a lot about nothing, or rather Jean-Felix talked and I listened. We ended up having a couple of drinks. I hadn't eaten and I felt a bit drunk; I think that was probably Jean-Felix's intention. He was trying his best to engage me, but the conversation was stilted — it was orchestrated, stage-managed. Everything that came out of his mouth seemed to start with "Wasn't it fun when" or "Do you remember that time we" — as if he'd rehearsed little reminiscences in the hope that they'd weaken my resolve and remind me how much history we had, how close we were. What he doesn't seem to realize is I've made my decision. And nothing he can say now will change that.

In the end, I'm glad I went. Not because I saw Jean-Felix — because I saw the play. *Alcestis* isn't a tragedy I've heard of — I suppose it's obscure because it's a smaller kind of domestic story, which is why I liked it so much. It was staged in the present day, in a small suburban house in Athens. I liked the scale of it. An intimate kitchen-sink tragedy. A man is condemned to die, and his wife, Alcestis, wants to save him. The actress playing Alcestis looked like a Greek statue, she had a wonderful face — I kept thinking about painting her. I thought about getting her details and contacting her agent. I nearly mentioned it to Jean-Felix, but I stopped myself. I don't want to involve him in my life anymore, on any level. I had tears in my eyes at the end — Alcestis dies and is reborn. She literally comes back from the dead. There's something there that I need to think about. I'm not sure exactly what yet. Of course, Jean-Felix had all kinds of reactions to the play, but none of them resonated with me, so I tuned him out and stopped listening.

I couldn't get Alcestis's death and resurrection out of my mind — I kept thinking about it as we walked back across the bridge to the station. Jean-Felix asked if I wanted to have another drink, but I said I was tired. There was another awkward pause. We stood outside the entrance to the station. I thanked him for the evening and said it had been fun.

"Just have one more drink," Jean-Felix said. "One more. For old times' sake?"

"No, I should go."

I tried to leave — and he grabbed my hand.

"Alicia," he said. "Listen to me. I need to tell you something."

"No, please don't, there's nothing to say, really —"

"Just listen. It's not what you think."

And he was right, it wasn't. I was expecting Jean-Felix to plead for our friendship, or try to make me feel guilty for leaving the gallery. But what he said took me totally by surprise.

"You need to be careful," he said. "You're way too trusting. The people around you . . . you trust them. Don't. Don't trust them."

I stared at him blankly. It took me a second to speak.

"What are you talking about? Who do you mean?"

Jean-Felix just shook his head and didn't say anything. He let go of my hand and walked off. I called after him but he didn't stop.

"Jean-Felix. Stop."

He didn't look back. I watched him disappear around the corner. I stood there, rooted to the spot. I didn't know what to think. What was he doing making a mysterious warning and then walking off like that? I guess he wanted to get the upper hand and leave me feeling unsure and wrong-footed. And he succeeded.

He also left me feeling angry. Now, in a way, he's made it easy for me. Now I'm determined to cut him out of my life. What did he mean about "people around me" — presumably that means Gabriel? But why?

No. I'm not doing this. This is exactly what Jean-Felix wanted — to fuck with my head. Get me obsessing about him. Come between me and Gabriel.

I won't fall for it. I won't give it another thought.

I went back home, and Gabriel was in bed, asleep. He had a five a.m. call for a shoot. But I woke him up, and we had sex. I couldn't get close enough to him or feel him deeply enough in me. I wanted to be fused with him. I wanted to climb inside him and disappear.

August 11
I saw that man again. He was a bit farther away this time — he was sitting on a bench farther into the park. But it was him, I could tell — most people are wearing shorts and T-shirts and light colors in this weather, and he was wearing a dark shirt and trousers, black sunglasses, and cap. His head was angled toward the house, looking at it.

I had a funny thought — maybe he's not a burglar, perhaps he's a *painter*. Perhaps he's a painter like me and he's thinking about

319

painting the street — or the house. But as soon as I thought this, I knew it wasn't true. If he were really going to paint the house, he wouldn't just be sitting there — he'd be making sketches.

I got myself into a state about it and I phoned Gabriel. That was a mistake. I could tell he was busy — the last thing he needed was me calling, freaking out because I think someone is watching the house. Of course, I'm only assuming the man is watching the house. He could be watching *me.*

August 13
He was there again.

It was soon after Gabriel left this morning. I had a shower and saw him out the bathroom window. He was closer this time. He was standing outside the bus stop. Like he was casually waiting for the bus.

I don't know who he thinks he's fooling.

I got dressed quickly and went into the kitchen to have a better look. But he was gone.

I decided to tell Gabriel about it when he got home. I thought he'd brush it off, but he took it seriously. He seemed quite worried.

"Is it Jean-Felix?" he said straightaway.

"No, of course not. How can you even think that?"

I tried to sound surprised and indignant. But in truth I had wondered that too. The man and Jean-Felix are the same build. It could be Jean-Felix, but even so — I just don't want to believe it. He wouldn't try to frighten me like that. Would he?

"What's Jean-Felix's number?" Gabriel said. "I'm calling him right now."

"Darling, don't, please. I'm sure it's not him."

"Positive?"

"Absolutely. Nothing happened. I don't know why I'm making such a big deal out of it. It's nothing."

"How long was he there for?"

"Not long — an hour or so — and then he vanished."

"What do you mean, vanished?"

"He just disappeared."

"Uh-huh. Is there any chance you could be imagining this?"

Something about the way he said that annoyed me. "I'm not imagining it. I need you to believe me."

"I do believe you."

But I could tell he didn't totally believe me. He only partly believed me. Part of him was just humoring me. Which makes me angry, if I'm honest. So angry I have to stop here — or I might write something I'll regret.

August 14
I jumped out of bed as soon as I woke up. I checked the window, hoping the man would be there again — so Gabriel could see him too — but there was no sign of him. So I felt even more stupid.

This afternoon I decided to go for a walk, despite the heat. I wanted to be in the park, away from the buildings and roads and other people — and be alone with my thoughts. I walked up to Parliament Hill, passing the bodies of sunbathers strewn around on either side of the path. I found a bench that was unoccupied, and I sat down. I stared out at London glinting in the distance.

While I was there, I was conscious the whole time of something. I kept looking over my shoulder — but couldn't see anyone. But someone was there, the whole time. I could feel it. I was being watched.

On my way back, I walked past the pond. I happened to look up — and there he was, the man. He was standing across the water on the other side, too far away to see clearly, but it was him. I knew it was him. He was standing perfectly still, motionless, staring right at me.

I felt an icy shiver of fear. I acted out of instinct:

"Jean-Felix?" I shouted. "Is that you? Stop it. Stop following me!"

He didn't move. I acted as fast as I could. I reached into my pocket, pulled out my phone, and took a photo of him. What good it will do, I have no idea. Then I turned and started walking quickly to the end of the pond, not letting myself look back until I reached the main path. I was scared he was going to be right behind me.

I turned around — and he was gone.

I hope it's not Jean-Felix. I really do.

When I got home, I was feeling on edge. I drew the blinds and turned off the lights. I peered out the window — and there he was:

The man was standing on the street, staring up at me. I froze — I didn't know what to do.

I nearly jumped out of my skin when someone called my name:

"Alicia? Alicia, are you there?"

It was that awful woman from next door. Barbie Hellmann. I left the window and went to the back door and opened it. Barbie had let herself in the side gate and was in the garden, clutching a bottle of wine.

"Hi, honey. I saw you weren't in your studio. I wondered where you were."

"I was out, I just got back."

"Time for a drink?" She said this in a baby voice she sometimes uses and that I find irritating.

"Actually, I should get back to work."

"Just a quick one. And then I have to go. I've got my Italian class tonight. Okay?"

Without waiting for a reply, she came in. She said something about how dark it was in the kitchen and started opening the blinds without asking me. I was about to stop her, but when I looked outside, no one was on the street. The man had gone.

I don't know why I told Barbie about it. I don't like her or trust her — but I was scared, I suppose, and I needed someone to talk to, and she happened to be there. We had a drink, which was unlike me, and I burst into tears. Barbie stared at me wide-eyed, silent for once. After I finished, she put down her bottle of wine and said, "This calls for something stronger." She poured us a couple of whiskeys.

"Here." She gave it to me. "You need this."

She was right — I needed it. I knocked it back and felt a kick from it. Now it was my turn to listen, while Barbie talked. She didn't want to scare me, she said, but it didn't sound good. "I've seen this on like a million TV shows. He's studying your house, okay? Before he makes his move."

"You think he's a burglar?"

Barbie shrugged. "Or a rapist. Does that matter? It's bad news, whatever it is."

I laughed. I felt relieved and grateful that someone was taking me seriously — even if it was just Barbie. I showed her the photo on my phone, but she wasn't impressed.

"Text it to me so I can look at it with my glasses on. It looks like a blurry smudge to me. Tell me. Have you mentioned this to your husband yet?"

I decided to lie. "No. Not yet."

Barbie gave me a funny look. "Why not?"

"I don't know, I suppose I worry Gabriel might think I'm exaggerating — or imagining it."

"Are you imagining it?"

"No."

Barbie looked pleased. "If Gabriel doesn't take you seriously, we'll go to the police together. You and me. I can be very persuasive, believe me."

"Thanks, but I'm sure that won't be necessary."

"It's already necessary. Take this seriously, honey. Promise me you'll tell Gabriel when he gets home?"

I nodded. But I had already decided not to say anything further to Gabriel. There was nothing to tell. I have no proof the man was following me or watching me. Barbie was right, the photo proves nothing.

It was all in my imagination — that's what Gabriel will say. Best not to say anything to him at all and risk upsetting him again. I don't want to bother him.

I'm going to forget all about it.

4:00 A.M.

It's been a bad night.

Gabriel came home, exhausted, at about ten. He'd had a long day and wanted to go to bed early. I tried to sleep too, but I couldn't.

Then a couple of hours ago, I heard a noise. It was coming from the garden. I got up and went to the back window. I looked out — I couldn't see anyone, but I felt someone's eyes on me. Someone was watching me from the shadows.

I managed to pull myself away from the window and ran to the bedroom. I shook Gabriel awake.

"The man is outside," I said, "he's outside the house."

Gabriel didn't know what I was talking about. When he understood, he started to get angry. "For Christ's sake. Give it a rest. I've got to be at work in three hours. I don't want to play this fucking game."

"It's not a game. Come and look. Please."

So we went to the window —

328

And of course, the man wasn't there. There was no one there.

I wanted Gabriel to go outside, to check, but he wouldn't. He went back upstairs, annoyed. I tried reasoning with him, but he said he wasn't talking to me and went to sleep in the spare room.

I didn't go back to bed. I've been sitting here since then, waiting, listening, alert to any sound, checking the windows. No sign of him so far.

Only a couple more hours to go. It will be light soon.

August 15
Gabriel came downstairs ready to go to the shoot. When he saw me by the window and realized I'd been up all night, he went quiet and started acting strange.

"Alicia, sit down. We need to talk."

"Yes. We do need to talk. About the fact that you don't believe me."

"I believe that you believe it."

329

"That's not the same thing. I'm not a fucking idiot."

"I never said you were an idiot."

"Then what are you saying?"

I thought we were about to get into a fight, so I was taken aback by what Gabriel said. He spoke in a whisper. I could barely hear him. He said:

"I want you to talk to someone. Please."

"What do you mean? A policeman?"

"No," Gabriel said, looking angry again. "Not a policeman."

I understood what he meant, what he was saying. But I needed to hear him say it. I wanted him to spell it out. "Then who?"

"A doctor."

"I'm not seeing a doctor, Gabriel —"

"I need you to do this for me. You need to meet me halfway." He said it again: "I need you to meet me halfway."

330

"I don't understand what you mean. Halfway where? I'm right here."

"No, you're not. You're not here!"

He looked so tired, so upset. I wanted to protect him. I wanted to comfort him. "It's okay, darling," I said. "It's going to be okay, you'll see."

Gabriel shook his head, like he didn't believe me. "I'm going to make an appointment with Dr. West. As soon as he can see you. Today if possible." He hesitated and looked at me. "Okay?"

Gabriel held out his hand for mine — I wanted to slap it away or scratch it. I wanted to bite him or hit him, or throw him over the table and scream, "You think I'm fucking crazy but I'm not crazy! I'm not, I'm not, I'm not!"

But I didn't do any of those things. Instead I nodded and took Gabriel's hand, and held it.

"Okay, darling," I said. "Whatever you want."

August 16
I went to see Dr. West today. Unwillingly, but I went.

331

I hate him, I've decided. I hate him and his narrow house, and sitting in that weird, small room upstairs, hearing his dog barking in the living room. It never stopped barking, the whole time I was there. I wanted to shout at it to shut up, and I kept thinking Dr. West would say something about it, but he acted like he couldn't hear it. Maybe he couldn't. He didn't seem to hear anything I was saying either. I told him what happened. I told him about the man watching the house, and how I had seen him following me into the park. I said all of this, but he didn't respond. He just sat there with that thin smile of his. He looked at me like I was an insect or something. I know he's supposedly a friend of Gabriel's, but I don't see how they ever could have been friends. Gabriel is so warm, and Dr. West is the opposite of warm. It's a strange thing to say about a doctor, but he has no kindness.

After I finished telling him about the man, he didn't speak for ages. The silence seemed to last forever. The only sound was that dog downstairs. I started to mentally tune in to the barking and go into a kind of trance. It took me by surprise when Dr. West actually spoke.

"We've been here before, Alicia, haven't we?"

I looked at him blankly. I wasn't sure what he meant. "Have we?"

He nodded. "Yes. We have."

"I know you think I'm imagining this. I'm not imagining it. It's real."

"That's what you said last time. Remember last time? Do you remember what happened?"

I didn't reply. I didn't want to give him the satisfaction. I just sat there, glaring at him, like a disobedient child.

Dr. West didn't wait for an answer. He kept talking, reminding me what happened after my father died, about the breakdown I suffered, the paranoid accusations that I made — the belief I was being watched, being followed, and spied upon. "So, you see, we've been here before, haven't we?"

"But that was different. It was just a *feeling.* I never actually saw someone. This time I *saw* someone."

"And who did you see?"

"I already told you. A *man.*"

"Describe him to me."

I hesitated. "I can't."

"Why not?"

"I couldn't see him clearly. I told you — he was too far away."

"I see."

"And — he was in disguise. He was wearing a cap. And sunglasses."

"A lot of people are wearing sunglasses in this weather. And hats. Are they all in disguise?"

I was starting to lose my temper. "I know what you're trying to do."

"And what is that?"

"You're trying to get me to admit I'm going crazy again — like after Dad died."

"Is that what you think is happening?"

"No. That time I was sick. This time I'm not sick. Nothing's the matter with me — apart from the fact that someone is spying on me and you won't believe me!"

Dr. West nodded but didn't say anything. He wrote a couple of things down in his notebook.

"I'm going to put you back on medication. As a precaution. We don't want to let this get out of hand, do we?"

I shook my head. "I'm not taking any pills."

"I see. Well, if you refuse the medication, it's important to be aware of the consequences."

"What consequences? Are you threatening me?"

"It's nothing to do with me. I'm talking about your husband. How do you think Gabriel feels about what he went through, last time you were unwell?"

I pictured Gabriel downstairs, waiting in the living room with the barking dog. "I don't know. Why don't you ask him?"

"Do you want him to have to go through it all again? Do you perhaps think there's a limit to how much he can take?"

"What are you saying? I'll lose Gabriel? That's what you think?"

Even saying it made me feel sick. The thought of losing him, I couldn't bear it. I'd do anything to keep him — even pretend I'm crazy when I know I'm not. So I gave in. I agreed to be "honest" with Dr. West about what I was thinking and feeling and tell him if I heard any voices. I promised to take the pills he gave me, and to come back in two weeks, for a checkup.

Dr. West looked pleased. He said we could go downstairs now and rejoin Gabriel. As he went downstairs in front of me, I thought about reaching forward and shoving him down the stairs. I wish I had.

Gabriel seemed much happier on the way home. He kept glancing at me as he was driving and smiling. "Well done. I'm proud of you. We're going to get through this, you'll see."

I nodded but didn't say anything. Because of course it's bullshit — "we" aren't going to get through this.

I'm going to have to deal with it alone.

It was a mistake telling anyone. Tomorrow I'm going to tell Barbie to forget all about it — I'll say I've put it behind me and I don't want to talk about it again. She'll think I'm odd and she'll be annoyed because I'll be denying her the drama, but if I act normally, she'll soon forget all about it. As for Gabriel, I'm going to put his mind at rest. I'm going to act like everything is back to normal. I'll give a brilliant performance. I won't let my guard slip for a second.

We went to the pharmacy on the way back, and Gabriel got my prescription. Once we were home again, we went into the kitchen.

He gave me the yellow pills with a glass of water. "Take them."

"I'm not a child. You don't need to hand them to me."

"I know you're not a child. I just want to make sure you'll take them — and not throw them away."

"I'll take them."

"Go on, then."

Gabriel watched me put the pills in my mouth and sip some water.

"Good girl," he said, and kissed my cheek. He left the room.

The moment Gabriel's back was turned, I spat out the pills. I spat them into the sink and washed them down the drain. I'm not taking any medication. The drugs Dr. West gave me last time nearly drove me crazy. And I'm not going to risk that again.

I need my wits about me now.

I need to be prepared.

August 17
I've started hiding this diary. There's a loose floorboard in the spare bedroom. I'm keeping it there, out of sight in the space underneath the floorboards. Why? Well, I'm being too honest here in these pages. It's not safe to leave it lying around. I keep imagining Gabriel stumbling across the notebook and fighting his curiosity but then opening it and starting to read. If he found out I'm not taking the medication, he'd feel so betrayed, so hurt — I couldn't bear that.

Thank God I have this diary to write in. It's keeping me sane. There's no one else I can talk to.

No one I can trust.

August 21
I've not been outside for three days. I've been pretending to Gabriel that I'm going for walks in the afternoons when he's out, but it's not true.

It makes me fearful, the thought of going outside. I'll be too exposed. At least here, in the house, I know I'm safe. I can sit by the window and monitor the passersby. I'm scanning each face that passes for that man's face — but I don't know what he looks like, that's the problem. He could have removed his disguise and be moving about in front of me, completely unnoticed.

That's an alarming thought.

August 22
Still no sign of him. But I mustn't lose focus. It's just a matter of time. Sooner or later he'll be back. I need to be ready. I need to take steps.

I woke up this morning and remembered Gabriel's gun. I'm going to move it from the spare room. I'll keep it downstairs where I can get to it easily. I'll put it in the kitchen cupboard, by the window. That way it will be there if I need it.

I know all this sounds crazy. I hope nothing comes of it. I hope I never see the man again.

But I have a horrible feeling I will.

Where is he? Why hasn't he been here? Is he trying to get me to lower my guard? I mustn't do that. I must continue my vigil by the window.

Keep waiting.

Keep watching.

August 23
I'm starting to think I imagined the whole thing. Maybe I did.

Gabriel keeps asking me how I'm doing — if I'm okay. I can tell he's worried, despite me insisting I'm fine. My acting doesn't seem to be convincing him anymore. I need to try harder. I pretend to be focused on work all day, whereas in fact work couldn't be further from my mind. I've lost any connection with it, any impetus to finish the paintings. As I write this, I can't honestly say I think I'll paint again. Not until all this is behind me, anyway.

I've been making excuses about why I don't want to go out, but Gabriel told me tonight I had no choice. Max has asked us out to dinner.

I can't think of anything worse than seeing Max. I pleaded with Gabriel to cancel, saying I needed to work, but he told me it would do me good to go. He insisted and I could tell he meant it, so I had no choice. I gave in and said yes.

I've been worrying all day, about tonight. Because as soon as my mind started turning on it, everything seemed to fall into place. Everything made sense. I don't know why I didn't think of it before, it's so obvious.

I understand now. The man — the man who's watching — it isn't Jean-Felix. Jean-Felix isn't dark or devious enough to do this kind of thing. Who else would want to torment me, scare me, punish me?

341

Max.

Of course it's Max. It has to be Max. He's trying to drive me crazy.

I'm dreading it, but I must work up the courage somehow. I'm going to do it tonight.

I'm going to confront him.

August 24
It felt strange and a little frightening to go out
last night, after so long inside the house.

The outside world felt huge — an empty space
around me, the big sky above. I felt very small
and held on to Gabriel's arm for support.

Even though we went to our old favorite, Augusto's, I didn't feel safe. It didn't feel comfort-
ing or familiar like it used to. The restaurant
seemed different somehow. And it smelled different — it smelled of something burning. I
asked Gabriel if something was on fire in the
kitchen, but he said he couldn't smell anything,
that I was imagining it.

"Everything's fine," he said. "Just calm down."

"I am calm. Don't I seem calm?"

342

Gabriel didn't respond. He just clenched his jaw, the way he does when he's annoyed. We sat down and waited for Max in silence.

Max brought his receptionist to dinner. Tanya, she's called. Apparently they've started dating. Max was acting like he was smitten with her, his hands all over her, touching her, kissing her — and all the time he kept staring at me. Did he think he was going to make me jealous? He's horrible. He makes me sick.

Tanya noticed something was up — she caught Max staring at me a couple of times. I should warn her about him really. Tell her what she's getting into. Maybe I will, but not right now. I've got other priorities at the moment.

Max said he was going to the bathroom. I waited a moment and then I seized my chance. I said I needed the bathroom too. I left the table and followed him.

I caught up with Max around the corner and grabbed hold of his arm. I gripped it hard.

"Stop it," I said. "Stop it!"

Max looked bemused. "Stop what?"

"You're spying on me, Max. You're watching me. I know you are."

"What? I have no idea what you are talking about, Alicia."

"Don't lie to me." I was finding it hard to control my voice. I wanted to scream. "I've seen you, okay? I took a photo. I took a picture of you!"

Max laughed. "What are you talking about? Let go of me, you crazy bitch."

I slapped his face. Hard.

And then I turned and saw Tanya standing there. She looked like she was the one who'd been slapped.

Tanya looked from Max to me but didn't say anything. She walked out of the restaurant.

Max glared at me, and before he followed her, he hissed, "I have no idea what you're talking about. I'm not fucking watching you. Now, get out of my way."

The way he said it, with such anger, such contempt, I could tell Max was speaking the truth. I believed him. I didn't want to believe

344

him — but I did.

But if it's not Max . . . who is it?

August 25
I just heard something. A noise outside. I checked the window. And I saw someone, moving in the shadows —

It's the man. He's outside.

I phoned Gabriel but he didn't pick up. Should I call the police? I don't know what to do. My hand is shaking so much I can barely —

I can hear him — downstairs — he's trying the windows, and the doors. He's trying to get in.

I need to get out of here. I need to escape.

Oh my God — I can hear him —

He's inside.

He's inside the house.

■ ■ ■ ■

PART FOUR

■ ■ ■ ■

The aim of therapy is not to correct the past, but to enable the patient to confront his own history, and to grieve over it.

— ALICE MILLER

CHAPTER ONE

I closed Alicia's diary and placed it on my desk.

I sat there, not moving, listening to the rain pelting outside the window. I tried to make sense of what I had just read. There was obviously a great deal more to Alicia Berenson than I had supposed. She had been like a closed book to me; now that book was open and its contents had taken me altogether by surprise.

I had a lot of questions. Alicia suspected she was being watched. Did she ever discover the man's identity? Did she tell anyone? I needed to find out. As far as I knew, she only confided in three people — Gabriel, Barbie, and this mysterious Dr. West. Did she stop there, or did she tell anyone else? Another question. Why did the diary end so abruptly? Was there more, written elsewhere? Another notebook, which she didn't give to me? And I wondered about

Alicia's purpose in giving me the journal to read. She was communicating something, certainly — and it was a communication of almost shocking intimacy. Was it a gesture of good faith — showing how much she trusted me? Or something more sinister?

There was something else; something I needed to check. Dr. West — the doctor who had treated Alicia. An important character witness, with vital information on her state of mind at the time of the murder. Yet Dr. West hadn't testified at Alicia's trial. Why not? No mention was made of him at all. Until I saw his name in her diary, it was as if he didn't exist. How much did he know? Why had he not come forward?

Dr. West.

It couldn't be the same man. It had to be a coincidence, surely. I needed to find out.

I put the diary in my desk drawer, locking it. Then, almost immediately, I changed my mind. I unlocked the drawer and took out the diary. Better keep it on me — safer not to let it out of my sight. I slipped it into the pocket of my coat.

I left my office. I went downstairs and walked along the corridor until I reached a door at the end.

I stood there for a moment, looking at it. A name was inscribed on a small sign on the door: DR. C. WEST.

I didn't bother to knock. I opened the door and went inside.

CHAPTER TWO

Christian was sitting behind his desk, eating takeaway sushi with chopsticks. He looked up and frowned.

"Don't you know how to knock?"

"I need a word."

"Not now, I'm in the middle of lunch."

"This won't take long. Just a quick question. Did you ever treat Alicia Berenson?"

Christian swallowed a mouthful of rice and gave me a blank look. "What do you mean? You know I do. I'm in charge of her care team."

"I don't mean here — I mean before she was admitted to the Grove."

I watched Christian closely. His expression told me all I needed to know. His face went red and he lowered the chopsticks.

"What are you talking about?"

I took out Alicia's diary from my pocket and held it up.

"You might be interested in this. It's

Alicia's journal. It was written in the months leading up to the murder."

Christian looked surprised and a little alarmed. "Where the hell did you get that?"

"Alicia gave it to me. I've read it."

"What's it got to do with me?"

"She mentions you in it."

"Me?"

"Apparently you were seeing her privately before she was admitted to the Grove. I wasn't aware of that."

"I — don't understand. There must be some mistake."

"I don't think so. You saw her as a private patient over several years. And yet you didn't come forward to testify at the trial — despite the importance of your evidence. Nor did you admit you already knew Alicia when you started working here. Presumably she recognized you straightaway — it's lucky for you she's silent."

I said this drily, but I was intensely angry. Now I understood why Christian was so against my trying to get Alicia to talk. It was in his every interest to keep her quiet.

"You're a selfish son of a bitch, Christian, you know that?"

Christian stared at me with an increasing look of dismay. "Fuck," he said under his breath. "Fuck. Theo. Listen — it's not what

353

it looks like."

"Isn't it?"

"What else does it say in the diary?"

"What else is there to say?"

Christian didn't answer the question. He held out his hand. "Can I have a look at it?"

"Sorry." I shook my head. "I don't think that's appropriate."

Christian played with his chopsticks as he spoke. "I shouldn't have done it. But it was entirely innocent. You've got to believe me."

"I'm afraid I don't. If it were innocent, why didn't you come forward after the murder?"

"Because I wasn't really Alicia's doctor — I mean, not officially. I only did it as a favor to Gabriel. We were friends. We were at university together. I was at their wedding. I hadn't seen him for years — until he called me, looking for a psychiatrist for his wife. She'd become unwell following her father's death."

"And you volunteered your services?"

"No, not at all. Quite the reverse. I wanted to refer him to a colleague, but he insisted I see her. Gabriel said Alicia was extremely resistant to the whole idea, and the fact I was a friend of his made it much more likely she'd cooperate. I was reluctant, obviously."

"I'm sure you were."

Christian shot me a hurt look. "There's no need to be sarcastic."

"Where did you treat her?"

He hesitated. "My girlfriend's house. But as I told you," he said quickly, "it was unofficial — I wasn't really her doctor. I rarely saw her. Every now and then, that's all."

"And on those rare occasions, did you charge a fee?"

Christian blinked and avoided my gaze. "Well, Gabriel insisted on paying, so I had no choice —"

"Cash, I presume?"

"Theo —"

"Was it cash?"

"Yes, but —"

"And did you declare it?"

Christian bit his lip and didn't reply. So the answer was no. That was why he hadn't come forward at Alicia's trial. I wondered how many other patients he was seeing "unofficially" and not declaring the income from them.

"Look. If Diomedes finds out, I — I could lose my job. You know that, don't you?" His voice had a pleading note, appealing to my sympathy.

But I had no sympathy for Christian. Only contempt. "Never mind the professor. What about the Medical Council? You'll lose your license."

"Only if you say something. You don't need to tell anyone. It's all water under the bridge at this point, isn't it? I mean, it's my career we're talking about, for fuck's sake."

"You should have thought of that before, shouldn't you?"

"Theo, please . . ."

Christian must have hated having to crawl to me like this, but watching him squirm provided me with no satisfaction, only irritation. I had no intention of betraying him to Diomedes — not yet anyway. He'd be much more use to me if I kept him dangling.

"It's okay," I said. "No one else needs to know. For the moment."

"Thank you. Seriously, I mean it. I owe you one."

"Yes, you do. Go on."

"What do you want?"

"I want you to talk. I want you to tell me about Alicia."

"What do you want to know?"

"Everything."

CHAPTER THREE

Christian stared at me, playing with his chopsticks. He deliberated for a few seconds before he spoke.

"There's not much to tell. I don't know what you want to hear — or where you want me to start."

"Start at the beginning. You saw her over a number of years?"

"No — I mean, yes — but I told you, not as frequently as you make it sound. I saw her two or three times after her father died."

"When was the last time?"

"About a week before the murder."

"And how would you describe her mental state?"

"Oh . . ." Christian leaned back in his chair, relaxing now that he was on safer ground. "She was highly paranoid, delusional — psychotic, even. But she'd been like this before. She had a long-standing pattern of mood swings. She was always up and down — typical borderline."

"Spare me the fucking diagnosis. Just give me the facts."

Christian gave me a wounded look but decided not to argue. "What do you want to know?"

"Alicia confided in you she was being watched, correct?"

Christian gave me a blank look. "Watched?"

"Someone was spying on her. I thought she told you about it?"

Christian looked at me strangely. Then, to my surprise, he laughed.

"What's so funny?"

"You don't really believe that, do you? The Peeping Tom spying through the windows?"

"You don't think it's true?"

"Pure fantasy. I should have thought that was obvious."

I nodded at the diary. "She writes about it pretty convincingly. I believed her."

"Well, of course she sounded convincing. I'd have believed her too if I hadn't known better. She was having a psychotic episode."

"So you keep saying. She doesn't sound psychotic in the diary. Just scared."

"She had a history — the same thing happened at the place they lived before Hampstead. That's why they had to move. She accused an elderly man across the street of spying on her. Made a huge fuss. Turned out the old guy was blind — couldn't even see her, let alone spy on her. She was always highly unstable, but it was her father's suicide that did it. She never recovered."

"Did she talk about him with you at all? Her father?"

Christian shrugged. "Not really. She would always insist that she loved him and they had a very normal relationship — as normal as it could be, considering her mother killed herself. To be honest, I was lucky to get anything out of Alicia at all. She was pretty uncooperative. She was — well, you know what she's like."

"Not as well as you, apparently." I went on before he could interrupt, "She attempted suicide after her father's death?"

Christian shrugged. "If you like. That's not what I would call it."

"What would you call it?"

"It was suicidal behavior, but I don't believe she intended to die. She was too narcissistic to ever really want to hurt herself. She took an overdose, more for show than anything else. She was 'communicating' her distress to Gabriel — she was always trying to get his attention, poor bastard. If I hadn't had to respect her

359

confidentiality, I'd have warned him to get the hell out."

"How unfortunate for him that you're such an ethical man."

Christian winced. "Theo, I know you're a very empathetic man — that's what makes you such a good therapist — but you're wasting your time with Alicia Berenson. Even before the murder, she had precious little capacity for introspection or mentalizing or whatever you want to call it. She was entirely consumed with herself and her art. All the empathy you have for her, all the kindness — she isn't capable of giving it back. She's a lost cause. A total bitch."

Christian said this scornfully — and with absolutely no detectable empathy for such a damaged woman. For a second, I wondered if perhaps Christian was borderline, not Alicia. That would make a lot more sense.

I stood up. "I'm going to see Alicia. I need some answers."

"From Alicia?" Christian looked startled. "And how do you intend to get them?"

"By asking her."

I walked out.

CHAPTER FOUR

I waited until after Diomedes disappeared into his office and Stephanie was in a meeting with the Trust. Then I slipped into the goldfish bowl and found Yuri.

"I need to see Alicia."

"Oh, yes?" Yuri gave me an odd look. "But — I thought the therapy was discontinued?"

"It was. I need to have a private conversation with her, that's all."

"Right, I see." Yuri looked doubtful. "Well, the therapy room is occupied — Indira is seeing patients there for the rest of the afternoon." He thought for a second. "The art room is free, if you don't mind meeting there? It'll have to be quick, though."

He didn't elaborate but I knew what he meant — we had to be fast, so no one noticed and reported us to Stephanie. I was grateful Yuri was on my side; he was obviously a good man. I felt guilty for having misjudged him when we first met.

"Thanks. I appreciate this."

Yuri grinned at me. "I'll have her there in ten minutes."

Yuri was as good as his word. Ten minutes later, Alicia and I were in the art room, sitting opposite each other, across the paint-splattered work surface.

I perched on a rickety stool, feeling precarious. Alicia looked perfectly poised as she sat down — as if she were posing for a portrait, or about to paint one.

"Thank you for this." I took out her diary and placed it in front of me. "For allowing me to read it. It means a great deal to me that you entrusted me with something so personal."

I smiled, only to be met by a blank expression. Alicia's features were hard and unyielding. I wondered if she regretted giving me the diary. Perhaps she felt a sense of shame at having exposed herself so completely?

I left a pause, then went on, "The diary ends abruptly, on a cliff-hanger." I flicked through the journal's remaining empty pages. "It's a little like our therapy together — incomplete, unfinished."

Alicia didn't speak. She just stared. I don't know what I'd expected, but not this. I'd assumed giving me the diary signaled a

362

change of some kind, representing an invitation, an opening, an entry point, yet here I was, back at square one, faced with an impenetrable wall.

"You know, I hoped that having spoken to me indirectly — through these pages — that you might go one step further and speak to me in person."

No response.

"I think you gave this to me because you wanted to communicate with me. And you did communicate. Reading this told me a great deal about you — how lonely you were, how isolated, how afraid — that your situation was a lot more complicated than I had previously appreciated. Your relationship with Dr. West, for instance."

I glanced at her as I said Christian's name. I hoped for some kind of reaction, a narrowing of the eyes, a clenched jaw — something, anything — but there was nothing, not even a blink.

"I had no idea you knew Christian West before you were admitted to the Grove. You saw him privately for several years. You obviously recognized him when he first came to work here — a few months after your arrival. It must have been confusing when he didn't acknowledge you. And probably quite upsetting, I imagine?"

I asked it as a question, but there was no reply. Christian seemed of little interest to her. Alicia looked away, bored, disappointed — as if I had missed some opportunity, gone down the wrong track. She had been expecting something from me, something I had failed to deliver.

Well, I wasn't done yet.

"There's something else. The diary raises certain questions — questions that need answering. Certain things don't make sense, don't fit with information I have from other sources. Now that you've allowed me to read it, I feel obliged to investigate further. I hope you understand that."

I gave Alicia back the diary. She took it and rested her fingers on it. We stared at each other for a moment.

"I'm on your side, Alicia," I said eventually. "You know that, don't you?"

She didn't say anything.

I took that as a yes.

CHAPTER FIVE

Kathy was getting careless. It was inevitable, I suppose. Having gotten away with her infidelity for so long, she started getting lazy.

I returned home to find her about to go out.

"I'm going for a walk," she said, pulling on her trainers. "I won't be long."

"I could use some exercise. Fancy some company?"

"No, I need to practice my lines."

"I can test you on them if you like."

"No." Kathy shook her head. "It's easier on my own. I just keep reciting the speeches — the ones I can't get my head around, you know, the ones in act two. I walk around the park, repeating them aloud. You should see the looks I get."

I had to give it to her. Kathy said all of this with perfect sincerity, while maintaining constant eye contact. She was a remarkable actress.

My acting was also improving. I gave her a warm, open smile. "Have a nice walk."

I followed her after she left the flat. I kept a careful distance, but she didn't even look back once. As I said, she was getting careless.

She walked for about five minutes, to the entrance of the park. As she neared it, a man emerged from the shadows. He had his back to me and I couldn't see his face. He had dark hair and was well built, taller than me. She went up to him and he pulled her close. They started kissing. Kathy devoured his kisses hungrily, surrendering herself to him. It was strange — to say the least — to see another man's arms around her. His hands groped and fondled her breasts through her clothes.

I knew I should hide. I was exposed and in plain sight — if Kathy turned around, she'd be sure to see me. But I couldn't move. I was transfixed, staring at a Medusa, turned to stone.

Eventually they stopped kissing and walked into the park, arm in arm. I followed. It was disorienting. From behind, from a distance, the man didn't look dissimilar to me — for a few seconds I had a confused, out-of-body experience, convinced I was watching myself walking in the park with Kathy.

Kathy led the man toward a wooded area. He followed her into it and they vanished.

I felt a sick feeling of dread in my stomach. My breathing was thick, slow, heavy. Every part of my body was telling me to leave, go, run, run away. But I didn't. I followed them into the woods.

I tried to make as little noise as possible, but twigs crunched under my feet, and branches clawed at me. I couldn't see them anywhere — the trees grew so closely together that I could only see a few feet in front of me.

I stopped and listened. I heard a rustling in the trees, but it could have been the wind. Then I heard something unmistakable, a low-pitched guttural sound I recognized at once.

It was Kathy moaning.

I tried to get closer, but the branches caught me and held me suspended, like a fly in a web. I stood there in the dim light, breathing in the musty smell of bark and earth. I listened to Kathy moaning as he fucked her. He grunted like an animal.

I burned with hate. This man had come from nowhere and invaded my life. He had stolen and seduced and corrupted the one thing in the world that was precious to me.

It was monstrous — supernatural. Perhaps he wasn't human at all, but the instrument of some malevolent deity intent on punishing me. Was God punishing me? Why? What was I guilty of — except falling in love? Was it that I loved too deeply, too needily? Too much?

Did this man love her? I doubted it. Not the way I did. He was just using her; using her body. There was no way he cared for her as I did. I would have died for Kathy.

I would have killed for her.

I thought of my father — I knew what he'd do in this situation. He'd murder the guy. *Be a man,* I could hear my father shouting. *Toughen up.* Was that what I should do? Kill him? Dispose of him? It was a way out of this mess — a way to break the spell, release Kathy and set us free. Once she had grieved his loss, it would be over, he'd just be a memory, easily forgotten, and we could go on as before. I could do it now, here, in the park. I'd drag him into the pond, plunge his head underwater. I'd hold it there until his body convulsed and went limp in my arms. Or I could follow him home on the Tube, stand right behind him on the platform, and — with a sharp shove — push him in the path of an oncoming train. Or creep up behind him on a deserted street, clutching a brick, and bash out his brains. Why not?

Kathy's moans grew louder suddenly, and I recognized the groans she made as she climaxed. Then there was a silence . . . interrupted by a muffled giggle I knew so well. I could hear the snapping of twigs as they tramped out of the woods.

I waited for a few moments. Then I snapped the branches around me and fought my way out of the trees, tearing and scratching my hands to shreds.

When I emerged from the wood, my eyes were half-blind with tears. I wiped them away with a bleeding fist.

I lurched off, going nowhere. I walked round and round like a madman.

CHAPTER SIX

"Jean-Felix?"

No one was at the reception desk, and no one came when I called. I hesitated for a moment, then went into the gallery.

I walked along the corridor to where the *Alcestis* was hanging. Once again, I looked at the painting. Once again, I tried to read it, and again I failed. Something about the picture defied interpretation — or else it had some kind of meaning that I had yet to comprehend. But what?

Then — a sharp intake of breath as I noticed something. Behind Alicia, in the darkness, if you squinted and looked hard at the painting, the darkest parts of the shadows came together — like a hologram that goes from two dimensions to three when you look at it from a certain angle — and a shape burst forth from the shadows . . . the figure of a man. *A man* — hiding in the dark. Watching. Spying on Alicia.

"What do you want?"

The voice made me jump. I turned around.

Jean-Felix didn't look particularly pleased to see me. "What are you doing here?"

I was about to point out the figure of the man in the painting and ask Jean-Felix about it, but something told me it might be a bad idea.

Instead I smiled. "I just had a couple more questions. Is now a good time?"

"Not really. I've told you everything I know. Surely there can't be anything else?"

"Actually, some new information has come up."

"And what is that?"

"Well, for one thing, I didn't know Alicia was planning on leaving your gallery."

There was a second's pause before Jean-Felix answered. His voice sounded tight, like a rubber band about to snap.

"What are you talking about?"

"Is it true?"

"What business is it of yours?"

"Alicia is my patient. It's my intention to get her talking again — but I see now it might be in your interest if she remains silent."

"What the hell is that supposed to mean?"

"Well, as long as no one knows of her wish

371

to leave, you can hold on to her artwork indefinitely."

"What exactly are you accusing me of?"

"I'm not accusing you at all. Merely stating a fact."

Jean-Felix laughed. "We'll see about that. I'll be contacting my lawyer — and making a formal complaint to the hospital."

"I don't think you will."

"And why is that?"

"Well, you see, I haven't told you how I heard Alicia was planning to leave."

"Whoever told you was lying."

"It was Alicia."

"What?" Jean-Felix looked stunned. "You mean . . . she spoke?"

"In a way. She gave me her diary to read."

"Her — diary?" He blinked a few times, as if he was having trouble processing the information. "I didn't know Alicia kept a diary."

"Well, she did. She describes your last few meetings in some detail."

I didn't say anything else. I didn't need to. There was a heavy pause. Jean-Felix was silent.

"I'll be in touch," I said. I smiled and walked out.

As I emerged onto the Soho street, I felt a little guilty for ruffling Jean-Felix's feathers

372

like that. But it had been intentional — I wanted to see what effect the provocation would have, how he'd react, what he would do.

Now I had to wait and see.

As I walked through Soho, I phoned Alicia's cousin, Paul Rose, to let him know I was coming. I didn't want to turn up at the house unannounced and risk a similar reception to last time. The bruise on my head still hadn't fully healed.

I cradled the phone between my ear and my shoulder as I lit a cigarette. I barely had time to inhale before the phone was answered, on the first ring. I hoped it would be Paul, not Lydia. I was in luck.

"Hello?"

"Paul. It's Theo Faber."

"Oh. Hello, mate. Sorry I'm whispering. Mum's having her nap, and I don't want to disturb her. How's your head?"

"Much better, thanks."

"Good, good. How can I help?"

"Well, I've received some new information about Alicia. I wanted to talk to you about it."

"What kind of information?"

I told him that Alicia had given me her diary to read.

373

"Her diary? I didn't know she kept one. What does it say?"

"It might be easier to talk in person. Are you free today at all?"

Paul hesitated. "It might be better if you don't come to the house. Mother isn't . . . well, she wasn't too happy about your last visit."

"Yes, I gathered that."

"There's a pub at the end of the road, by the roundabout. The White Bear —"

"Yes, I remember it. That sounds fine. What time?"

"Around five? I should be able to get away then for a bit."

I heard Lydia shouting in the background. Evidently she had woken up.

"I have to go. I'll see you later." Paul hung up.

A few hours later, I was on my way back to Cambridge. On the train, I made another phone call — to Max Berenson. I hesitated before calling. He'd already complained to Diomedes once, so he wouldn't be pleased to hear from me again. But I knew I had no choice.

Tanya answered. Her cold sounded better, but I could hear the tension in her voice when she realized who I was. "I don't think

374

— I mean, Max is busy. He's in meetings all day."

"I'll call back."

"I'm not sure that's a good idea. I —"

I could hear Max in the background saying something, and Tanya's reply: "I'm not saying that, Max."

Max grabbed the phone and spoke to me directly: "I just told Tanya to tell you to fuck off."

"Ah."

"You've got a nerve calling here again. I already complained once to Professor Diomedes."

"Yes, I'm aware of that. Nonetheless some new information has come to light, and it concerns you directly — so I felt I had no choice but to get in touch."

"What information?"

"It's a journal Alicia kept in the weeks leading up to the murder."

There was silence at the other end of the line. I hesitated.

"Alicia writes about you in some detail, Max. She said you had romantic feelings for her. I was wondering if —"

There was a click as he hung up. So far so good. Max had taken the bait — and now I had to wait to see how he'd react.

I realized I was a little afraid of Max Berenson, just as Tanya was afraid of him. I remembered her whispered advice to me, to talk to Paul, to ask him something — what? Something about the night after the accident that killed Alicia's mother. I remembered the look on Tanya's face when Max had appeared, how she fell silent and presented him with a smile. No, I thought, Max Berenson was not to be underestimated.

That would be a dangerous mistake.

CHAPTER SEVEN

As the train approached Cambridge, the landscape flattened and the temperature dropped. I did up my coat as I left the station. The wind cut into my face like a volley of icy razor blades. I made my way to the pub to meet Paul.

The White Bear was a ramshackle old place — it looked as if several extensions had been added onto the original structure over the years. A couple of students were braving the wind, sitting outside with their pints in the beer garden, wrapped up in scarves, smoking. Inside, the temperature was much warmer, thanks to several roaring fires, which provided a welcome relief from the cold.

I got a drink and looked around for Paul. Several small rooms led off from the main bar and the lighting was low. I peered at the figures in the shadows, unsuccessfully trying to spot him. A good place for an illicit rendezvous, I thought. Which, I suppose, is what this was.

I found Paul alone in a small room. He was facing away from the door, sitting by the fire. I recognized him at once, on account of his sheer size. His huge back nearly blocked the fire from sight.

"Paul?"

He jumped up and turned around. He looked like a giant in the tiny room. He had to stoop slightly to avoid hitting the ceiling.

"All right?" he said. He looked like he was bracing himself for bad news from a doctor. He made some room for me, and I sat down in front of the fire, relieved to feel its warmth on my face and hands.

"It's colder than London here. That wind doesn't help."

"Comes straight from Siberia, that's what they say." Paul continued without pausing, clearly in no mood for small talk, "What's this about a diary? I never knew Alicia kept a diary."

"Well, she did."

"And she gave it to you?"

I nodded.

"And? What does it say?"

"It specifically details the last couple of months before the murder. And there are a couple of discrepancies I wanted to ask you about."

"What discrepancies?"

"Between your account of events and hers."

"What are you talking about?" He put down his pint and gave me a long stare. "What do you mean?"

"Well, for one thing, you told me you hadn't seen Alicia for several years before the murder."

Paul hesitated. "Did I?"

"In the diary, Alicia says she saw you a few weeks before Gabriel was killed. She says you came to the house in Hampstead."

I stared at him, sensing him deflate inside. He looked like a boy suddenly, in a body that was much too big for him. Paul was afraid, it was obvious. He didn't reply for moment. He shot me a furtive glance.

"Can I have a look? At the diary?"

I shook my head. "I don't think that would be appropriate. Anyway, I didn't bring it with me."

"Then how do I even know it exists? You could be lying."

"I'm not lying. But you were — you lied to me, Paul. Why?"

"It's none of your business, that's why."

"I'm afraid it is my business. Alicia's well-being is my concern."

"Her well-being has got nothing to do with it. I didn't hurt her."

"I never said you did."

"Well, then."

"Why don't you tell me what happened?"

Paul shrugged. "It's a long story." He hesitated, then gave in. He spoke quickly, breathlessly. I sensed his relief at finally telling someone. "I was in a bad way. I had a problem, you know — I was gambling and borrowing money, and not able to pay it back. I needed some cash to . . . to put everyone straight."

"And so you asked Alicia? Did she give you the money?"

"What does the diary say?"

"It doesn't."

Paul hesitated, then shook his head. "No, she didn't give me anything. She said she couldn't afford to."

Again he was lying. Why?

"How did you get the money, then?"

"I — I took it out of my savings. I'd appreciate it if you kept this between us — I don't want my mother to find out."

"I don't think there's any reason to involve Lydia in this."

"Really?" Some color came back into Paul's expression. He looked more hopeful.

380

"Thanks. I appreciate that."

"Did Alicia ever tell you she suspected she was being watched?"

Paul lowered his glass and gave me a puzzled look. I could see she hadn't. "Watched? What do you mean?"

I told him the story I had read in the diary — about Alicia's suspicions she was being watched by a stranger, and finally her fears that she was under attack in her own home.

Paul shook his head. "She wasn't right in the head."

"You think she imagined it?"

"Well, it stands to reason, doesn't it?" Paul shrugged. "You don't think someone was stalking her? I mean, I suppose it's possible —"

"Yes, it is possible. So I presume she said nothing to you about it?"

"Not a word. But Alicia and I never talked much, you know. She was always pretty silent. We all were, as a family. I remember Alicia saying how weird it was — she'd go to friends' houses and see other families laugh and joke and have conversations about things, and our house was so silent. We never talked. Apart from my mum, giving orders."

"And what about Alicia's father? Vernon?

381

What was he like?"

"Vernon didn't really talk much. He wasn't right in the head — not after Eva died. He was never the same after that. Neither was Alicia, come to that."

"That reminds me. There was something I wanted to ask you — something Tanya mentioned to me."

"Tanya Berenson? You spoke to her?"

"Only briefly. She suggested I talk to you."

"Tanya did?" Paul's cheeks colored. "I — I don't know her well, but she's always been very kind to me. She's a good, very good person. She visited me and Mum a couple of times." A smile appeared on Paul's lips and he looked faraway for a moment.

He has a crush on her, I thought. I wondered how Max felt about that.

"What did Tanya say?" he asked.

"She suggested I ask you about something — that happened the night after the car accident. She didn't go into detail."

"Yes, I know what she means — I told her during the trial. I asked her not to tell anyone."

"She didn't tell me. It's up to you to tell me. If you wish to. Of course, if you don't want to . . ."

Paul drained his pint and shrugged. "It's probably nothing, but — it might help you

382

understand Alicia. She . . ." He hesitated and fell silent.

"Go on."

"Alicia . . . the first thing Alicia did, when she got home from the hospital — they kept her in for a night after the crash — was she climbed up onto the roof of the house. I did too. We sat up there all night, pretty much. We used to go there all the time, Alicia and me. It was our secret place."

"On the roof?"

Paul hesitated. He looked at me for a second, deliberating. He made a decision.

"Come on." He stood up. "I'll show you."

CHAPTER EIGHT

The house was in darkness as we approached.

"Here it is," Paul said. "Follow me."

An iron ladder was attached to the side of the house. We made our way over to it. The mud was frozen beneath our feet, sculpted into hard ripples and ridges. Without waiting for me, Paul started climbing up.

It was getting colder by the minute. I was wondering if this was such a good idea. I followed him and gripped the first rung — icy and slippery. It was overgrown with some kind of climbing plant; ivy, perhaps.

I made my way up, rung by rung. By the time I reached the top, my fingers were numb and the wind was slashing my face. I climbed over, onto the roof. Paul was waiting for me, grinning in an excited, adolescent way. The razor-thin moon hung above us; the rest was darkness.

Suddenly Paul rushed at me, a strange

expression on his face. I felt a flicker of panic as his arm reached out toward me — I swerved to avoid it, but he grabbed hold of me. For a terrifying second I thought he was going to throw me off the roof.

Instead he pulled me toward him. "You're too close to the edge. Stay in the middle here. It's safer."

I nodded, catching my breath. This was a bad idea. I didn't feel remotely safe around Paul. I was about to suggest climbing down again — then he pulled out his cigarettes and offered me one. I hesitated, then I accepted. My fingers were shaking as I took out my lighter and lit the cigarettes.

We stood there and smoked in silence for a moment.

"This is where we would sit. Alicia and me. Every day, pretty much."

"How old were you?"

"I was about seven, maybe eight. Alicia couldn't have been more than ten."

"You were a bit young to be climbing ladders."

"I suppose so. Seemed normal to us. When we were teenagers, we'd come up and smoke and drink beers."

I tried to picture a teenage Alicia, hiding from her father and her bullying aunt; Paul, her adoring younger cousin, following up the ladder, pestering her when she'd much rather be silent, alone with her thoughts.

"It's a good hiding place," I said.

Paul nodded. "Uncle Vernon couldn't make it up the ladder. He had a big build, like Mum."

"I could barely make it up myself. That ivy is a death trap."

"It's not ivy, it's jasmine." Paul looked at the green vines that curled over the top of the ladder. "No flowers yet — not until the spring. Smells like perfume then, when there's a lot of it." He seemed lost in a memory for a moment. "Funny that."

"What?"

"Nothing." He shrugged. "The things you remember . . . I just was thinking about the jasmine — it was in full bloom that day, the day of the accident, when Eva was killed."

I looked around. "You and Alicia came up here together, you said?"

He nodded. "Mum and Uncle Vernon were looking for us down there. We could hear them calling. But we didn't say a word. We stayed hiding. And that's when it happened."

He stubbed out his cigarette and gave me an odd smile. "That's why I brought you here. So you can see it — the scene of the crime."

"The crime?"

Paul didn't answer, just kept grinning at me.

"What crime, Paul?"

"Vernon's crime. Uncle Vernon wasn't a good man, you see. No, not at all."

"What are you trying to say?"

"Well, that's when he did it."

"Did what?"

"That's when he killed Alicia."

I stared at Paul, unable to believe my ears. "Killed Alicia? What are you talking about?"

Paul pointed at the ground below. "Uncle Vernon was down there with Mum. He was drunk. Mum kept trying to get him to go back inside. But he stood down there, yelling for Alicia. He was so angry with her. He was so mad."

"Because Alicia was hiding? But — she was a child — her mother had just died."

"He was a mean bastard. The only person he ever cared about was Auntie Eva. I suppose that's why he said it."

"Said what?" I was losing patience. "I don't understand what you're saying to me. What exactly happened?"

"Vernon was going on about how much he loved Eva — how he couldn't live without her. 'My girl,' he kept saying, 'my poor girl, my Eva . . . Why did she have to die? Why did it have to be her? *Why didn't Alicia die instead?'* "

I stared at Paul for a second, stunned. I wasn't sure I understood. " 'Why didn't Alicia die instead?' "

"That's what he said."

"Alicia heard this?"

"Yeah. And Alicia whispered something to me — I'll never forget it. 'He killed me,' she said. 'Dad just — killed me.' "

I stared at Paul, speechless. A chorus of bells started ringing in my head, clanging, chiming, reverberating. This was what I'd been looking for. I'd found it, the missing piece of the jigsaw, at last — here on a roof in Cambridge.

All the way back to London, I kept thinking about the implications of what I had heard. I understood now why *Alcestis* had struck a chord with Alicia. Just as Admetus had physically condemned Alcestis to die, so had Vernon Rose psychically condemned his daughter to death. Admetus must have loved Alcestis, on some level, but there was no love in Vernon Rose, just hate. He had committed psychic infanticide — and Alicia knew it.

"He killed me," she said. "Dad just killed me."

388

Now, at last, I had something to work with. Something I knew about — the emotional effects of psychological wounds on children, and how they manifest themselves later in adults. Imagine it — hearing your father, the very person you depend upon for your survival, wishing you dead. How terrifying that must be for a child, how traumatizing — how your sense of self-worth would implode, and the pain would be too great, too huge to feel, so you'd swallow it, repress it, bury it. Over time you would lose contact with the origins of your trauma, dissociate the roots of its cause, and forget. But one day, all the hurt and anger would burst forth, like fire from a dragon's belly — and you'd pick up a gun. You'd visit that rage not upon your father, who was dead and forgotten and out of reach — but upon your husband, the man who had taken his place in your life, who loved you and shared your bed. You'd shoot him five times in the head, without possibly even knowing why.

The train raced through the night back to London. At last, I thought — at last I knew how to reach her.

Now we could begin.

CHAPTER NINE

I sat with Alicia in silence.

I was getting better at these silences, better at enduring them, settling into them and toughing it out; it had become almost comfortable, sitting in that small room with her, keeping quiet.

Alicia held her hands in her lap, clenching and unclenching them rhythmically, like a heartbeat. She was facing me, not looking at me, but gazing out of the window through the bars. It had stopped raining, and the clouds momentarily parted to reveal a pale blue sky; then another cloud appeared, obscuring it with gray. Then I spoke.

"There's something I have become aware of. Something your cousin told me."

I said this as gently as I could. She didn't react, so I went on.

"Paul said that when you were a child, you overheard your father say something devastating. After the car accident that killed your mother . . . you heard him say that he wished you had died, instead of her."

I was certain there would be a knee-jerk physical reaction, an acknowledgment of some kind. I waited, but none came.

"I wonder how you feel about Paul telling me this — it might seem like a betrayal of confidence. But I believe he had your best interests in mind. You are, after all, in my care."

No response. I hesitated.

"It might help you if I tell you something. No — perhaps that's being disingenuous — perhaps it's me it would help. The truth is I understand you better than you think. Without wishing to disclose too much, you and I experienced similar kinds of childhoods, with similar kinds of fathers. And we both left home as soon as we could. But we soon discovered that geographical distance counts for little in the world of the psyche. Some things are not so easily left behind. I know how damaging your childhood was. It's important you understand how serious this is. What your father said is tantamount to psychic murder. He *killed* you."

This time she reacted.

She looked up sharply — straight at me. Her eyes seemed to burn right through me. If looks could kill, I would have dropped dead. I met her murderous gaze without flinching.

"Alicia. This is our last chance. I'm sitting here now without Professor Diomedes's knowledge or permission. If I keep breaking the rules like this for your sake, I'm going to get fired. That's why this will be the last time you see me. Do you understand?"

I said this without any expectation or emotion, drained of hope or feeling. I was sick of bashing my head against a wall. I didn't expect any kind of response. And then . . .

I thought I imagined it at first. I thought I was hearing things. I stared at her, breathless. I felt my heart thudding in my chest. My mouth was dry when I spoke.

"Did — did you just . . . say something?"

Another silence. I must have been mistaken. I must have imagined it. But then . . . it happened again.

Alicia's lips moved slowly, painfully; her voice cracked a little as it emerged, like a creaking gate that needed oiling.

"What . . ." she whispered. Then she stopped. And again: "What . . . what —"

For a moment we just stared at each other. My eyes slowly filled with tears — tears of disbelief, excitement, and gratitude.

"What do I want? I want you to keep talking. . . . Talk — talk to me, Alicia —"

Alicia stared at me. She was thinking about something. She came to a decision. She slowly nodded. "Okay," she said.

CHAPTER TEN

"She said *what?*"

Professor Diomedes stared at me with a look of stunned amazement. We were outside, smoking. I could tell he was excited because he had dropped his cigar on the ground without even noticing. "She spoke? Alicia really spoke?"

"She did."

"Incredible. So you were right. You were right. And I was wrong."

"Not at all. It was wrong of me to see her without your permission, Professor. I'm sorry, I just had an instinct . . ."

Diomedes waved away my apology and finished my sentence for me. "You followed your gut. I would have done the same, Theo. Well done."

I was unwilling to be too celebratory. "We mustn't count our chickens yet. It's a breakthrough, yes. But there's no guarantee — she might revert or regress at any point."

Diomedes nodded. "Quite right. We must organize a formal review and interview Alicia as soon as possible — get her in front of a panel — you and me and someone from the Trust — Julian will do, he's harmless enough —"

"You're going too fast. You're not listening to me. That's too soon. Anything like that will scare her. We need to move slowly."

"Well, it's important the Trust knows —"

"No, not yet. Maybe this was a one-off. Let's wait. Let's not make any announcements. Not just yet."

Diomedes nodded, taking this in. His hand reached for my shoulder and gripped it. "Well done. I'm proud of you."

I felt a small flicker of pride — a son congratulated by his father. I was conscious of my desire to please Diomedes, justify his faith in me and make him proud. I felt a little emotional. I lit a cigarette to disguise it. "What now?"

"Now you keep going. Keep working with Alicia."

"And if Stephanie finds out?"

"Forget Stephanie — leave her to me. You focus on Alicia."

And so I did.

During our next session, Alicia and I talked

nonstop. Or rather, Alicia talked and I listened. Listening to Alicia was an unfamiliar and somewhat disconcerting experience, after so much silence. She spoke hesitantly at first, tentatively — trying to walk on legs that hadn't been used in a while. She soon found her feet, picking up speed and agility, tripping through sentences as if she had never been silent, which in a way, she hadn't.

When the session ended, I went to my office. I sat at the desk, transcribing what had been said while it was still fresh in my mind. I wrote down everything, word for word, capturing it as precisely and accurately as possible.

As you will see, it's an incredible story — of that there is no doubt.

Whether you believe it or not is up to you.

396

CHAPTER ELEVEN

Alicia sat in the chair opposite me in the therapy room.

"Before we begin, I have some questions for you. A few things I'd like to clarify . . ."

No reply. Alicia looked at me with that unreadable look of hers.

"Specifically, I want to understand your silence. I want to know why you refused to speak."

Alicia seemed disappointed by the question. She turned and looked out the window.

We sat like that in silence for a minute or so. I tried to contain the suspense I was feeling. Had the breakthrough been temporary? Would we now go on as before? I couldn't let that happen.

"Alicia. I know it's difficult. But once you start talking to me, you'll find it easier, I promise."

No response.

"Try. Please. Don't give up when you've

made such progress. Keep going. Tell me . . . tell me why you wouldn't speak."

Alicia turned back and stared at me with a chilly gaze. She spoke in a low voice:

"Nothing . . . nothing to say."

"I'm not sure I believe that. I think there was too much to say."

A pause. A shrug. "Perhaps. Perhaps . . . you're right."

"Go on."

She hesitated. "At first, when Gabriel . . . when he was dead — I couldn't, I tried . . . but I couldn't . . . talk. I opened my mouth — but no sound came out. Like in a dream . . . where you try to scream . . . but can't."

"You were in a state of shock. But over the next few days, you must have found your voice returning to you . . . ?"

"By then . . . it seemed pointless. It was too late."

"Too late? To speak in your defense?"

Alicia held me in her gaze, a cryptic smile on her lips. She didn't speak.

"Tell me why you started talking again."

"You know the answer."

"Do I?"

"Because of you."

"Me?" I looked at her with surprise.

"Because you came here."

"And that made a difference?"

"All the difference — it made . . . all the difference." Alicia lowered her voice and stared at me, unblinking. "I want you to understand — what happened to me. What it felt like. It's important . . . you understand."

"I want to understand. That's why you gave me the diary, isn't it? Because you want me to understand. It seems to me the people who mattered most to you didn't believe your story about the man. Perhaps you're wondering . . . if I believe you."

"You believe me." This was not a question but a simple statement of fact.

I nodded. "Yes, I believe you. So why don't we start there? The last diary entry you wrote described the man breaking into the house. What happened then?"

"Nothing."

"Nothing?"

She shook her head. "It wasn't him."

"It wasn't? Then who was it?"

"It was Jean-Felix. He wanted — he had come to talk about the exhibition."

"Judging by your diary, it doesn't seem you were in the right state of mind for visitors."

Alicia acknowledged this with a shrug.

"Did he stay long?"

"No. I asked him to leave. He didn't want to — he was upset. He shouted at me a bit — but he went after a while."

"And then? What happened after Jean-Felix left?"

Alicia shook her head. "I don't want to talk about that."

"No?"

"Not yet."

Alicia's eyes looked into mine for a moment. Then they darted to the window, considering the darkening sky beyond the bars. Something in the way she was tilting her head was almost coquettish, and the beginning of a smile was forming at the corner of her mouth. She's enjoying this, I thought. Having me in her power.

"What do you want to talk about?" I asked.

"I don't know. Nothing. I just want to talk."

So we talked. We talked about Lydia and Paul, and about her mother, and the summer she died. We talked about Alicia's childhood — and mine. I told her about my father, and growing up in that house; she seemed curious to know as much as possible about my past and what had shaped me and made me who I am.

I remember thinking, There's no going

back now. We were crashing through every last boundary between therapist and patient. Soon it would be impossible to tell who was who.

CHAPTER TWELVE

The next morning, we met again. Alicia seemed different that day somehow — more reserved, more guarded. I think it's because she was preparing herself to talk about the day of Gabriel's death.

She sat opposite me and, unusually for her, looked straight at me and maintained eye contact throughout. She started speaking without being prompted; slowly, thoughtfully, choosing each phrase with care, as if cautiously applying brushstrokes to a canvas.

"I was alone that afternoon. I knew I had to paint, but it was so hot, I didn't think I could face it. But I decided to try. So I took the little fan I'd bought down to the studio in the garden, and then . . ."

"And then?"

"My phone rang. It was Gabriel. He was calling to say he'd be back late from the shoot."

"Did he normally do that? Call to say he'd be late?"

Alicia gave me an odd look, as if it struck her as a strange question. She shook her head. "No. Why?"

"I wondered if he might be calling for another reason. To see how you were feeling? Judging from your diary, it sounds like he was concerned about your mental state."

"Oh." Alicia pondered this, taken aback. She slowly nodded. "I see. Yes, yes, possibly . . ."

"I'm sorry — I interrupted you. Go on. What happened after the phone call?"

Alicia hesitated. "I saw him."

"Him?"

"The man. I mean, I saw his reflection. Reflected in the window. He was inside — inside the studio. Standing right behind me."

Alicia shut her eyes and sat quite still. There was a long pause.

I spoke gently. "Can you describe him? What did he look like?"

She opened her eyes and stared at me for a moment. "He was tall. . . . Strong. I couldn't see his face — he had put on a mask, a black mask. But I could see his eyes — they were dark holes. No light in them at all."

403

"What did you do when you saw him?"

"Nothing. I was so scared. I kept looking at him. He had a knife in his hand. I asked what he wanted. He didn't speak. And I said I had money in the kitchen, in my bag. And he shook his head and said, 'I don't want money.' And he laughed. A horrible laugh, like breaking glass. He held the knife up to my neck. The sharp end of the blade was against my throat, against my skin. . . . He told me to go with him into the house."

Alicia shut her eyes as she remembered it. "He led me out of the studio, onto the lawn. We walked toward the house. I could see the gate to the street, just a few meters away — I was so close to it. . . . And something in me took over. It was — it was my only chance to escape. So I kicked him hard and broke away from him. And I ran. I ran for the gate." Her eyes opened and she smiled at the memory. "For a few seconds, I was free."

Her smile faded.

"Then — he jumped on me. On my back. We fell to the ground. . . . His hand was over my mouth, and I felt the cold blade against my throat. He said he'd kill me if I moved. We lay there for a few seconds, and I could feel his breath on my face. It stank. Then he pulled me up — and dragged me

404

into the house."

"And then? What happened?"

"He locked the door. And I was trapped."

Alicia's breathing was heavy and her cheeks were flushed. I was concerned she was becoming distressed, and I was wary of pushing her too hard.

"Do you need a break?"

She shook her head. "Let's keep going. I've waited long enough to say this. I want to get it over with."

"Are you sure? It might be a good idea to take a moment."

She hesitated. "Can I have a cigarette?"

"A cigarette? I didn't know you smoked."

"I don't. I — I used to. Can you give me one?"

"How do you know I smoke?"

"I can smell it on you."

"Oh." I smiled, feeling a little embarrassed. "Okay." I stood up. "Let's go outside."

CHAPTER THIRTEEN

The courtyard was populated with patients. They were huddled about in their usual groups, gossiping, arguing, smoking; some were hugging themselves and stamping their feet to keep warm.

Alicia put a cigarette to her lips, holding it between her long thin fingers. I lit it for her. As the flame caught the tip of her cigarette, it crackled and glowed red. She inhaled deeply, her eyes on mine. She seemed almost amused.

"Aren't you going to smoke? Or is that inappropriate? Sharing a cigarette with a patient?"

She's making fun of me, I thought. But she was right to — no regulation prohibited a member of staff and a patient from having a cigarette together. But if staff smoked, they tended to do it covertly, sneaking to the fire escape at the back of the building. They certainly didn't do it in front of the patients. To stand here in the courtyard and smoke with her did feel like a transgression. I was probably imagining it, but I felt we were being watched. I sensed Christian spying on us from the window. His words came back to me: "Borderlines are so seductive." I looked into Alicia's eyes. They weren't seductive; they weren't even friendly. A fierce mind was behind those eyes, a sharp intelligence that was only just waking up. She was a force to be reckoned with, Alicia Berenson. I understood that now.

Perhaps that's why Christian had felt the need to sedate her. Was he scared of what she might do — what she might say? I felt a little scared of her myself; not scared, exactly — but alert, apprehensive. I knew I had to watch my step.

"Why not?" I said. "I'll have one too."

I put a cigarette in my mouth and lit it. We smoked in silence for a moment, maintaining eye contact, only inches from each other, until I felt a strange adolescent embarrassment and averted my gaze. I tried to cover it by gesturing at the courtyard.

"Shall we walk and talk?"

Alicia nodded. "Okay."

We started walking around the wall, along the perimeter of the courtyard. The other patients watched us. I wondered what they

407

were thinking. Alicia didn't seem to care. She didn't even seem to notice them. We walked in silence for a moment.

Eventually she said, "Do you want me to go on?"

"If you want to, yes . . . Are you ready?"

Alicia nodded. "Yes, I am."

"What happened once you were inside the house?"

"The man said . . . he said he wanted a drink. So I gave him one of Gabriel's beers. I don't drink beer. I didn't have anything else in the house."

"And then?"

"He talked."

"What about?"

"I don't remember."

"You don't?"

"No."

She lapsed into silence.

I waited as long as I could bear before prompting her, "Let's keep going. You were in the kitchen. How were you feeling?"

"I don't . . . I don't remember feeling anything at all."

I nodded. "That's not uncommon in these situations. It's not just a case of flight-or-fight responses. There's a third, equally common response when we're under attack — we freeze."

408

"I didn't freeze."

"No?"

"No." She shot me a fierce look. "I was preparing myself. I was getting ready . . . ready to fight. Ready to — kill him."

"I see. And how did you intend to do that?"

"Gabriel's gun. I knew I had to get to the gun."

"It was in the kitchen? You had put it there? That's what you wrote in the diary."

Alicia nodded. "Yes, in the cupboard by the window." She inhaled deeply and blew out a long line of smoke. "I told him I needed some water. I went to get a glass. I walked across the kitchen — it took forever to walk a few feet. Step by step, I reached the cupboard. My hand was shaking. . . . I opened it. . . ."

"And?"

"The cupboard was empty. The gun was gone. And then I heard him say, 'The glasses are in the cupboard to your right.' I turned around, and the gun was there — in his hand. He was pointing it at me, and laughing."

"And then?"

"Then?"

"What were you thinking?"

"That it had been my last chance to

409

escape, and now — now he was going to kill me."

"You believed he was going to kill you?"

"I knew he was."

"But then why did he delay? Why not do it as soon as he broke into the house?"

Alicia didn't answer. I glanced at her. To my surprise, a smile was on her lips.

"When I was young, Aunt Lydia had a kitten. A tabby cat. I didn't like her much. She was wild, and she'd go for me sometimes with her claws. She was unkind — and cruel."

"Don't animals act out of instinct? Can they be cruel?"

Alicia looked at me intently. "They can be cruel. She was. She would bring in things from the field — mice or little birds she'd caught. And they were always half-alive. Wounded, but alive. She'd keep them like that and play with them."

"I see. It sounds like you're saying you were this man's prey? That he was playing some kind of sadistic game with you. Is that right?"

Alicia dropped the end of her cigarette on the ground and stepped on it. "Give me another one."

I handed her the pack. She took one and lit the cigarette herself. She smoked for a

410

moment. "Gabriel was coming home at eight. Two more hours. I kept staring at the clock. 'What's the matter?' he said. 'Don't you like spending time with me?' And he stroked my skin with the gun, running it up and down my arm." She shivered at the memory. "I said Gabriel was going to be home any minute. 'And what then?' he asked. 'He'll rescue you?' "

"And what did you say?"

"I didn't say anything. I just kept staring at the clock . . . and then my phone rang. It was Gabriel. He told me to answer it. He held the gun against my head."

"And? What did Gabriel say?"

"He said . . . he said the shoot was turning into a nightmare, so I should go ahead and eat without him. He wouldn't get back until ten at the earliest. I hung up. 'My husband is on his way home,' I said. 'He'll be here in a few minutes. You should go, now, before he gets back.' The man just laughed. 'But I heard him say he won't be back until ten,' he said. 'We've got hours to kill. Get me some rope,' he said, 'or tape or something. I want to tie you up.'

"I did as he asked. I knew it was hopeless now. I knew how it was going to end."

Alicia stopped talking and looked at me. I could see the raw emotion in her eyes. I

411

wondered if I was pushing her too hard.

"Maybe we should take a break."

"No, I need to finish. I need to do this."

She went on, speaking faster now. "I didn't have any rope, so he took the wire I had for hanging canvases. He made me go in the living room. He pulled out one of the upright chairs from the dining table. He told me to sit down. He started wrapping the wire around my ankles, tying me to the chair. I could feel it cutting into me. 'Please,' I said, 'please —' But he didn't listen. He tied my wrists behind my back. I was sure then that he was going to kill me. I wish . . . *I wish he had.*"

She spat this out. I was startled by her vehemence.

"Why do you wish that?"

"Because what he did was worse."

For a second I thought Alicia was going to cry. I fought a sudden desire to hold her, take her in my arms, kiss her, reassure her, promise her she was safe. I restrained myself. I stubbed out my cigarette on the redbrick wall.

"I feel that you need to be taken care of. I find myself wanting to take care of you, Alicia."

"No." She shook her head firmly. "That's not what I want from you."

412

"What do you want?"

Alicia didn't answer. She turned and walked back inside.

"What do you want?"

Alicia didn't answer. She turned and walked back inside.

CHAPTER FOURTEEN

I turned on the light in the therapy room and shut the door. When I turned around, Alicia had already sat down — but not in her chair. She was sitting in my chair.

Normally I would have explored the meaning of this telling gesture with her. Now, however, I said nothing. If sitting in my chair signified she had the upper hand — well, she did. I was impatient to get to the end of her story, now that we were so close to it. So I just sat down and waited for her to speak. She half shut her eyes and was perfectly still.

Eventually she said, "I was tied to the chair, and every time I squirmed, the wire cut deeper into my legs, and they were bleeding. It was a relief to focus on the cutting instead of my thoughts. My thoughts were too scary. . . . I thought I would never see Gabriel again. I thought I was going to die."

"What happened next?"

"We sat there for what seemed like forever. It's funny. I've always thought of fear as a cold sensation, but it's not — it burns like fire. It was so hot in that room, with the windows closed and the blinds drawn. Still, stifling, heavy air. Beads of sweat were dripping down my forehead and into my eyes, stinging them. I could smell the alcohol on him and the stink of his sweat while he drank and talked — he kept talking. I didn't listen to a lot of it. I could hear a big fat fly, buzzing between the blind and the window — it was trapped and thudding against the glass, thud, thud, thud. He asked questions about me and Gabriel — how we met, how long we'd been together, if we were happy. I thought if I could keep him talking, I had a better chance of staying alive. So I answered his questions — about me, Gabriel, my work. I talked about whatever he wanted. Just to buy time. I kept focusing on the clock. Listening to it tick. And then suddenly it was ten o'clock. . . . And then . . . ten-thirty. And still Gabriel hadn't come home.

" 'He's late,' he said. 'Maybe he's not coming.'

" 'He's coming,' I said.

" 'Well, it's a good thing I'm here to keep

you company.'

"And then the clock struck eleven, and I heard a car outside. The man went to the window and looked out. 'Perfect timing,' he said."

What happened next — Alicia said — happened fast.

The man grabbed Alicia and swung her chair around, so she faced away from the door. He said he would shoot Gabriel in the head if she spoke one word or made a single sound. Then he disappeared. A moment later the lights fused and everything went dark. In the hallway, the front door opened and closed.

"Alicia?" Gabriel called out.

There was no reply, and he called her name again. He walked into the living room — and saw her by the fireplace, sitting with her back to him.

"Why are you sitting in the dark?" Gabriel asked. No reply. "Alicia?"

Alicia fought to remain silent — she wanted to cry out, but her eyes had become accustomed to the dark and she could see in front of her, in the corner of the room, the man's gun glinting in the shadows. He was pointing it at Gabriel. Alicia kept silent for his sake.

"Alicia?" Gabriel walked toward her. "What's wrong?"

Just as Gabriel reached out his hand to touch her, the man leaped from the darkness. Alicia screamed, but it was too late — and Gabriel was knocked to the floor, the man on top of him. The gun was raised like a hammer and brought down onto Gabriel's head with a sickening thud — once, twice, three times — and he lay there, unconscious, bleeding. The man pulled him up and sat Gabriel on a chair. He tied him to it, using the wire. Gabriel stirred as he regained consciousness.

"What the fuck? What —"

The man raised the gun and aimed it at Gabriel. There was a gunshot. And another. And another. Alicia started screaming. The man kept firing. He shot Gabriel in the head six times. Then he tossed the gun to the floor.

He left without saying a word.

CHAPTER FIFTEEN

So there you have it. Alicia Berenson didn't kill her husband. A faceless intruder broke into their home and, in an apparently motiveless act of malice, shot Gabriel dead before vanishing into the night. Alicia was entirely innocent.

That's if you believe her explanation.

I didn't. Not a word of it.

Apart from her obvious inconsistencies and inaccuracies — such as that Gabriel was not shot six times, but only five, one of the bullets being fired at the ceiling; nor was Alicia discovered tied to a chair, but standing in the middle of the room, having slashed her wrists. Alicia made no mention to me of the man's untying her, nor did she explain why she hadn't told the police this version of events from the start. No, I knew she was lying. I was annoyed that she had lied, badly and pointlessly, to my face. For a second I wondered if she was testing me, seeing whether I accepted the story? If so, I was determined to give nothing away.

I sat there in silence.

Unusually, Alicia spoke first. "I'm tired. I want to stop."

I nodded. I couldn't object.

"Let's carry on tomorrow," she said.

"Is there more to say?"

"Yes. One last thing."

"Very well. Tomorrow."

Yuri was waiting in the corridor. He escorted Alicia to her room, and I went up to my office.

As I have said, it's been my practice for years to transcribe a session as soon as it's ended. The ability to accurately record what has been said during the past fifty minutes is of paramount importance to a therapist — otherwise much detail is forgotten and the immediacy of the emotions lost.

I sat at my desk and wrote down, as fast as I could, everything that had transpired between us. The moment I finished, I marched through the corridors, clutching my pages of notes.

I knocked on Diomedes's door. There was no response, so I knocked again. Still no answer. I opened the door a crack — and there was Diomedes, fast asleep on his narrow couch.

"Professor?" And again, louder: "Professor Diomedes?"

He woke with a start and sat up quickly. He blinked at me.

"What is it? What's wrong?"

"I need to talk to you. Should I come back later?"

Diomedes frowned and shook his head. "I was having a brief siesta. I always do, after lunch. It helps me get through the afternoon. It becomes a necessity as you get older." He yawned and stood up. "Come in, Theo. Sit down. By the looks of you, it's important."

"I think it is, yes."

"Alicia?"

I nodded. I sat in front of the desk. He sat down behind it. His hair was sticking up to one side, and he still looked half-asleep.

"Are you sure I shouldn't come back later?"

Diomedes shook his head. He poured himself a glass of water from a jug. "I'm awake now. Go on. What is it?"

"I've been with Alicia, talking. . . . I need some supervision."

Diomedes nodded. He was looking more awake by the second, and more interested. "Go on."

I started reading from my notes. I took

420

him through the entire session. I repeated her words as accurately as I could and relayed the story she had told me: how the man who'd been spying on her broke into the house, took her prisoner, and shot and killed Gabriel.

When I finished, there was a long pause. Diomedes's expression gave little away. He pulled a box of cigars out of his desk drawer. He took out a little silver guillotine. He popped the end of a cigar into it and sliced it off.

"Let's start with the countertransference. Tell me about your emotional experience. Start at the beginning. As she was telling you her story, what kind of feelings were coming up?"

I thought about it for a moment. "I felt excited, I suppose. . . . And anxious. Afraid."

"Afraid? Was it your fear, or hers?"

"Both, I imagine."

"And what were you afraid of?"

"I'm not sure. Fear of failure, perhaps. I have a lot riding on this, as you know."

Diomedes nodded. "What else?"

"Frustration too. I feel frustrated quite frequently during our sessions."

"And angry?"

"Yes, I suppose so."

"You feel like a frustrated father, dealing

with a difficult child?"

"Yes. I want to help her — but I don't know if she wants to be helped."

He nodded. "Stay with the feeling of anger. Talk more about it. How does it manifest itself?"

I hesitated. "Well, I often leave the sessions with a splitting headache."

Diomedes nodded. "Yes, exactly. It has to come out one way or another. 'A trainee who is not anxious will be sick.' Who was it who said that?"

"I don't know." I shrugged. "I'm sick *and* anxious."

Diomedes smiled. "You're also no longer a trainee — although those feelings never go away entirely." He picked up his cigar. "Let's go outside for a smoke."

We went onto the fire escape. Diomedes puffed on his cigar for a moment, mulling things over. Eventually he reached a conclusion.

"She's lying, you know."

"You mean about the man killing Gabriel? I thought so too."

"Not just that."

"Then what?"

"All of it. The whole cock-and-bull story. I don't believe a single word of it."

I must have looked rather taken aback. I had suspected he'd disbelieve some elements of Alicia's tale. I hadn't expected him to reject the whole thing.

"You don't believe in the man?"

"No, I don't. I don't believe he ever existed. It's a fantasy. From start to finish."

"What makes you so sure?"

Diomedes gave me a strange smile. "Call it my intuition. Years of professional experience with fantasists." I tried to interrupt but he forestalled me with a wave of his hand. "Of course, I don't expect you to agree, Theo. You're in deep with Alicia, and your feelings are bound up with hers like a tangled ball of wool. That is the purpose of a supervision like this — to help you unpick the strands of wool — to see what is yours and what is hers. And once you gain some distance, and clarity, I suspect you will feel rather differently about your experience with Alicia Berenson."

"I'm not sure what you mean."

"Well, to be blunt, I fear she has been performing for you. Manipulating you. And it's a performance that I believe has been tailored specifically to appeal to your chivalric . . . and, let's say, romantic instincts. It was obvious to me from the start that you intended to rescue her. I'm quite sure it was

423

obvious to Alicia too. Hence her seduction of you."

"You sound like Christian. She hasn't seduced me. I am perfectly capable of withstanding a patient's sexual projections. Don't underestimate me, Professor."

"Don't underestimate *her*. She's giving an excellent performance." Diomedes shook his head and peered up at the gray clouds. "The vulnerable woman under attack, alone, in need of protection. Alicia has cast herself as the victim and this mystery man as the villain. Whereas in fact Alicia and the man are one and the same. She killed Gabriel. She was guilty — and she is still refusing to accept that guilt. So she splits, dissociates, fantasizes — Alicia becomes the innocent victim and you are her protector. And by colluding with this fantasy you are allowing her to disown all responsibility."

"I don't agree with that. I don't believe she is lying, consciously, anyway. At the very least, Alicia believes her story to be true."

"Yes, she believes it. Alicia is under attack — but from her own psyche, not the outside world."

I knew that wasn't true, but there was no point in arguing further. I stubbed out my cigarette.

"How do you think I should proceed?"

"You must force her to confront the truth. Only then will she have a hope of recovery. You must refuse point-blank to accept her story. Challenge her. Demand she tell you the truth."

"And do you think she will?"

He shrugged. "That" — he took a long drag on his cigar — "is anyone's guess."

"Very well. I'll talk to her tomorrow. I'll confront her."

Diomedes looked slightly uneasy and opened his mouth as if he was about to say something further. But he changed his mind. He nodded and stamped out his cigar with an air of finality. "Tomorrow."

CHAPTER SIXTEEN

After work, I followed Kathy to the park again. Sure enough, her lover was waiting at the same spot where they met last time. They kissed and groped each other like teenagers.

Kathy glanced in my direction, and for a second I thought she saw me, but no. She only had eyes for him. I tried to get a better look at him this time. But I still didn't see his face properly, though something about his build was familiar. I had the feeling I'd seen him before somewhere.

They walked toward Camden and disappeared into a pub, the Rose and Crown, a seedy-looking place. I waited in the café opposite. About an hour later, they came out. Kathy was all over him, kissing him. They kissed for a while by the road. I watched, feeling sick to my stomach, burning with hate.

She eventually said goodbye to him, and

they left each other. She started walking away. The man turned and walked in the opposite direction. I didn't follow Kathy.

I followed him.

He waited at a bus stop. I stood behind him. I looked at his back, his shoulders; I imagined lunging at him — shoving him under the oncoming bus. But I didn't push him. He got on the bus. So did I.

I assumed he would go directly home, but he didn't. He changed buses a couple of times. I followed him from a distance. He went to the East End, where he disappeared into a warehouse for half an hour. Then another journey, on another bus. He made a couple of phone calls, speaking in a low voice and chuckling frequently. I wondered if he was talking to Kathy. I was feeling increasingly frustrated and disheartened. But I was also stubborn and refused to give up.

Eventually he made his way home — getting off the bus and turning onto a quiet tree-lined street. He was still talking on his phone. I followed him, keeping my distance. The street was deserted. If he had turned around, he would have seen me. But he didn't.

I passed a house with a rock garden and succulent plants. I acted without thinking

— my body seemed to move on its own. My arm reached over the low wall into the garden and picked up a rock. I could feel its weight in my hands. My hands knew what to do: they had decided to kill him, crack open the worthless scumbag's skull. I went along with this, in a mindless trance, creeping after him, silently gaining ground, getting nearer. Soon I was close enough. I raised the rock, preparing to smash it down on him with all my strength. I'd knock him to the ground and bash his brains out. I was so close; if he weren't still talking on his phone, he'd have heard me.

Now: I raised the rock, and —

Right behind me, on my left, a front door opened. A sudden buzz of conversation, loud *Thank you*s and *Goodbye*s as people left the house. I froze. Right in front of me, Kathy's lover stopped and looked in the direction of the noise, at the house. I stepped aside and hid behind a tree. He didn't see me.

He started walking again, but I didn't follow. The interruption had startled me out of my reverie. The rock fell from my hand and it thudded to the ground. I watched him from behind the tree. He strolled up to the front door of a house, unlocked it, and let himself inside.

A few seconds later, a light went on in the kitchen. He was standing in profile, a little way from the window. Only half of the room was visible from the street. He was talking to someone I couldn't see. While they talked, he opened a bottle of wine. They sat down and ate a meal together. Then I caught a glimpse of his companion. It was a woman. Was it his wife? I couldn't see her clearly. He put his arm around her and kissed her.

So I wasn't the only one being betrayed. He had returned home, after kissing my wife, and ate the meal this woman had prepared for him, as if nothing had happened. I knew I couldn't leave it here — I had to do something. But what? Despite my best homicidal fantasies, I wasn't a murderer. I couldn't kill him.

I'd have to think of something cleverer than that.

CHAPTER SEVENTEEN

I planned to have it out with Alicia first thing in the morning. I intended to make her admit she had lied to me about the man killing Gabriel and force her to confront the truth.

Unfortunately, I never got the chance.

Yuri was waiting for me in reception. "Theo, I need to talk to you —"

"What is it?"

I took a closer look at him. His face seemed to have aged overnight; he looked shrunken, pale, bloodless. Something bad had happened.

"There's been an accident. Alicia — she took an overdose."

"What? Is she — ?"

Yuri shook his head. "She's still alive, but —"

"Thank God —"

"But she's in a coma. It doesn't look good."

"Where is she?"

Yuri took me through a series of locked corridors into the intensive care ward. Alicia was in a private room. She was hooked up to an ECG machine and a ventilator. Her eyes were closed.

Christian was there with another doctor. He looked ashen in contrast to the emergency-room doctor, who had a deep suntan — she'd obviously just gotten back from holiday. But she didn't look refreshed. She looked exhausted.

"How is Alicia?" I said.

The doctor shook her head. "Not good. We had to induce coma. Her respiratory system failed."

"What did she take?"

"An opioid of some kind. Hydrocodone, probably."

Yuri nodded. "There was an empty bottle of pills on the desk in her room."

"Who found her?"

"I did," Yuri said. "She was on the floor, by the bed. She didn't seem to be breathing. I thought she was dead at first."

"Any idea how she got hold of the pills?"

Yuri glanced at Christian, who shrugged. "We all know there's a lot of dealing going on in the wards."

"Elif is dealing," I said.

431

Christian nodded. "Yes, I think so too."

Indira came in. She looked close to tears. She stood by Alicia's side and watched her for a moment. "This is going to have a terrible effect on the others. It always sets the patients back months when this sort of thing happens." She sat down and reached for Alicia's hand and stroked it. I watched the ventilator rise and fall. There was silence for a moment.

"I blame myself," I said.

Indira shook her head. "It's not your fault, Theo."

"I should have taken better care of her."

"You did your best. You helped her. Which is more than anyone else did."

"Has anybody told Diomedes?"

Christian shook his head. "We've not been able to get hold of him yet."

"Did you try his mobile?"

"And his home phone. I've tried a few times."

Yuri frowned. "But — I saw Professor Diomedes earlier. He was here."

"He was?"

"Yes, I saw him early this morning. He was at the other end of the corridor, and he seemed in a rush — at least, I think it was him."

"That's odd. Well, he must have gone

home. Try him again, will you?"

Yuri nodded. He looked far away somehow; dazed, lost. He seemed to have taken it badly. I felt sorry for him.

Christian's pager went off, startling him — he quickly left the room, followed by Yuri and the doctor.

Indira hesitated and spoke in a low voice. "Would you like a moment alone with Alicia?"

I nodded, not trusting myself to speak. Indira stood up and squeezed my shoulder for a second. Then she walked out.

Alicia and I were alone.

I sat down by the bed. I reached out and took Alicia's arm. A catheter was attached to the back of her hand. I gently held her hand, stroking her palm and the inside of her wrist. I stroked her wrist with my finger, feeling the veins under her skin, and the raised, thickened scars from her suicide attempts.

So this was it. This was how it was going to end. Alicia was silent again, and this time her silence would last forever.

I wondered what Diomedes would say. I could imagine what Christian would tell him — Christian would find a way to blame me somehow: the emotions I stirred up in therapy were too much for Alicia to contain

433

— she got hold of the hydrocodone as an attempt to self-soothe and self-medicate. The overdose might have been accidental, I could hear Diomedes saying, but the behavior was suicidal. And that would be that.

But that was not that.

Something had been overlooked. Something significant, something no one had noticed — not even Yuri, when he found Alicia unconscious by the bed. An empty pill bottle was on her desk, yes, and a couple of pills were on the floor, so of course it was assumed she had taken an overdose.

But here, under my fingertip, on the inside of Alicia's wrist, was some bruising and a little mark that told a very different story.

A pinprick along the vein — a tiny hole left by a hypodermic needle — revealing the truth: Alicia didn't swallow a bottle of pills in a suicidal gesture. She was injected with a massive dose of morphine. This wasn't an overdose.

It was attempted murder.

CHAPTER EIGHTEEN

Diomedes turned up half an hour later. He had been in a meeting with the Trust, he said, then got stuck on the Underground, delayed by a signal failure. He asked Yuri to send for me.

Yuri found me in my office. "Professor Diomedes is here. He's with Stephanie. They're waiting for you."

"Thanks. I'll be right there."

I made my way to Diomedes's office, expecting the worst. A scapegoat would be needed to take the blame. I'd seen it before, at Broadmoor, in cases of suicide: whichever member of staff was closest to the victim was held accountable, be it therapist, doctor, or nurse. No doubt Stephanie was baying for my blood.

I knocked on the door and went inside. Stephanie and Diomedes were standing on either side of the desk. Judging by the tense silence, I'd interrupted a disagreement.

Diomedes spoke first. He was clearly agitated, and his hands flew all over the place. "Terrible business. Terrible. Obviously it couldn't have come at a worse time. It gives the Trust the perfect excuse to shut us down."

"I hardly think the Trust is the immediate concern," Stephanie said. "The safety of the patients comes first. We need to find out exactly what happened." She turned to me. "Indira mentioned you suspected Elif of dealing drugs? That's how Alicia got hold of the hydrocodone?"

I hesitated. "Well, I've no proof. It's something I've heard a couple of the nurses talking about. But actually there's something else I think you should know —"

Stephanie interrupted me with a shake of her head. "We know what happened. It wasn't Elif."

"No?"

"Christian happened to be passing the nurses' station, and he saw the drugs cabinet was left wide-open. There was no one in the station. Yuri had left it unlocked. Anyone could have gone in and helped themselves. And Christian saw Alicia lurking around the corner. He wondered what she was doing there at the time. Now of course it makes sense."

"How fortunate Christian was there to see all this."

My voice had a sarcastic tone. But Stephanie chose not to pick up on it. "Christian isn't the only person who's noticed Yuri's carelessness. I've often felt Yuri is far too relaxed about security. Too friendly with the patients. Too concerned with being popular. I'm surprised something like this didn't happen sooner."

"I see." I did see. I understood now why Stephanie was being cordial to me. It seemed I was off the hook; she had chosen Yuri as the scapegoat.

"Yuri always seems so meticulous," I said, glancing at Diomedes, wondering if he'd intervene. "I really don't think —"

Diomedes shrugged. "My personal opinion is Alicia has always been highly suicidal. As we know, when someone wants to die, despite your best efforts to protect them, it's often impossible to prevent it."

"Isn't that our job?" Stephanie snapped. "To prevent it?"

"No." Diomedes shook his head. "Our job is to help them heal. But we are not God. We do not have the power over life and death. Alicia Berenson wanted to die. At some point she was bound to succeed. Or at least partly succeed."

I hesitated. It was now or never.

"I'm not so sure that's true," I said. "I don't think it was a suicide attempt."

"You think it was an accident?"

"No. I don't think it was an accident."

Diomedes gave me a curious look. "What are you trying to say, Theo? What other alternative is there?"

"Well, to start with, I don't believe Yuri gave Alicia the drugs."

"You mean Christian is mistaken?"

"No," I said. "Christian is lying."

Diomedes and Stephanie stared at me, shocked. I went on before they could recover their power of speech.

I quickly told them everything that I had read in Alicia's diary: that Christian had been treating Alicia privately before Gabriel's murder; that she was one of several private patients he saw unofficially, and not only had he not come forward to testify at the trial, he had pretended not to know Alicia when she was admitted to the Grove. "No wonder he was so against any attempt to get her talking again," I said. "If she did speak, she would be in a position to expose him."

Stephanie stared at me blankly. "But — what are you saying? You can't seriously be suggesting that he —"

438

"Yes, I am suggesting it. It wasn't an overdose. It was an attempt to murder her."

"Where is Alicia's diary?" Diomedes asked me. "You have it in your possession?"

I shook my head. "No, not anymore. I gave it back to Alicia. It must be in her room."

"Then we must retrieve it." Diomedes turned to Stephanie. "But first, I think we should call the police. Don't you?"

CHAPTER NINETEEN

From then on things moved fast.

Police officers swarmed all over the Grove, asking questions, taking photographs, sealing off Alicia's studio and her room. The investigation was led by Chief Inspector Steven Allen, heavyset, bald, with large reading glasses that distorted his eyes, magnifying them, making them seem bigger than life, bulging with interest and curiosity.

Allen listened with careful interest to my story; I told him everything I had said to Diomedes, and I showed him my supervision notes.

"Thank you very much indeed, Mr. Faber."

"Call me Theo."

"I'd like you to make an official statement, please. And I'll be talking to you more in due course."

"Yes, certainly."

Inspector Allen had commandeered Diomedes's office. He showed me out. After I made my statement to a junior officer, I hung around in the corridor, waiting. Soon enough, Christian was led to the door by a police officer. He looked uneasy, scared — and guilty. I felt satisfied he would soon be charged.

There was nothing else to do now, except wait. On my way out of the Grove, I passed the goldfish bowl. I glanced inside — and what I saw stopped me in my tracks.

Elif was being slipped some drugs by Yuri, and he was pocketing some cash.

Elif charged out and fixed me with her one eye. A look of contempt and hatred.

"Elif," I said.

"Fuck off." She marched off, disappearing around the corner.

Yuri emerged from the goldfish bowl. As soon as he saw me, his jaw dropped. He stuttered with surprise. "I — I didn't see you there."

"Obviously not."

"Elif — forgot her medication. I was just giving it to her."

"I see."

So Yuri was dealing and supplying Elif. I wondered what else he was up to — perhaps I had been a little too hasty to defend him

441

so determinedly to Stephanie. I'd better keep an eye on him.

"I wanted to ask you," he said, leading me away from the goldfish bowl. "What should we do about Mr. Martin?"

"What do you mean?" I looked at him, surprised. "You mean Jean-Felix Martin? What about him?"

"Well, he's been here for hours. He came this morning to visit Alicia. And he's been waiting since then."

"What? Why didn't you tell me? You mean he's been here all this time?"

"Sorry, it slipped my mind with everything that happened. He's in the waiting room."

"I see. Well, I'd better go and talk to him."

I hurried downstairs to reception, thinking about what I'd just heard. What was Jean-Felix doing here? I wondered what he wanted; what it meant.

I went into the waiting room and looked around.

But no one was there.

CHAPTER TWENTY

I left the Grove and lit a cigarette. I heard a man's voice calling my name. I looked up, expecting it to be Jean-Felix. But it wasn't him.

It was Max Berenson. He was getting out of a car and charging toward me.

"What the fuck?" he shouted. "What happened?" Max's face was bright red, contorted with anger. "They just called and told me about Alicia. What happened to her?"

I took a step backward. "I think you need to calm down, Mr. Berenson."

"Calm down? My sister-in-law is lying in there in a fucking coma because of your negligence —"

Max's hand was clenched in a fist. He raised it. I thought he was going to throw a punch at me.

But he was interrupted by Tanya. She hurried over, looking just as angry as he was — but angry with Max, not me. "Stop it, Max!

443

For Christ's sake. Aren't things bad enough? It's not Theo's fault!"

Max ignored her and turned back to me. His eyes were wild.

"Alicia was in your care," he shouted. "How did you let it happen? How?"

Max's eyes filled with angry tears. He was making no attempt to disguise his emotions. He stood there crying. I glanced at Tanya; she obviously knew about his feelings for Alicia. Tanya looked dismayed and drained. Without another word, she turned and went back to their car.

I wanted to get away from Max as fast as possible. I kept walking.

He kept shouting abuse. I thought he was going to follow, but he didn't — he was rooted to the spot, a broken man, calling after me, yelling piteously:

"I hold you responsible. My poor Alicia, my girl . . . my poor Alicia . . . You'll pay for this! You hear me?"

Max kept on shouting, but I ignored him. Soon his voice faded into silence. I was alone.

I kept walking.

CHAPTER TWENTY-ONE

I walked back to the house where Kathy's lover lived. I stood there for an hour, watching. Eventually the door opened, and he emerged. I watched him leave. Where was he going? To meet Kathy? I hesitated, but decided not to follow him. Instead I stayed watching the house.

I watched his wife through the windows. As I watched, I felt increasingly sure I had to do something to help her. She was me, and I was her: we were two innocent victims, deceived and betrayed. She believed this man loved her — but he didn't.

Perhaps I was wrong, assuming she knew nothing about the affair? Perhaps she did know. Perhaps they enjoyed a sexually open relationship and she was equally promiscuous? But somehow I didn't think so. She looked innocent, as I had once looked. It was my duty to enlighten her. I could reveal the truth about the man she was living with, whose bed she shared. I had no choice. I had to help her.

Over the next few days, I kept returning. One day, she left the house and went for a walk. I followed her, keeping my distance. I was worried she saw me at one point, but even if she did, I was just a stranger to her. For the moment.

I went away and made a couple of purchases. I came back again. I stood across the road, watching the house. I saw her again, standing by the window.

I didn't have a plan, as such, just a vague, unformed idea of what I needed to accomplish. Rather like an inexperienced artist, I knew the result I wanted — without knowing quite how to achieve it. I waited awhile, then walked up to the house. I tried the gate — it was unlocked. It swung open and I stepped into the garden. I felt a sudden rush of adrenaline. An illicit thrill at being an intruder on someone else's property.

Then I saw the back door opening. I looked for somewhere to hide. I noticed the little summerhouse across the grass. I raced silently across the lawn and slipped inside. I stood there for a second, catching my breath. My heart was pounding. Had she seen me? I heard her footsteps approaching.

Too late to back out now. I reached into my back pocket and took out the black balaclava I'd bought. I pulled it over my head. I put on a pair of gloves.

She walked in. She was on the phone: "Okay, darling. I'll see you at eight. Yes . . . I love you too."

She ended the call and switched on an electric fan. She stood in front of the fan, her hair blowing in the breeze. She picked up a paintbrush and approached a canvas on an easel. She stood with her back to me. Then she caught sight of my reflection in the window. I think she saw my knife first. She stiffened and slowly turned around. Her eyes were wide with fear. We stared at each other in silence.

This was the first time I came face-to-face with Alicia Berenson.

The rest, as they say, is history.

■ ■ ■ ■

PART FIVE

■ ■ ■ ■

If I justify myself, mine own mouth shall
condemn me.

— Job 9:20

CHAPTER ONE

Alicia Berenson's Diary

February 23
Theo just left. I am alone. I'm writing this as fast as I can. I haven't got much time. I've got to get this down while I still have the strength.

I thought I was crazy at first. It was easier to think I was crazy than believe it was true. But I'm not crazy. I'm not.

That first time I met him in the therapy room, I wasn't sure — there was something familiar about him, but different — I recognized his eyes, not just the color but the shape. And the same smell of cigarettes and smoky after-shave. And the way he formed words, and the rhythm of his speech — but not the tone of his voice, it seemed different somehow. So I wasn't sure — but the next time we met, he gave himself away. He said the same words

— the exact same phrase he'd used at the house, burned into my memory:

"I want to help you — I want to help you see clearly."

As soon as I heard that, something in my brain clicked and the jigsaw came together — the picture was complete.

It was him.

And something in me took over, some kind of wild animal instinct. I wanted to kill him, kill or be killed — I leaped on him and tried to strangle him and scratch his eyes out, bash his skull to pieces on the floor. But I didn't succeed in killing him, and they held me down and drugged me and locked me up. And then — after that I lost my nerve. I started to doubt myself again — maybe I'd made a mistake, maybe I was imagining it, maybe it wasn't him.

How could it possibly be Theo? What purpose could he have in coming here to taunt me like this? And then I understood. All that bullshit about wanting to help me — that was the sickest part of it. He was getting a kick out of it, he was getting off on it — that's why he was here. He had come back to gloat.

"I want to help you — I want to help you see clearly."

Well, now I saw. I saw clearly. I wanted him to know that I knew. So I lied about the way Gabriel died. As I was talking, I could see he knew I was lying. We looked at each other and he saw it — that I had recognized him. And there was something in his eyes I'd never seen before. Fear. He was afraid of me — of what I might say. He was scared — of the sound of my voice.

That's why he came back a few minutes ago. He didn't say anything this time. No more words. He grabbed my wrist and stuck a needle in my vein. I didn't struggle. I didn't fight back. I let him do it. I deserve it — I deserve this punishment. I am guilty — but so is he. That's why I'm writing this — so he won't get away with it. So he will be punished.

I've got to be quick. I can feel it now — the stuff he injected me with is working. I'm so drowsy. I want to lie down. I want to sleep. . . . But no — not yet. I've got to stay awake. I've got to finish the story. And this time, I'll tell the truth.

That night, Theo broke into the house and tied

me up — and when Gabriel came home, Theo knocked him out. At first I thought he'd killed him — but then I saw Gabriel was breathing. Theo pulled him up and tied him to the chair. He moved it so Gabriel and I were sitting back-to-back, and I couldn't see his face.

"Please," I said. "Please don't hurt him. I'm begging you — I'll do anything, anything you want."

Theo laughed. I'd come to hate his laugh so much — it was cold, empty. Heartless. "Hurt him?" He shook his head. "I'm going to kill him."

He meant it. I felt such terror, I lost control of my tears. I wept and pleaded. "I'll do anything you want, anything — please, please let him live — he deserves to live. He's the kindest and the best of men — and I love him, I love him so much —"

"Tell me, Alicia. Tell me about your love for him. Tell me, do you think he loves you?"

"He loves me," I said.

I heard the clock ticking in the background. There seemed to be an age before he replied.

"We'll see," he said. His black eyes stared at me for a second and I felt consumed by darkness. I was in the presence of a creature that wasn't even human. He was evil.

He walked around the chair and faced Gabriel. I turned my head as far as I could, but I couldn't see them. There was a horrible dull thud — I flinched as I heard him strike Gabriel across the face. He hit him again and again, until Gabriel started spluttering and woke up.

"Hello, Gabriel," he said.

"Who the fuck are you?"

"I'm a married man. So I know what it's like to love someone. And I know what it's like to be let down."

"What the fuck are you talking about?"

"Only cowards betray the people who love them. Are you a coward, Gabriel?"

"Fuck you."

"I was going to kill you. But Alicia pleaded for your life. So instead, I'm going to give you a choice. Either you die — or Alicia does. You decide."

The way he spoke was so cool and calm and in control. No emotion. Gabriel didn't reply for a second. He sounded out of breath, like he'd been punched.

"No —"

"Yes. Alicia dies, or you die. Your choice, Gabriel. Let's find out how much you love her. Would you die for her? You have ten seconds to decide. . . . Ten . . . nine —"

"Don't believe him," I said. "He's going to kill us both — I love you —"

"— eight . . . seven —"

"I know you love me, Gabriel —"

"— six . . . five —"

"You love me —"

"— four . . . three —"

"Gabriel, say you love me —"

"— two —"

And then Gabriel spoke. I didn't recognize his voice at first. Such a tiny voice, so far away — a little boy's voice. A small child — with the power of life and death at his fingertips.

"I don't want to die," he said.

Then there was silence. Everything stopped. Inside my body, every cell deflated; wilting cells, like dead petals falling from a flower. Jasmine flowers floating to the ground. Can I smell jasmine somewhere? Yes, yes, sweet jasmine — on the windowsill perhaps . . .

Theo stepped away from Gabriel and started talking to me. I found it hard to focus on his words. "You see, Alicia? I knew Gabriel was a coward — fucking my wife behind my back. He destroyed the only happiness I've ever had." Theo leaned forward, right in my face. "I'm sorry to do this. But quite frankly, now you know the truth . . . you're better off dead."

He raised the gun and pointed it at my head. I shut my eyes. I heard Gabriel screaming — *"Don't shoot don't shoot don't —"*

A click. And then a gunshot — so loud that it

blew away all other sound. There was silence for a few seconds. I thought I was dead.

But I wasn't so lucky.

I opened my eyes. Theo was still there — pointing the gun at the ceiling. He smiled. He put his finger to his lips, telling me to keep quiet.

"Alicia?" Gabriel shouted. "Alicia?"

I could hear Gabriel writhing in his chair, trying to turn around to see what had happened.

"What did you do to her, you bastard? You fucking bastard. Oh, Jesus —"

Theo untied my wrists. He dropped the gun to the floor. Then he kissed me, ever so gently, on the cheek. He walked out, and the front door slammed after him.

Gabriel and I were alone. He was sobbing, crying, barely able to form words. He just kept calling my name, wailing, "Alicia, Alicia —"

I remained silent.

"Alicia? Fuck, fuck, oh, fuck —"

I remained silent.

"Alicia, answer me, Alicia — oh, God —"

I remained silent. How could I talk? Gabriel had sentenced me to death.

The dead don't talk.

I untied the wire around my ankles. I got up from the chair. I reached down to the floor. My fingers closed around the gun. It was hot and heavy in my hand. I walked around the chair, and I faced Gabriel. Tears were streaming down his cheeks. His eyes widened.

"Alicia? You're alive — thank God you're —"

I wish I could say I struck a blow for the defeated — that I was standing up for the betrayed and brokenhearted — that Gabriel had a tyrant's eyes, my father's eyes. But I'm past lying now. The truth is Gabriel had my eyes, suddenly — and I had his. Somewhere along the way we had swapped places.

I saw it now. I would never be safe. Never be loved. All my hopes, dashed — all my dreams, shattered — leaving nothing, nothing. My father was right — I didn't deserve to live. I was — nothing. That's what Gabriel did to me.

That's the truth. I didn't kill Gabriel. He killed me.

All I did was pull the trigger.

CHAPTER TWO

"There is nothing so pitiful," Indira said, "as seeing all someone's possessions in a cardboard box."

I nodded. I looked around the room sadly.

"Surprising, really," Indira went on, "how few things Alicia had. When you think how much junk the other patients accumulate . . . All she had were some books, a few drawings, her clothes."

Indira and I were clearing out Alicia's room on Stephanie's instructions. "It's unlikely she'll ever wake up," Stephanie had said, "and quite frankly we need the bed." We worked in silence mostly, deciding what to put in storage and what to throw away. I carefully looked through her belongings. I wanted to make sure there was nothing incriminating — nothing that might trip me up.

I wondered how Alicia had managed to keep her diary hidden and out of sight for

461

so long. Each patient was allowed to bring a small amount of personal items with them upon admittance to the Grove. Alicia had brought a portfolio of sketches, which I presume was how she had smuggled in the diary. I opened the portfolio and flicked through the drawings — they were mostly unfinished pencil sketches and studies. A few casual lines thrown onto a page, immediately coming to life, brilliantly evocative, capturing an unmistakable likeness.

I showed a sketch to Indira. "It's you."

"What? It's not."

"It is."

"Is it?" Indira looked delighted and studied it closely. "Do you think so? I never noticed her drawing me. I wonder when she did it. It's good, isn't it?"

"Yes, it is. You should keep it."

Indira pulled a face and handed it back. "I couldn't do that."

"Of course you can. She wouldn't mind." I smiled. "No one will ever know."

"I suppose — I suppose not." She glanced at the painting upright on the floor, leaning against the wall — the painting of me and Alicia on the fire escape of the burning building, which had been defaced by Elif.

"What about that?" Indira asked. "Will you take it?"

I shook my head. "I'll call Jean-Felix. He can take charge of it."

Indira nodded. "Shame you can't keep it."

I looked at it for a moment. I didn't like it. Of all of Alicia's paintings, it was the only one I didn't like. Strange, considering it had me as its subject.

I want to be clear — I never thought Alicia would shoot Gabriel. This is an important point. I never intended nor expected her to kill him. All I wanted was to awaken Alicia to the truth about her marriage, as I had been awakened. I intended to show her that Gabriel didn't love her, that her life was a lie, their marriage a sham. Only then would she have a chance, as I had, to build a new life from the rubble; a life based on truth, not lies.

I had no idea about Alicia's history of instability. Had I known, I never would have pushed things so far. I had no idea she would react like that. And when the story was all over the press and Alicia was on trial for murder, I felt a deep sense of personal responsibility, and the desire to expiate my guilt and prove that I was not responsible for what had happened. So I applied for the job at the Grove. I wanted to help her through the aftermath of the murder — help her understand what had happened, work

463

through it — and be free. If you were cynical, you might say I revisited the scene of the crime, so to speak, to cover my tracks. That's not true. Even though I knew the risks of such an endeavor, the real possibility that I might get caught, that it might end in disaster, I had no choice — because of who I am.

I am a psychotherapist, remember. Alicia needed help — and only I knew how to help her.

I was nervous she might know me, despite my having worn the mask and disguised my voice. But Alicia didn't seem to recognize me, and I was able to play a new part in her life. Then, that night in Cambridge, I finally understood what I had unwittingly re-enacted, the long-forgotten land mine on which I had trodden. Gabriel was the second man to condemn Alicia to death; bringing up this original trauma was more than she could bear — which is why she picked up the gun and visited her long-awaited revenge not upon her father, but upon her husband. As I suspected, the murder had much older, deeper origins than my actions.

But when she lied to me about how Gabriel died, it was obvious Alicia had recognized me and she was testing me. I was forced to take action, to silence Alicia forever. I had Christian take the blame — a poetic justice, I felt. I had no qualms about framing him. Christian had failed Alicia when she needed him the most; he deserved to be punished.

Silencing Alicia wasn't so easy. Injecting her with morphine was the hardest thing I've ever done. That she didn't die, but is asleep, is better — this way, I can still visit her every day and sit by her bed and hold her hand. I haven't lost her.

"Are we done?" asked Indira, interrupting my thoughts.

"I think so."

"Good. I have to go, I have a patient at twelve."

"Go ahead," I said.

"See you at lunch?"

"Yes."

Indira gave my arm a squeeze and left.

I looked at my watch. I thought about leaving early, going home. I felt exhausted. I was about to turn off the light and leave when a thought occurred to me and I felt my body stiffen.

The diary. Where was it?

My eyes flickered around the room, neatly packed and boxed up. We'd gone through it all. I had looked at and considered each and every one of her personal items.

And it wasn't there.

How could I have been so careless? Indira and her fucking endless inane chatter had distracted me and made me lose focus.

Where was it? It had to be here. Without the diary there was precious little evidence to convict Christian. I had to find it.

I searched the room, feeling increasingly frantic. I turned the cardboard boxes upside down, scattering their contents on the floor. I rummaged through the debris, but it wasn't there. I tore apart her clothing but found nothing. I ripped open the art portfolio, shaking the sketches to the floor, but the diary wasn't among them. Then I went through the cupboards and pulled out all the drawers, checking that they were empty, then hurling them aside.

But it wasn't there.

CHAPTER THREE

Julian McMahon from the Trust was waiting for me in reception. He had a big build, curly ginger hair, and a fondness for phrases such as *between you and me* or *at the end of the day* or *the bottom line,* which frequently popped up in his conversation, often in the same sentence. He was essentially a benign figure — the friendly face of the Trust. He wanted to have a word with me before I went home.

"I've just come from Professor Diomedes. I thought you should know — he's resigned."

"Ah. I see."

"He took early retirement. Between you and me, it was either that or face an inquiry into this mess." Julian shrugged. "I can't help but feel sorry for him — not a particularly glorious end to a long and distinguished career. But at least this way he'll be spared the press and all the hoo-ha. Incidentally, he mentioned you."

"Diomedes?"

"Yes. He suggested we give you his job." Julian winked. "He said you were the perfect man for it."

I smiled. "That's very kind."

"Unfortunately, at the end of the day, given what happened to Alicia, and Christian's arrest, there's simply no question of keeping the Grove open. We're closing it down permanently."

"I can't say I'm surprised. So in fact there's no job to be had?"

"Well, the bottom line is this — we're planning to open a new, much more cost-effective psychiatric service here in the next few months. And we'd like you to consider running it, Theo."

It was hard to conceal my excitement. I agreed with pleasure. "Between you and me," I said, borrowing one of his phrases, "it's the kind of opportunity that I dream about." And it was — a chance to actually help people, not just medicate them; help them the way I believe they should be helped. The way Ruth helped me. The way I tried to help Alicia.

Things have worked out well for me — I'd be ungrateful not to acknowledge that.

468

It seems I've gotten everything I wanted. Well, almost.

Last year, Kathy and I moved out of central London to Surrey — back to where I grew up. After my father died, he left me the house; although it remained my mother's to live in until she died, she decided to give it to us, and she moved into a care facility.

Kathy and I thought the extra space and a garden would be worth the commute into London. I thought it would be good for us. We promised ourselves we would transform the house and made plans to redecorate and exorcise. But nearly a year since we moved in, the place remains unfinished, half-decorated, the pictures and convex mirror we bought in Portobello Market still propped up against unpainted walls. It remains very much the house I grew up in. But I don't mind the way I thought I would. In fact, I feel quite at home, which is ironic.

I arrived at the house and let myself in. I quickly took off my coat — it was sweltering, like a greenhouse. I turned down the thermostat in the hallway. Kathy loves being hot, while I much prefer being cold, so temperature is one of our little battlegrounds. I could hear the TV from the hallway. Kathy seems to watch a lot of TV these days. A never-ending sound track of garbage that underscores our life in this house.

I found her in the living room, curled up on the sofa. She had a giant bag of prawn cocktail crisps on her lap and was fishing them out with sticky red fingers and shoveling them into her mouth. She's always eating crap like that; it's not surprising she's gained weight recently. She hasn't been working much in the past couple of years, and she's become quite withdrawn, depressed even. Her doctor wanted to put her on antidepressants, but I discouraged it. Instead I advocated her getting a therapist and talking through her feelings; I even offered to find her a shrink myself. But Kathy doesn't want to talk, it seems.

Sometimes I catch her looking at me strangely — and wonder what she's thinking. Is she trying to summon up the courage to tell me about Gabriel and the affair? But she doesn't say a word. She just sits in silence, the way Alicia used to. I wish I could help her — but I can't seem to reach her.

That's the terrible irony: I did all this to keep Kathy — and I've lost her anyway.

I perched on the armrest and watched her a moment. "A patient of mine took an

470

overdose. She's in a coma." No reaction. "It looks as though another member of the staff may have administered the overdose deliberately. A colleague." No reaction. "Are you listening to me?"

Kathy gave a brief shrug. "I don't know what to say."

"Some sympathy might be nice."

"For who? For you?"

"For her. I've been seeing her for a while, in individual therapy. Her name is Alicia Berenson." I glanced at Kathy as I said this. She didn't react. Not even a flicker of emotion.

"She's famous, or infamous. Everyone was talking about her a few years ago. She killed her husband . . . remember?"

"No, not really." Kathy shrugged and changed the channel.

So we continue our game of "Let's pretend."

I seem to do a lot of pretending, these days — for a lot of people, including myself. Which is why I'm writing this, I suppose. An attempt to bypass my monstrous ego and access the truth about myself — if that's possible.

I needed a drink. I went into the kitchen and poured myself a shot of vodka from the freezer. It burned my throat as I swallowed it. I poured another.

I wondered what Ruth would say if I went to find her again — as I did six years ago — and confessed all this to her? But I knew it was impossible. That I was altogether a different creature now, a guiltier thing, less capable of honesty. How could I sit opposite that frail old lady and look into those watery blue eyes that held me safe for so long — and gave me nothing but decency, kindness, truth — and reveal how foul I am, how cruel, how vengeful and perverse, how unworthy I am of Ruth and everything she tried to do for me? How could I tell her that I have destroyed three lives? That I have no moral code, that I'm capable of the worst kind of acts without remorse, and my only concern is for my own skin?

Even worse than the shock or repulsion, or possibly even fear, in Ruth's eyes as I told her this would be the look of sadness, disappointment, and self-reproach. Because not only had I let her down, I know she would be thinking she had let *me* down — and not just me, but the talking cure itself. For no therapist ever had a better shot at it than Ruth — she had years to work with someone who was damaged, yes, but so young, just a boy, and so willing to change, to get better, to heal. Yet, despite hundreds of hours of psychotherapy, talking and listening and analyzing, she was unable to save his soul. Perhaps I was wrong. Perhaps some of us are simply born evil, and despite our best efforts we remain that way.

The doorbell rang, rousing me from my thoughts. It wasn't a common occurrence, an evening visitor, not since we moved to Surrey; I couldn't even remember the last time we'd had friends over.

"Are you expecting someone?" I called out, but there was no reply. Kathy probably couldn't hear me over the TV.

I went to the front door and opened it. To my surprise, it was Chief Inspector Allen. He was wrapped up in a scarf and coat, and his cheeks were flushed.

"Good evening, Mr. Faber."

"Inspector Allen? What are you doing here?"

"I happened to be in the neighborhood and thought I'd pop in. A couple of developments I wanted to tell you about. Is now convenient?"

I hesitated. "To be honest, I'm just about to cook dinner, so —"

"This won't take long."

Allen smiled. He clearly wasn't going to take no for an answer, so I stepped aside and let him enter. He looked happy to be inside. He pulled off his gloves and his coat. "It's getting bloody cold out there. Cold enough to snow, I'd bet." His glasses had steamed up and he took them off and wiped them with his handkerchief.

"I'm afraid it's rather warm in here," I said.

"Not for me. Can't be too warm for my liking."

"You'd get on with my wife."

Right on cue, Kathy appeared in the hallway. She looked from me to the inspector quizzically. "What's going on?"

"Kathy, this is Chief Inspector Allen. He's in charge of the investigation about the patient I mentioned."

"Good evening, Mrs. Faber."

"Inspector Allen wants to talk to me about something. We won't be long. Go upstairs and have your bath, and I'll call you when dinner's ready." I nodded at the inspector to go into the kitchen. "After you."

Inspector Allen glanced at Kathy again before he turned and went into the kitchen. I followed, leaving Kathy lingering in the hallway, before I heard her footsteps slowly going upstairs.

"Can I get you something to drink?"

"Thank you. That's very kind. A cup of tea would be lovely." I saw his eyes go to the bottle of vodka on the counter.

I smiled. "Or something stronger if you prefer?"

"No, thank you. A cup of tea suits me just fine."

"How do you take it?"

"Strong, please. Just enough milk to color it. No sugar, I'm trying to give it up."

As he spoke, my mind drifted — wondering what he was doing here, and if I should be nervous. His manner was so genial it was hard not to feel safe. Besides, there was nothing that could trip me up, was there?

I switched on the kettle and turned to face him.

"So, Inspector? What was it you wanted to talk to me about?"

"Well, about Mr. Martin, mainly."

"Jean-Felix? Really?" That surprised me. "What about him?"

"Well, he came to the Grove to collect Alicia's art materials, and we got talking about one thing and another. Interesting man, Mr. Martin. He's planning a retrospective of Alicia's work. He seems to think now is a good time to reevaluate her as an artist. Given all the publicity, I daresay he's right." Allen gave me an appraising look. "You might want to write about her, sir. I'm sure there'll be interest in a book, or something like that."

"I hadn't considered it. . . . What exactly has Jean-Felix's retrospective got to do with me, Inspector?"

"Well, Mr. Martin was particularly excited to see the new painting — he didn't seem concerned that Elif defaced it. He said it added a special quality to it — I can't remember the exact words he used — I don't know much about art myself. Do you?"

"Not really." I wondered how long it was going to take the inspector to get to the point, and why I was feeling increasingly uneasy.

"Anyway, Mr. Martin was admiring the picture. And he picked it up to look at it more closely, and there it was."

"What was?"

"This."

The inspector pulled out something from inside his jacket. I recognized it at once.

The diary.

The kettle boiled and a shriek filled the air. I switched it off and poured some boiling water into the mug. I stirred it and noticed my hand was trembling slightly.

"Oh, good. I wondered where it was."

"Wedged in the back of the painting, in the top-left corner of the frame. It was jammed in tight."

So that's where she hid it, I thought. The back of the painting that I hated. The one place I didn't look.

The inspector stroked the creased, faded black cover and smiled. He opened it and looked through the pages. "Fascinating. The arrows, the confusion."

I nodded. "A portrait of a disturbed mind."

Inspector Allen flicked through the pages to the end. He started reading from it aloud:

" '. . . he was scared — of the sound of my voice. . . . He grabbed my wrist and stuck a needle in my vein.' "

I felt a sudden rising panic. I didn't know those words. I hadn't read that entry. It was the incriminating evidence I had been looking for — and it was in the wrong hands. I wanted to snatch the diary from Allen and tear out the pages — but I couldn't move. I was trapped. I started stammering —

"I — I really think it's better if I —"

I spoke too nervously, and he heard the fear in my voice. "Yes?"

"Nothing."

I made no further attempt to stop him. Any action I took would be viewed as incriminating anyway. There was no way out. And the strangest thing is, I felt relieved.

"You know, I don't believe you happened to be in my neighborhood at all, Inspector." I handed him his tea.

"Ah. No, you're quite right. I thought it best not to announce the intention of my visit on the doorstep. But the fact is, this puts things in rather a different light."

"I'm curious to hear it," I heard myself saying. "Will you read it aloud?"

"Very well."

I felt strangely calm as I sat in the chair by the window.

He cleared his throat and began. " 'Theo just left. I am alone. I'm writing this as fast as I can. . . .' "

As I listened, I looked up at the white clouds drifting past. Finally, they had opened — it had started to snow — snowflakes were falling outside. I opened the window and reached out my hand. I caught a snowflake. I watched it disappear, vanish from my fingertip. I smiled.

And I went to catch another one.

ACKNOWLEDGMENTS

I'm hugely indebted to my agent, Sam Copeland, for making all this happen. And I'm especially grateful to my editors — Ben Willis in the United Kingdom and Ryan Doherty in the United States — for making the book so much better. I also want to thank Hal Jensen and Iván Fernandez Soto for their invaluable comments; Brett Kahr and Kate White for years of showing me how good therapy works; the young people and staff at Northgate and everything they taught me; Diane Medak for letting me use her house as a writing retreat; Uma Thurman and James Haslam for making me a better writer. And for all their helpful suggestions, and encouragement, Emily Holt, Victoria Holt, Vanessa Holt, Nedie Antoniades, and Joe Adams.

ABOUT THE AUTHOR

Alex Michaelides was born in Cyprus in 1977 to a Greek father and English mother. He studied English literature at Cambridge University and got his MA in screenwriting at the American Film Institute in Los Angeles. He wrote the film *The Devil You Know* (2013) starring Rosamund Pike and cowrote *The Con Is On* (2018), starring Uma Thurman, Tim Roth, Parker Posey and Sofia Vergara. *The Silent Patient* is his first novel.